In 1968 she went in search of America.
. . . America didn't want to be found.

# THE OTHER SIDE *of* THE WIND

A NOVEL

## WILLIAM JOHN ROSTRON

CARPATHIA PUBLISHING

*To all the strong women in my life who served as role models for the character of Maria:*

*Filomena Longo Cippitelli*
*Lucia Cippitelli Paradiso*
*Josephine Paradiso Rostron*
*Marilyn Daniele Rostron*
*Brittany Caitlin Rostron*
*Erin Broderick Rostron*
*Heather Brauer Rostron*
*Karen Rostron Lauria*
*Robin Rostron Tarzia*
*Robina Pilling Rostron*

# CONTENTS


PROLOGUE                                                                1

Part I
"OUR TIME IN THE SUN"
 1. "Oh, So Very Young"                                                  7
 2. "Frankie and Johnny"                                               10
 3. "Johnny Angel"                                                     15
 4. "Catch the Wind"                                                   20
 5. "Pretty Flamingo"                                                  23
 6. "Slow Dancin'"                                                     26
 7. "Love Hurts"                                                       30
 8. "How Long Before You Break My Heart"                               32
 9. "Giving Up"                                                        35

Part II
"CHICAGO"
10. "She's Leaving Home"                                               45
11. "Cross Roads Blues"                                                50
12. "Take Me Out to the Ballgame"                                      55
13. "Abraham, Martin, and John"                                        58
14. "You Can't Always Get What You Want"                               63
15. "Broken Dreams"                                                    66
16. "Leavin' in Your Eyes"                                             69
17. "I Can't Keep From Cryin' Sometimes"                               72
18. "Ball of Confusion"                                                77
19. "For What It's Worth"                                              80
20. "Paint It Black"                                                   88

Part III
"DANCING ON THE OTHER SIDE OF THE
WIND"
21. "The Way"                                                         93

22. "On the Road Again" 99
23. "Magical Mystery Tour" 105
24. "Eight Miles High" 110
25. "I'm a Man" 116
26. "Hello. Goodbye" 122

## Part IV
## "SAN FRANCISCO NIGHTS"

27. "San Francisco (Be Sure to Wear Flowers in Your Hair)" 127
28. "Do You Want to Know a Secret? "(Reprise) 131
29. "We Built This City on Rock and Roll" 135
30. "Time in a Bottle" 140
31. "Revolution" 143
32. "Sympathy for the Devil" 147
33. "It's All Over Now" 150

## Part V
## "VIVA, LAS VEGAS"

34. "Devil in Disguise" 157
35. "Strange Brew" 161
36. "Foxy Lady" 167
37. "Peaceful, Easy Feeling" 169
38. "Pretty Flamingo" (Reprise) 173
39. "Bad To The Bone" 175
40. "Highway to Hell" 178

## Part VI
## "BORN TO RUN"

41. "Leavin' Las Vegas" 189
42. "Free Fallin'" 192
43. "Take It Easy" 194
44. "Don't You Go Talkin' to Strangers" 198
45. "Horse With No Name" 203
46. "Turn the Page" 207

## Part VII
## "OB-LA-DI, OB-LA-DA"

47. "In My Life" 219

48. "Shot Through the Heart" 223

49. "Strangers When We Meet" 228

50. "Sunday Bloody Sunday" 231

51. "I Love You More Than You'll Ever Know" 233


Part VIII

"THE EVE OF DESTRUCTION"

52. "My City of Ruins" 239

53. "Reason To Believe" 242

54. "Goodnight Saigon" 248


Part IX

"THE END OF THE LINE"

55. "If the Sun Comes Up Without Me Tomorrow (You'll Be Fine)" 253

56. "Tomorrow Never Comes" 256

57. "Lean on Me" 261

58. "Time to Say Goodbye" 265

59. "And So It Goes" 267

60. "The Story in Your Eyes" 270

61. "Midnight Confession" 278

Epilogue 281

Epilogue Scene 1 282

Epilogue Scene 2 288

Epilogue Scene 3 291

*Author's Note* 293

*About the Author* 299

"Everything will be okay in the end. If it's not okay, it's not the end."

*- John Lennon*

# PROLOGUE

**"Do You Want to Know a Secret?"**
*- The Beatles*
December 2012

At least two organized crime families want me dead—one in New York and one in Las Vegas.

What can I say? That's just some of the mystery I have held back from everyone who knows me. I can write my story in this memoir because I don't believe anyone will ever read it…except, perhaps, my two children…and I haven't even decided about them yet. They are the ones who encouraged me to tell my tale. They wanted to know the details of my life before I met and fell in love with their father, Jason Carlson. However, I'm not particularly proud of many of my early…ah-hem experiences. It's not the kind of story you tell your children and expect them to look at you the same.

The big question out there is, why didn't I go to the authorities?

Why didn't I use the witness protection program to ensure my further existence on this planet? Well, that might have been difficult. At a certain point in my life, there were warrants for my arrest in at least four jurisdictions. (There still might be!)

I don't believe I did anything *morally* wrong. It's just that the Chicago, Seattle, San Francisco, and Las Vegas police departments may disagree. It is a good thing that most of the warrants are made out for "Jane Doe" and one of them for "Becky Simon," a smartly chosen pseudo-name.

It's hard to believe that I started with a fairly typical, indeed boring, childhood and am now the very definition of middle-class stability. Oh, but those years from 1968 to 1972, when I took off in search of America, and got lost (both literally and figuratively). Those were such extraordinary times that I tend to think of them as my Magical Mystery Tour. (The name may have also had to do with some of the drugs ingested during that period.)

In the end, I found myself and emerged as a much stronger person because of my experiences. But it wasn't pretty…or easy. I have come to realize that my four-year sabbatical from normalcy was all because of love. I don't use that to rationalize my behavior or justify my rap sheet.

I only gave a damn about four men in my life. One disappeared, two cheated on me, and three died. I can count—the number is still four because two of those who cheated on me also died. (No, I didn't kill either one!) One of those who cheated and then died would be my recently departed husband. I did love him most of the time. Well, at least until I caught him with "Bitch-Slut #1." Yes, the numerical ranking does indeed indicate that there were Bitch-Sluts #2 and #3. I don't think this is a revelation to my children.

Our love soured after that, but watching his slow and painful death from a mysterious cancer still tore me apart. He had inhaled toxic fumes while sifting through the rubble of the 9/11 terrorist attack—never worrying about what the carcinogenic debris might do to him. He was a selfless, brave man who paid the price for that. Unfortunately, he passed away a few weeks ago. We had some good years…happy years. However, I must think about what I am going to write next because I don't want to disrespect Jason's memory, even so…

I've never felt the mind-boggling, out-of-control passion for Jason as I did for my first love, Johnny Cipp…the one who disappeared. Maybe this memoir will help me accept or reject that concept after all these years. In all the years since Johnny left me behind, there has never been a day that I have not thought of him.

# PART I

# "OUR TIME IN THE SUN"

## - CHRIS DELANEY AND THE BROTHERHOOD BLUES BAND

*"Our days seemed to go on forever,
It was our time in the sun."*

New York
(1949 to 1968)

# "OH, SO VERY YOUNG"

## - CAT STEVENS

*J*amaica—the land of sunny Caribbean beaches, reggae music, and Rastafarian culture. Wrong! If that's what you thought, you were obviously not from New York. No, *the* Jamaica, in my life, was the bustling but grimy transportation hub of Southeast Queens. It was the terminal point of all rapid forms of transportation traveling eastbound within the city of New York. It is where the elevated trains and subway systems came to die, and the Long Island Railroad merely passed through on its way to the promised land of the suburbs. It was as if the city planners had decided nothing past this point was worth traveling to.

The Queens hamlet of Jamaica did not even get its name from the same native words as its namesake vacation destination. However, it is notable for the birth of one Maria Theresa Romano in Queens General Hospital on a sunny June morning in 1949.

I didn't live there. It was just that Jamaica held the nearest hospital to Cambria Heights, where I would spend the first sixteen years of my life. Later, I would discover the supreme irony of the fact that the first real love of my life, John Cippitelli (henceforth

Johnny Cipp), was born a day later in the same hospital. Our cribs could have been side by side. Hell, we might have held hands before we could talk. If we had stayed together, we could have literally told people that we knew each other from the cradle to the grave. But, alas, though only three blocks separated us in that Queens neighborhood, we never met until we were fourteen years old.

There were several reasons I could give for this oddity. First, there was a shitload of kids on the streets of Cambria Heights. You could spend your entire existence merely playing with the friends who lived on your actual block, never needing to expand your circle of acquaintances beyond twenty or so boys and girls whose houses you could see from your front door. Second, Johnny went to the local Catholic school while I went to PS 147. The third and most important reason for our lack of contact was "Rusty."

When I became old enough to venture to Cambria's main drag of Linden Boulevard, there were many routes we could take from my cul-de-sac off Springfield Boulevard. I never took the path that led me down 217th Street. That was where the hated Rusty could be found. He was a huge Irish setter dog who always seemed to break free from the constraints of his owner and, without fail, make a beeline for any strangers like me who darkened his turf. He didn't seem vicious, but he scared me so intensely for three years that I never came anywhere near that block.

This ritual of detouring lasted until the day I was late for meeting friends at the Cambria Movie Theater. We were going to have a quick egg cream at Newcombe's and then catch the latest matinee. However, chores at home put me behind schedule. Unable to take the roundabout route, my path took me toward "Rusty's Revenge," as we called 217th street. Sure enough, no sooner did I clear the cobblestone hill that led from my house to the danger zone than the red monster spied me and took giant strides to get to me. I froze, and he seemed mystified about why I hadn't run. He couldn't understand why I wasn't playing the chase game. Finally, his mouth opened, and huge gobs of saliva tickled my ankles.

This boy, who looked about my age, ran up to the bemused dog and the panicked girl. Grabbing him by the collar, he muttered some harsh words to the dog, resulting in Rusty depositing an equally large dose of saliva in the boy's hand.

"Sorry, what can I do?" stuttered the boy.

"Keep him on a leash," I yelled at him and walked away. Unfortunately, some of the emotion of my point was lost because I couldn't resist turning and smiling at him—he was cute. However, this twelve-year-old boy seemed too shy to notice that I was flirting. Of all the reasons mentioned, his shyness was probably the deciding factor why Johnny and I would not formally go out for another three years.

Little did I know that this harmless encounter would be the beginning of a half-century roller coaster ride of emotions for me that would turn my life upside down on more than one occasion.

# "FRANKIE AND JOHNNY"

## - JOHNNY CASH

Who was Johnny? You'll see that I will make quite a few references to him in this memoir. I did have a life before and after him. However, it seems as if my brief but passionate love for him has shaped my life in both good and bad ways. It made me do things I probably never would have done if our paths had not crossed.

Before we met, my life was not much different than thousands, if not millions, of teenage girls all over America. As a little kid, I have great memories of playing the street games prevalent in my Queens neighborhood of Cambria Heights. We played punchball, hide-go-seek, and so many others. There were many kids to play with on my block—both boys and girls. Of course, when puberty hit, those same boys now wanted to play different games with me. I was naïve, young, and most of all, Catholic. Yeah, I really was a pure, go-to-mass-every-Sunday-and-wait-until-you-get-married-for-sex-Catholic. That was okay with Johnny, at least for as long as I knew him. Perhaps it might not have worked out if the whole thing had gone on longer.

But Johnny wasn't my first boyfriend. No, a guy named Frank

had that honor. He was an absolute asshole. Of course, I didn't find this out until after we had broken up. I was stupid and allowed myself to be "fixed up" with him by my parents simply because they were friends with his parents. As you read this memoir, you will find that my mother, and especially my father were racist, misogynistic, control freaks. Therefore, the fruits of their labors were bound to be poisonous.

I was more in love with the concept of being in love than I was actually in love with Frank. Okay, that is not a great sentence for a retired English teacher. I mean, three "in loves" in the same sentence? What's with that? Anyway, you get the point. Yet looking back, I understood the physical attraction. Frank was tall, fairly-good looking—with straight blonde hair and blue eyes. He displayed a dry sense of humor that made me giggle at times. However, there was no doubt who was the boss in our relationship —his parents. I found this out towards the end of our time together.

Frank attended a commuter military academy, an attempt by his parents to give their son a boost up the social ladder. I think it was *their* attempt to social climb using their son. They hoped to jump from the lower class, blue-collar trash to acceptable society in one generation.

To digress here, we never used the word blue-collar trash to describe ourselves, but people outside our area sometimes did describe us that way simply because our economic level was lower. For those living in Cambria (especially the western section), it was a hard life that offered limited means of advancement. I realize that some kids from the neighborhood went on to college—I just didn't know any of them. Certainly, no females, but that is my story, and I'll get to that later. Back to Frank.

We were going out in the sense that young teens in the sixties went out. Not much happened, just some short dates, light kissing, and a lot of talk. Remember, I had that whole Catholic thing going on. However, Frank knew all the right things to say to keep me interested. His hoity-toity military school was going to have a *cotillion*. I had no idea what that word meant, except it was a fancy dance that would allow me to get all dressed up in a gown and, along with all the other dates, be arm candy for the military students in full dress uniform. Beautiful gown—sign me up. We talked about it often…until we didn't. As the time grew near and my parents asked about details, Frank's parents said nothing. So finally, I confronted Frank.

"What's up? My mom wants to take me for a gown, but you aren't giving up any details."

"We're not going."

"Oh, I'm so sorry. Did they cancel it? Or did something come up in your family?"

He was tongue-tied. I could tell he was having difficulty speaking. However, I was not going to let up.

"Well?"

"I'm going…you're not."

I was caught by surprise. What the hell did that mean?

"My parents decided."

"Decided what? Well? It's your parents and mine that encouraged us to go out. Now they decide I'm not good enough for you? Why?"

"My parents want me to present a classy image…you know…so that I can go places in life."

"It's not like I'm your wife or anything. But, wait…they think I'm holding you back…at fifteen years old?"

"Well, they…they think I need to present a cleaner, upper-class image."

"What the hell does that mean?"

"You're…you know…"

"No, I don't know."

"A guinea."

I thought about that conversation for the rest of my life. It was an awakening to the ignorance of certain people. We lived in a neighborhood of predominantly Irish, Italian, Jewish, and German second and third-generation immigrant families. We all got along. The indelible memory of my youth is that we joked about our differences in a way that today's attitude would not allow. We understood our slight differences and still chose to be close friends.

Frank's family was more primitive...perhaps Neanderthal in their worldview. I don't know if that is even a good description. They were a throwback to a time when only really white people were allowed in acceptable society. I don't even know Frank's background except that he always referred to it as "real American," as in, they had been here a long time.

I thought about what all this meant to me. I was full-blooded Italian with an olive complexion and long black hair, but I never thought of myself in the terms Frank now described me. Stunned, I walked away that day and only saw Frank once more—the day after the cotillion. He told me his family was moving to Nassau County, the next month. It seemed only fitting that his family was one of the first families in the "white flight" movement of the mid-sixties from Cambria Heights.

It made sense. If Frank's parents couldn't handle an olive-skinned Italian, they certainly couldn't handle African Americans' integration into the neighborhood. (People they called a variety of less kind names and wouldn't even submit to calling them "black.")

But this is my story, and despite the hurt that Frank inflicted on me, there was a more significant long-term effect of their racism. I had long understood that my parents were also racist. Before the falling out between my family and Frank's, they often talked about the neighborhood getting "bad." I knew that "bad" was code for integration. Not long after Frank's family left for the suburbs, my parents put our house up for sale—changing my life in ways I could never dream of.

# 3

# "JOHNNY ANGEL"

## - SHELLEY FABARES

However brief and ugly my relationship with Frank was, it did lead to me meeting Johnny. This isn't Johnny's story; this is mine. But my life was so affected by him that he will find his way into this memoir many times. He was the reason I went to college…and also why I dropped out. He was why I wasted four years of my life on a "Magical Mystery Tour" of America…and why I survived it. He was the reason I broke the law in 1990…and he was the reason I would gladly do it again. But mainly, he taught me how to love.

While writing this in 2012, it is hard to imagine that in the last 46 years, I have only seen Johnny once. Yet the memories are still there. So I think perhaps the feelings might still be there too.

I met Johnny through Frank, but it's not like Frank meant it to happen. He hated Johnny. That seems like a crazy statement considering they were in a band together. Frank had brought me to his band's practice, and it did not take long to realize that there was a toxic rivalry between Frank and another guitarist in the group. It also did not take long to notice that rivalry was with the dark-haired, handsome guitarist who interestingly was also Rusty's shy master.

He had filled out nicely, and more than once, Frank caught me looking at him just a bit too long. I often sat behind the band during their practices—just to look at Johnny's ass. (Time to go to confession?). I was brought up as a nice, honest girl—that whole Catholic thing again. Therefore, I would never two-time anyone, even Frank, the asshole (before I realized he fit that category). No, if I was ever going to be with Johnny, I would have to make a clean break with Frank. The whole "guinea" thing eventually took care of that matter. However, we had a relationship before Johnny and I ever dated, kissed, or anything, and it was based on the Q3A bus schedule.

Both Johnny and I commuted to Catholic high schools— different ones because all Catholic high schools were single-sex situations. Then, one day, I stayed late to have a conference with a nun, never knowing that that meeting would change my life. It's a long story, and I'll try to make it brief because I don't know if anyone born later than 1970 will even understand what happened.

My high school was a product of an America that no longer exists. My generation was the last vestige of a misogynistic, patriarchal society that deemed women inferior to men. It was a time when the dying remnants of a post-war culture believed that women were supposed to be funneled into submissive career choices —if they had careers at all. For example, women were not supposed to be doctors. Oh sure, a nurse who assisted a doctor was fine. They could be saleswomen but not managers. They were not executives, but they could be the secretary who obediently did what their boss ordered them to do. These old attitudes were in their death throes, but we didn't know.

My parents had sent me to a school where I would learn to be a secretary. I would then get a decent job for a few years and marry. Ultimately, I was destined to stay home and cater to every whim of my husband and multiple children. This lifestyle was the tract that my parents insisted I take. Become a secretary, make a little money, and then marry some fine young executive who would support me. The true threshold of being a successful man was believed to be having a wife who did not need to work. It never occurred to people that a woman might want to work, think, or want to be something other than an accessory to her husband.

Was there anyone who hadn't watched "Father's Knows Best" or "Leave it Beaver" in the sixties? In those shows, the wife was always in a dress with dinner prepared and just waiting for her husband to arrive. In the more risqué shows, "the Mrs." had a cocktail waiting for her hard-working man.

One very progressive nun (yes, all my teachers were nuns) decided to offer classes after school every day to those who *did* want to go to college. With an extra two-and-half-hour block after an already long day, she would supply us with the academic credentials for further education. It would be difficult, but I decided to think about it. I didn't know what to do. I felt that I wanted to go to college, and the extra work didn't bother me. However, my parents were going to give me hell. They would tell me that it was un-American, irreligious, and even communistic for women to work after getting married and having children. I am required to mention that they totally believed that shit. All this was going through my mind when I ran to catch the Q3A bus home at 4:30 in the afternoon. On that bus was Johnny. This was his regular schedule because he stayed after school for his fall baseball workouts.

I want to write that I was a truly liberated woman, a true daughter of Seneca Falls. I want to convince everyone that I knew that college was the road I should take, no matter the cost in time and aggravation. I would be lying. My first thought was that if I followed the study plan, I would be on the same bus as Johnny every day! I didn't have any devious intentions to cheat on Frank. I just wanted to get to know Johnny.

On that very first day, he changed my life. First, we talked about his baseball stuff, and I pretended to know and understand what he was talking about. Eventually, the conversation got around to why I was on the bus.

"I have to decide if I want to take extra classes to be able to go to college."

"Why extra? Don't you go to school full-time?" (He was half kidding.)

"Yeah, but I take typing, stenography, and transcription instead of math and foreign language."

"That stuff sounds like a foreign language to me." (His smile melted me)

"Don't get me wrong, those courses are just as hard, but they won't let me in college without the math and language requirements."

"I think you must decide if you want to attend college...and why." From a male, I thought this was a trick question designed to see if I was a normal-minded girl—suitable for dating and marriage... or was I some sort of weird duck?

"I think I do."

"Why?"

"To become a better person...to do something special. To have a career, not just a job,"

"When I watch a football game on TV, I am always amused by the cheerleaders."

"Yeah, because they're pretty," I responded, *and had big boobs*, I thought but didn't say to him.

"No, I always wonder if they wouldn't rather play the game instead of cheering for those who were?"

"That's silly. One of those girls playing football?"

"Is it?" He replied very seriously.

I looked at him, confused.

"Not everyone can make a football team or a baseball team. But why should anyone assume that the best anyone can do is cheer for others who do? Why shouldn't a woman have the same ambitions as men? I say if you want more, go for it."

I realized that I had never met a boy like Johnny. I am sure they were out there, but I hadn't seen or known them.

About two or three years before this incident, a singer named Shelley Fabares sang a song called "Johnny Angel." I now came to realize I had met him—my Johnny Angel.

4

---

# "CATCH THE WIND"

## - DONOVAN

*I* find the words lacking. But I'll try. Johnny was so many things to me that I fear I will not be able to do justice to what we had. All I can say is he made me laugh, cry, and want to live each day to the fullest. But, most of all, he made me feel so deeply and completely about everything like I never had before or after he came into my life. Sadly, this includes the years that I was married.

It all started so innocently. (Okay, there was the whole *staring at his ass* at band practice, but he didn't know about that.) Our innocuous cat-and-mouse game went on for about two months. The more I talked to him on the bus, the more I fell in love with him. Yes, I understand that we were very young. However, now that I have had a lifetime to consider the situation, I'll stick by my statement.

From the first day I said goodbye to Frank and hello to Johnny, it was magic. It's weird because I can't tell you about romantic dinners or getaway vacations. There were none. We were kids. Our entire relationship had to do with just being with each other. Sometimes it was just walking in a park where we would sneak a kiss or two. Actually, much of the making-out stuff happened in the back row of the Cambria Theater or under the boardwalk at Rockaway Beach.

That was great, but more importantly, I remember simply gazing into his beautiful green eyes as he told me fantastical stories of the future. He would always use the phrase from one of his favorite songs, "Catch the Wind," to explain that, somehow, we were both going to make it in life, and we were going to do it together.

"You and me, Maria, we are going to catch the wind out of here and to a beautiful life," I believed him. He had a dream. Better yet, he had many dreams. He was going to be a baseball star. He was going to go with me to college. But those were his backup plans. His real goal was to make music and be successful enough for us to get away from my parents. He would support me in whatever I wanted to do in my life, but first, we had to get out of the grip of my parents. His music would allow us to catch that wind until I could go to college and be what I wanted.

Our life was a fantasy for a while until the world started to throw shit at us. I tried for so long to forget all the bad things that happened in those days, and I am afraid that perhaps I succeeded to some extent.

Our first year was full of beautiful memories. It was young love at its best, and if that had been all, it might only have been categorized as simply puppy love. But as things grew tougher, we grew closer and closer, the trials and tribulations bonding us together for life. Even though Johnny suffered setback after setback, I would still hear the "Catch the Wind" speech. Even when Johnny fractured his hand, effectively ending his baseball dreams...you guessed it—*the* speech.

He lost faith in our future only once, and it cost us dearly. My parents' decision to move us to a lily-white neighborhood far from Cambria came when both Johnny and I were just turning seventeen. Because New York City residents were not allowed to drive until eighteen, Johnny and I knew we had a serious roadblock to seeing each other. On top of that, my parents wanted me to make a clean break with the city and everyone in it (i.e., Johnny). I still think I might have used a little Daddy's little girl charm to at least occasionally see Johnny…until Johnny lost his temper that one and only time.

There were so many roadblocks set before us, and still, we could think of nothing but each other. First, there was Frank and my foolish loyalty to him despite his arrogance. Then, there were my parents, who did not like Johnny from day one. They still believed I needed to put myself out there for some rich executive type to scoop up. They forbade me to see him once we had moved away. That's when Johnny's one moment of anger came at the expense of us seeing each other. Yes, it was all because of the flamingos.

# "PRETTY FLAMINGO"

## - MANFRED MANN

Our good times ended abruptly on a hot August night in 1966. I was moving the next day, and Johnny and I tried to see each other one last time. He came by in the afternoon during a break from his band practice, and my father made me tell him that I was busy packing. So we arranged to see each other after his practice, and that's when it all went to hell.

My father intercepted that rendezvous and told Johnny basically to get lost. As I looked out the window and mouthed the words "I love you," Johnny put up with insults from my father. To his credit, Johnny kept his cool (at least for a while). Then, as he turned to leave, my father hurled one final insult that Johnny could not take.

"Leave my daughter alone."

"Why? I just want to know why?"

"Because you're trash. You're not good enough for my little girl."

"I never did anything to make you think that."

"The fact that you and your family still choose to live in this neighborhood even though it is being overrun with mulanyans tells me everything I need to know."

I watched as Johnny's fury grew and his fists clenched, but he held back for my sake. He ignored my father and looked at me in the window. I again mouthed, "I love you."

Johnny would have made it off the block without incident, but my father couldn't resist one final dig as he walked back into the house. He meant for Johnny to hear it.

"Shitty parents raise shitty kids," remarked my father as he closed the door. I have not mentioned that Johnny's parents were the sweetest, most loving people I had ever met. They would end up being accomplices in allowing Johnny and me to see each other secretly for another year. I also might add that my parents had never met them and based their judgment on their choice to stay in a rapidly integrating neighborhood.

And that's where the flamingos come in.

In better times, Johnny and I would sneak good night kisses in front of my house, just out of the sight of my front windows. In the middle of my lawn stood a plastic pink flamingo. Why my father put it there, I have no idea. It does say a great deal about the lack of class in my gene pool. However, for Johnny and I, it provided comic relief. Johnny named him Fred and often had conversations with the plastic bird.

"I'm watching you." (Johnny in a falsetto bird voice)

"Nosey." (Johnny, in his own voice)

"Well, someone has to watch out for my girl Maria." (falsetto bird voice)

"She's perfectly safe with me." (Johnny)

"Yeah, sez who?" (falsetto bird voice)

"Me!" (I interrupted)

"See, I told you so." (Johnny petting the plastic head)

"You just make sure you take care of my girl." (plastic bird)

"Always." (Johnny)

But that last day, the Fred the Flamingo/Johnny relationship took a turn for the worse, and Johnny took out his anger at my father on Fred.

"I know what you're thinking, you dumb-shit bird brain. I don't care if he is your master; he's an asshole."

Silence (from the bird)

"No avian wisdom from you today?"

Silence (from the bird)

"What's the matter? Plastic cat got your plastic tongue? (Johnny)

Silence (from the bird)

As I watched from my bedroom window, Johnny laid a fierce kick on the flamingo and sent him flying twenty feet from our property and into the street. My father eventually found the crippled flamingo (he had a significant dent and had lost one of his metal legs) and placed it back on our lawn. He vocalized nothing, but we both knew who had done it.

The following day, we found that over three dozen other plastic flamingos had joined Fred on our property. Johnny and his band friends had collected all the plastic birds from the neighborhood… and placed them on my lawn. Later, he told me they called it the "Great Flamingo Round-up of 1966."

My father knew who had done it. I considered it Johnny's supreme act of defiance to my father …and love for me. (Okay, and maybe just a little "I'm sorry" to Fred.)

I will never forget Johnny's gesture, and neither did my father. He would not even let me glimpse Johnny as we left the neighborhood for good. I was forbidden ever to see him again.

At least Fred was happy for the company.

# "SLOW DANCIN'"

## - JOHNNY RIVERS

My family left our home in Cambria and moved to the suburbs. I never saw Fred (or all his new friends) again. However, despite my father's best efforts, I did see Johnny secretly for the following year. I was still in the same high school, and so was he, so we would meet at the bus terminal, spend some time, and then take separate buses home. Sometimes, I would go to my old neighborhood friend Diane's house, and Johnny would meet me there. The bottom line was that we did see each other—just not as much as we wanted. However, our love grew stronger.

Johnny's band was on the brink of financial and musical success, and we had planned to use that success as an opportunity to get away from my parents. I never forgave them for that last day in Cambria. As a parent now, I understand what they were trying to do, but they were wrong. They only drove us closer together by demanding that I stop seeing Johnny. If they had let us be, maybe we would have tired of each other or realized how young we were. I don't think that would have happened, but I guess we'll never know. The more they kept us apart, the more we wanted to be with each other. Our love went underground.

Would it be a cliché for a former English teacher to quote Dickens and say, "It was the best of times, and it was the worst of times?" We found ways, and that's all I will say. The year was challenging, and it was beautiful. I can't and won't try to recap all that happened. I can only try to make my story understood by explaining our last two times together.

On June 3, 1967, I told my parents that Diane and I were going to a dance at a local church hall. I didn't tell them that Johnny's band was playing there. The night was the pinnacle of our relationship. I could not know how bad things would be afterward, but that night was beautiful.

However, that night was about more than us.

A big shot was coming to see Johnny's band, and if he approved, they would have a good shot at a record contract and steady work. The band was exceptional that night, and when Mr. Big Shot gave the band the news, all hell broke loose. First, Diane and I went up to the stage and celebrated with the guys, and Johnny and I snuck away for some celebratory passionate kisses. Then, when it was time for the band to come back from their break, I was surprised to find Johnny in my arms. The band had told him to be with me while they played a romantic song for us to dance to.

I will never hear that tune again without thinking of those moments in Johnny's arms. I know every word of the song that was the first and last dance of our lives, "Slow Dancin'" by Johnny Rivers. Though Johnny was not a great singer (actually, he was horrible), he spoke the words in my ear as he held me tightly.

*And we're slow dancin', swayin' to the music*
*Slow dancin', just me and my girl*
*Slow dancin', swayin' to the music*
*No one else in the whole wide world just you, girl*

I melted in his arms and never wanted the moment to end. As it was sung by Johnny's best buddy and lead singer, Gio, every lyric had so much meaning and sent shivers down my spine. Johnny separated ever so slightly so that he could look me in the eyes. He mouthed the words...

*As we dance together in the dark*
*So much love in this heart of mine*
*You whisper to me, hold you tight*
*You're the one I thought I'd never find*

We snuck in an illicit kiss that the patrolling nuns and priests did not see, and tears of happiness filled my eyes. Finally, we were going to make it. Despite my parents and all the other obstacles we faced, we knew our love would get us through. And, as if the song had been written just for us, the lyrics came to its dramatic tempo change. As Gio sang the words, I whispered them to Johnny as I looked into his eyes…

*Hold me, oh, hold me,*
*No, never let me go.*

And Johnny did just that. He held me so tight that I thought I would burst with joy…and love…and… happiness…and whatever else a human being could feel.

And then that dance was over. I could not know then that it would be the only dance I would ever have with Johnny. I would only see him one more time before he would disappear from my life and the world as we knew it.

As I write this memoir in 2012, it is hard to imagine that in the last 45 years, I have only seen Johnny once since he disappeared. Yet the memories are still there. I think perhaps the feelings might also still be there.

When I saw him for that brief period in 1990, I read the journal he had written. It was heartbreaking. I wanted to take him in my arms and make the pain disappear. I didn't. I was married, and I loved my family. I went on to live my life, and he went on to live his. I have not heard from him, and I don't expect to. Johnny was such a good person that he would never do anything that would affect the happiness of others—including my husband and children. He might have felt something. Hell, I might have felt something, but we did nothing. And so, I will continue my tale—understanding that I have no idea what happened to him after those few weeks in 1990—never knowing what could have been in 1967, 1990, or now.

Most of the thoughts that swirled in my head after our brief encounter revolved around reading his journal. The "Journal of Johnny Cipp," as he called it, was a heart-wrenching account of his life up until that point. I guess the thoughts and feelings he conveyed will somehow find their way into the pages of this memoir.

As I wrote, Johnny liked to speak in song titles and lyrics. He said that they created a soundtrack for his life. He didn't have a name for this feeling when we were young, but by the time he wrote his journal, he was imbuing a magical quality to someone called the Music Doctor. He was this imaginary person who stood looking over his shoulder and whispered the titles to him. Hey, Music Doctor, do you want to join my Magical Mystery Tour? Do you want to title my memoir entries?

After all, I tried to "Catch the Wind" too—just not with Johnny.

# "LOVE HURTS"

## - EVERLY BROTHERS

ohnny disappeared in September 1967. Though I felt all the emotions of abandonment—anger, frustration, and confusion, my overriding feeling was one of fear. Soon after our last dance, Johnny's band, Those Born Free, had been invited for one final head-to-head competition with another band, with the prize being a permanent music gig and a record contract. Johnny's band won easily, but then things went tragically wrong.

I don't think I can bring myself to recount the horrors of that time. Three band members died under mysterious circumstances during that long, hot summer of 1967. Only Johnny and Gio were still around by the fall, and then, in September, they also disappeared. It would be more than two decades before I discovered that Johnny had fled. I know now that Johnny also ran to save *my* life. I didn't know that then, so I grieved for his life and my abandonment.

After our dance, I only saw Johnny one last time. Diane's family had invited mine over for a Fourth of July BBQ, and we had snuck off while our parents were getting drunk and weren't looking.

Johnny was waiting for me. He tried to give me a tiny silver ring to symbolize our bond. He wanted a physical commitment so that I would know that no matter what happened, he would stand by me. I didn't take that ring because the romantic in me thought I didn't need outward symbols to prove that I loved him. Sadly, I remember the exact words I said to him that day.

"Johnny, I will wait as long as you want for us to be together. No ring is going to change that. I've told you before that I want you to come to me when your journey is over. I will take that ring when you have found your way in the world. Your way…get it? Only then will I know that you are okay. Only then can I join you."

He tried to answer me, but I tenderly ended that attempt with a kiss. Then, I placed the ring back on his pinkie.

However, I didn't wait forever for him. Instead, I went off the deep end, and that is the story that follows. The day after our meeting, the first member of his band died under questionable circumstances. Two more deaths in two months, and Johnny was gone.

# "HOW LONG BEFORE YOU BREAK MY HEART"

## - MIKE DELGUIDICE

The rest of 1967 is a blur. I fought with my parents constantly and was angry at everyone and everything on this whole god-damned planet. Probably not the way to start college and hope for a new life. I had no friends. I went to Queens College, a commuter school, and had almost no interaction with anyone before heading home each day to continue bickering with my parents.

I probably only stayed as long as that one semester because I had worked hard to get there and needed to prove that I could do it. My long extra classes in high school earned me admission into one of the finest free schools in America. However, when I thought of those long afternoons of additional classes, my thoughts always returned to the bus ride home with Johnny. This led to more depression.

After the first week of my second semester, my whole point of view started to change…started to evolve. It all began when I arrived home one day and found a stranger sitting with my parents. As I entered the front door, my father quickly engaged me. Let me rephrase that—my father jumped all over me.

"I told this cop…excuse me…this police officer, that you have not seen that Johnny Cipp character in over a year and a half—since we got out of that nightmare neighborhood," ranted my father before I had even taken off my coat.

"Is that true?" asked this plain-clothes detective sitting in my den. This would be my first but by no means last encounter with Richie Shea, police detective…and somehow incredulously mob-connected criminal. He would insert himself into my life in the ensuing years and even decades. His red hair was slicked back, and the suit adorning his large body seemed just a bit too expensive for a civil servant's budget. It is not that I was any kind of expert on men's attire, but this had a fit and design like nothing I had ever seen.

"Tell him, Maria," interjected my mother.

I hesitated. I had hidden my meetings with Johnny for more than a year from their watchful eyes—only getting caught once. Should I tell them that we had remained incredibly close until he disappeared four months ago? I probably should have shocked them with my long history of sneaking off to see Johnny. I should have thrown in their face my deceit—just to tick them off. I would have…had not been for one significant factor—I didn't trust this red-headed liar sitting across from my parents. And I confirmed that he was lying with his next statement.

"We are looking into Cipp concerning the possible murder of Gio De Angelis," Shea revealed with a voice of authority. *Liar, liar, liar.*

"See! I told you that Johnny was no good. Now, do you see that you should listen to your parents? We always know what's right," screeched my father with an air of vindication.

Shea stared me down—his piercing blues eyes attempting to cut through to my soul. His provocative statement had been meant solely to view my reaction. I was very proud of my stone-cold demeanor in answering him. My father blathered on as Shea and I continued our stare-down confrontation.

"And what would make you say that? Why would you blame Johnny for Gio's…what?…his kidnapping…his death?" I curtly and softly broke the silence.

"Oh, we had reports of a disagreement between the two of them about a band and a girl."

"From whom did you get these reports?" I asked as I ignored the background chatter of my mom and dad.

"I'm sorry. That's confidential," Shea quickly responded.

"You're lying," I replied with confidence. *I almost gave him precisely what he wanted by saying that I was Johnny's girl and there had been no fighting over me.* Fortunately, I quickly recognized that was what he wanted me to say. I walked out of the room to the dissatisfaction of both my parents and the lying son-of-a-bitch cop.

I knew that Johnny and Gio had been the greatest of friends until the very end. As I now suspected, if Johnny had run away, he probably had done it *with* Gio.

Twenty-three years later, upon reading Johnny's journal, I would find out the real truth. On that long ago September 1967 day, Gio had died saving Johnny's life.

9

# "GIVING UP"

## - THE HASSLES

I've tried hard *not* to talk too much about Johnny Cipp in this memoir. I loved him so much that it may have affected all my relationships for the rest of my life. Everything about our time together was beautiful…until he disappeared without a word. Then, I met him again years after my wild and crazy years on the road. I probably could have run away with him and finally fulfilled the fantasies that I had had for over two decades. He wanted it. I wanted it.

However, I was married, and my family was important to me. So, case closed. That did not stop the fantasies from creeping into my thoughts and feelings. Perhaps my attitude might have differed if we had broken up like typical teenage romances often did. I never had closure. I had to move on without knowing whether Johnny was still alive or not—or if he still cared for me.

However, the fact that this detective was searching for him, officially or unofficially, meant that he believed that Johnny was alive. Yet my glance at his displayed credentials told me he was a homicide detective. So why was he looking for a "missing" person?

The facts just weren't adding up, and for the first time, I started to think about investigating Johnny's disappearance myself. Of course, I would later find out exactly why Shea was on the case. However, at that time, I only had vague suspicions.

Until January 1968, I was in college and living at home. I had not engaged in social life since Johnny's disappearance four months before. This is unusual for any 18-year-old, but it bordered on absurdity for me, a college freshman. I had done less than nothing to broaden my horizons. I had made no new friends in college and was as lonely as hell.

On campus, I had seen Johnny's non-band best friend, DJ Spinelli. I know he had tried to make contact with me, but I had successfully eluded him so far. Maybe it was time to see if he knew anything about Johnny that I did not. I finally met with him during the first week of the second semester. We talked after class, and he knew slightly more than I did about his friend's disappearance. He had the nerve to go to Johnny's house and see his parents. As he explained their emotional breakdown and lack of knowledge of Johnny's whereabouts, it made me comprehend the severity of the situation. For Johnny to abandon them, the most loving and supportive people I knew, he had no other choice. He was either dead or on the run. But where?

The day after my talk with DJ, I immediately thought about where Johnny might run (if he could run at all). I began to play with the idea of searching for him for the first time or at least thinking about the fact that he would never be found.

"Giving Up." It was a little-known song by a little-known Long Island group named The Hassles. Well, that's not entirely true. Gladys Knight sang the song in 1964. So I don't know if I am unconsciously being racist when I say the song meant nothing to me until I heard it sung by The Hassles.

Toward the first semester's end, I started talking to a girl named Val. She had missed some classes (actually, more than some), and often asked if she could borrow my notes. She didn't come across as a user, just someone who was overwhelmed. When we again found ourselves in the same class the second semester, she approached me about getting a coffee together in the student center. It was time for me to join the human race. I accepted. After a few minutes, I realized why she had missed so many classes.

"What are you doing Saturday night?" she asked totally out of the blue. She didn't strike me as the party animal type, but this was college.

"Nothing. My social calendar is empty," I blurted out but realized that I might sound desperate, so I added, "And I like it that way."

"Nobody, I mean absolutely nobody, likes to be alone."

"You've never seen me in action, or rather inaction. I perfected the art of sitting in my room and staring at a wall better than anyone you know."

"You're nuts, but I like you," was all she responded, and I thought that was the end of the conversation. To be honest, I was disappointed. I liked talking to her and was warming up to the idea of getting out there.

She reached into her pocket and pulled out a wad of tickets to some event. She peeled off two and handed them to me. They were for a show at My Father's Place, obviously a music concert hall. At first, I recoiled because the thought of listening to any band play brought back memories of Johnny and his band and all our wonderful times. I could not help but associate music and Johnny, and therefore music and heartbreak. Even as she slipped the tickets into my hand, I couldn't tell Val all this. Then, finally, I noticed the price of the tickets and reacted—$10 each.

"Val, that's a lot of money, and I may not...I probably won't use them," I murmured, trying to give them back.

"First of all, I owe you so much more than this for all the help you have given me this semester. And second, these didn't cost me anything."

"What's that mean?"

"They're comped because...well... my band, Hour Tyme, is the opening act for The Hassles. They're up-and-coming superstars."

"Wait a minute. You play in a band?"

"Yup, why do you think I missed so many classes? Did you think I was just a cut-up—a loser?" Quickly, her serious, faux-angry rant was followed by a broad smile. "When you're playing until two or three in the morning, it is hard to get up for an 8 o'clock class."

"You must be pretty good if they charge that much for tickets."

"We are pretty good. But no one is paying that money to see us. We are just 'arm candy' for the guys in the crowd to enjoy while waiting to see the stars."

"So..."

"You got it. All four of us are female...and proud of it."

"Arm candy?" I knew Val was beautiful and now had to assume so were the rest of her group.

"Use what you got," she boasted, laughing in an unassuming way that told me she knew exactly what she and her band had. Yet she was not obnoxiously vain. "Hey, I know this band gig will not last forever—and to be perfectly honest, I guess neither will my looks. That's why I'm in college—to make something of myself."

Maybe Val and I could have become good friends...if I hadn't taken her up on her offer and gone to see Hour Tyme...and the Hassles.

In reality, it is stupid for a single girl to go to a club alone. I didn't have the confidence Val had in my looks, but I can glance into a damn mirror and know I like what I see. Unfortunately, being unaccompanied by anyone made me one of the top targets of a wide variety of pickup artists. After all, I was not burdened by another female that the pickup artist would have to convince his wingman to be interested in. It was amazing how well I knew the game for someone who had never played it.

After Val's band finished their set (they were very good), she came to my rescue. She led me over to a table where two guys sat— the only two guys in the club that I did not need to worry about. They were the boyfriends of the drummer, Christine, and bass guitarist, Val herself.

"Maria, this is Jimmy, Christine's guy, and this is Billy, who belongs to me."

"Hey, being a male groupie is tough enough to start with but… 'belongs to me' is a bit much," and this good-looking guy got up to walk away. He got about three steps away and turned around with a big smile."

"He does this all the time," whispered Val to me, and ran and jumped into his arms. It was quite a passionate kiss that followed. Soon we were all sitting at the table, and I enjoyed the company. It was good to get out and do something and be with people. Inexplicably, I quickly put a negative spin on the whole affair. I had thought that maybe I had a friendship developing with Val. I know she would be great in helping me reacquaint myself with society. However, she barely had time for her band career and college—and now you throw in a full-time serious boyfriend in the mix? There are only so many hours in the day. Ironically, I must add that Val was the bass guitar in the group, just like Johnny had been in his group. And how did that work out?

As depression reared its ugly head and started seeping into my mood's fringes, I tried desperately to remain upbeat.

The Hassles began to play.

"Wait until you hear this keyboard player on the Hammond organ," yelled Val over the din of the group's opening song, appropriately named "Warming Up."

"You've seen them before?" I asked.

"Well, this isn't the first time we've opened for them. The whole basement of this place is a sort of dressing room for both groups before we come on. So we got to know each other a bit."

I listened as the crowd cheered on their favorite songs like "You Got Me Hummin'" and "Every Step I Take," and I realized that the group had a certain star power. Nevertheless, as I write this in 2012, I know they never made it. Except for those two minor hits, stardom avoided their grasp. Well, at least for four of the five.

"Wait until you hear this," gushed Val enthusiastically. "It's my favorite by them… and the keyboard player takes over the lead singing. If you ask me, he's better than their front man."

"What's his name?" I asked.

"Billy Joe, no Billy Joel."

Okay, I led you right into that little tangent of my story. However, it had a purpose. When *the* Billy Joel sang the next song, it changed my life.

---

It was an unusual beginning to this very slow and melodic song. The organ powerfully hit variations of two chords while the drummer followed by doing a roll on the ceiling. Well, not the ceiling per se but a beam that hung from the ceiling, thus creating a unique wooden sound punctuating the organ chords. It's hard for me to explain this song to someone who has never heard it. But it worked. My emotions were drawn into the whole attitude of "Giving Up."

Billy Joel started to sing,

*Givin' up…*
*Is hard to do*
*when you really love someone.*

My mind began to swirl, and a haze came over me. I forgot Val, her Billy, and all the others at the table and was transfixed by the singing of another Billy who someday would become world-famous. His voice was so emotional, and I felt he was singing only to me. This was so true that I twisted all the pronouns I heard to fit my story.

*His warm and tender touch,*
*His kiss and his caress,*
*That used to mean so much*
*And bring me happiness*

Giving up was all that I could think of. Johnny, you left me. You gave up.

*The light of hope burns dim,*
*but in my heart, I pray.*
*My love and faith in him,*
*Will bring him back someday.*

Giving up is so hard to do. But I did. I gave up that day. I gave up that very moment. Without a word to Val, I got up from the table and left.

When I got home, my parents were waiting. The pressure was constant—the nagging insufferable.

"Do something! Do something! Do something." They harassed and badgered me. So, I did something…I left home.

After they were asleep, I quietly packed a bag, took some money I had hidden under my bed, and left. I took a cab to New York City and a train to Chicago from there. I fooled myself at first into thinking I was seeking out Johnny by picking a destination where I might find him. Later, I would understand the reality that I was giving up on him. Instead, I was searching for something, anything, to give my life purpose and meaning.

# PART II

# "CHICAGO"

## - CROSBY, STILLS, NASH, AND YOUNG

*"We change the world,
Rearrange the world."*

The Windy City
(1968)

10

# "SHE'S LEAVING HOME"

## - THE BEATLES

Chicago? Was I freaking kidding? Yet that was where I ended up. I know that I was there because of Johnny. But was it because he made me stronger or weaker?

He had always encouraged me to follow my dreams no matter the cost. He had made me a more independent individual. Johnny had been the one who encouraged me to go to college. In fact, with the demise of his band, we were set to start Queens College together. Then without a word, he was gone.

I can't help but think that my weakness also led me to be here in Chicago. Was I such a love-struck, immature little girl that I gave up when Johnny left? I threw away all the work I put into getting into college. I left my family and friends. Scratch that. My family was one of the reasons I took off. They were obsessive about controlling my life, about telling me what to do. They had forbidden me from seeing Johnny while he was around and had no sympathy for me when he was gone. And friends…I had none.

And that's why I boarded a Greyhound bus and traveled to Chicago. Johnny always talked about how this was the Mecca for blues music. He used to dream that someday he would like to hear the Chicago blues sound. He was a student of music and made me aware that this "Chicago style" was just Mississippi Delta blues that black performers like Muddy Waters, Howlin' Wolf, and others had brought to the North. He wanted to experience it. Therefore, I reasoned that he might be here. When I ran, I had to go somewhere. Chicago is as good as any.

I was amazed at my ability to adapt and control the world around me. I had always been so sheltered in my existence. When I was young, my parents taught me that someone would always care for me. Though I left without any thought to this, I learned how to deal with everything thrown my way.

I found a room to rent. It wasn't much, but I had brought my life savings with me, including money that dated back to first communion gifts. I used this money as a stake for all the essentials in life while I figured out my next move. I was very proud of myself.

I eventually got a job. Johnny would have found it ironic that I spent my days at Wrigley Field, home of the Chicago Cubs, and my nights at blues clubs, both searching for him and soaking in the music. Music and baseball were his two loves (besides me).

Not a glorious job. I cleaned the stadium in preparation for the upcoming season. Perhaps, the worst part of the job was cleaning the troughs. The stadium was so ancient that they did not even have urinals in the men's room, but rather 20-foot-long metal basins. I was glad this was not baseball season, and the urinals were not in daily use. It was disgusting.

I did meet some of the people who I would come to call friends there. We laughed and told jokes and poured out our hearts to each other. We shared our youth, our crummy job, and one other thing —a love of music. While working, we sang and talked about the current crop of pop stars. We also decided to explore the world of blues music together. And so, we hit the clubs, especially the blues clubs on the South Side. Probably, not the safest place for naïve young white kids, but we threw caution to the wind and decided to go where we wanted to go.

Sara became my best friend. She was the only one in the group from Chicago. A beautiful girl with long blonde hair and blue eyes, she had an endearing smile and a devoted love of her city. Working with her, I realized the pain and anguish she suffered as a Cubs fan. As a Yankee and Met fan (yes, I could be both), I tried hard to sympathize with her plight. I mean, the Cubs had not won a World Series since before our grandparents were born.

As a Yankee fan, I was mortified that the Yanks had not been in the series for three years and hadn't won in five. As a Met fan, I knew they were a relatively new team (1962), and I had to have patience. Little did I know then that they would perform a miracle and win the championship of baseball the following year, only their seventh year of existence. Also, little did I know that by then, I would be on to the next phase of my life and would not even know of their impressive feat. Nonetheless, Sara had humor about her plight as a fan of the Cubs and often wore a tee-shirt throughout that spring of 1968 that simply stated, "Chicago Cubs—Rebuilding since 1908."

Lars and Jesse were brothers who were tall, strong, and handsome. In the manner of the times, they proffered a shaggy look in both the length of their blonde hair and budding facial hair. They had come from Minnesota in search of excitement in the big city. While they found their way, they cleaned the troughs just like me and hit the blues clubs at night.

Lars was by far the more outgoing of the two and displayed a sharp sense of humor. He was the de facto leader of our little group. Jesse was younger and shorter than his brother but the better-looking of the two. He was my best male friend in the group. We talked long into the night on many an occasion. He would have been the one if I had been looking for a love interest. But, instead, I was still hooked on the long-gone Johnny.

Though others came and went in our little crew, Dax Lightfeather was the only other core member of our group. The son of a black mother and Lakota Sioux father, he had a deep, brooding personality. He was our social conscience, our call to arms when the shit hit the fan—and the shit hit the fan quite often in Chicago in 1968.

Physically, he was an enigma. He was tall and robust but decidedly looked both Native American and black simultaneously. This fit in with his conflicted mental state, often leading him to switch his racial profile as he saw fit. In other words, sometimes he acted as a black man and sometimes as a Native American. We didn't care which Dax showed up on any given day. He was a true friend…no matter what persona he was in.

The five of us did many things together. We worked hard, and we played even harder. We laughed often and cried sometimes.

Many other friends came and went into our little group, but the five of us remained the closest. That may be because we all worked together at Wrigley Field. Many more people were working there, but we were the "Young-uns," as some older workers referred to us. That was okay because they mostly liked us.

We worked well together and joked our way through the days. Each night found us at the rock or blues clubs throughout Chicago. The music bound us together, and though our fellow workers called us the "Young-uns," we alternately called ourselves the "Wrigley Rockers." It was not like we were a gang…or a club or anything. It was easier to say things like, "Let's get all the Wrigley Rockers together tonight," or "Do you think the Wrigley Rockers will want to go to this or that club?" As I said, sometimes our numbers swelled to double digits, but only the five of us were charter members.

As rooms became available in the Trelawney Building, we all started to gravitate there. It was an easy train ride to both work and the clubs. We could afford these decent accommodations because Sara and I had become roommates, and the brothers, Lars and Jesse Johansen had tripled up with Dax. So now we were all living, working, and clubbing together. This would lead to some interesting hookups in the future…but that's getting ahead of my story.

The only time that the group was not together was when I split off to spend more time searching for Johnny at the more obscure blues clubs of the city. The gang loved me but told me they could only take so much of the blues over rock.

More and more, I realized that my search for Johnny was futile. I had been in enough clubs on enough nights that I would have run into him if he had been here. I worked very hard to get over him, or at least put thoughts of him on the back burner of my life. Though I used Johnny as an excuse, I realized I was getting into the music of the blues clubs, especially the Biloxi Blues Club.

# 11

# "CROSS ROADS BLUES"

## - ROBERT JOHNSON

*"I'm standin' at the crossroads.
I believe I'm sinkin' down."*

He was old. Damn, he was ancient—at least in the eyes of the nineteen-year-old version of me. Nevertheless, somehow, we struck up a friendship. His name was Smokey Joe Watson, and it was evident how he got his name. An unfiltered cigarette dangled from his lips 24/7. Though Smokey Joe would never tell his age, many guessed him to be in his late eighties. Still, his beaten and abused appearance could have resulted from a younger man who had endured a tortured past.

He was like a kindly old uncle, or great-uncle, or even great-great-uncle to me. I looked forward to our talks in between his sets at the Biloxi Blues Club, and I enjoyed his long sets of Mississippi Delta Blues songs. For a time, I forgot about Johnny and my own story of abandonment. But, I had not hidden it well enough for Smokey Joe not to notice.

"How old is you?" I was surprised by his question.

"19," I answered without much thought.

"You is too young to have a lifetime of blues inside you."

"I guess," was my stupid answer.

"It is what drew me to you. The blues can always see the blues."

"I'm too young to have had a hard life," I told him, thinking it was a wise answer.

"You is never too young for nothin'."

I told him my story, and I was afraid that it was silly. But he just looked at me and shook his head.

"You is never too young …to be feelin'."

"Feeling what?"

"Feelin' your heart." I felt that he wanted to hug me, but Smokey had grown up in the Jim Crow South. He knew that black men did not touch white girls, at least not in public—and live to tell about it.

"Yeah, Johnny and me had something special," I mumbled and let my first smile show at that revelation.

"I knowed it. You is still holdin' your blood."

"What's that mean?" I looked at him in total confusion.

"You is…you is a virgin."

"Well, yeah, Johnny and I were old fashioned…and Catholic. We were waiting to be married. But how did you know?"

"You stick out like a black man at a KKK meeting. You don't have to worry about people like me. I's too old, but you watch for some of the young studs like him." He nodded toward Trio Walker, a newcomer to the scene who could play the guitar and sing with incredible skill.

"Why?"

"He only cares about three things: women, whiskey, and playin' the blues…and he's got the devil in him."

"Oh so, he's some kind of bad boy?"

"No, he just not bad…he got the devil in him. I only know'd

one other person in my life who be like that…my friend Robert Johnson.

Now I knew that Robert Johnson, the first heralded star of the genre, had died in 1938 at a very young age, and many had considered him the first great blues star. The fact that Smokey Joe had played with him was amazing. So I had to know more.

"Me and him did the whole circuit of juke joints in the South through the 30s. Now here's the part you want to listen to really careful like. Robert Johnson weren't no good at the guitar until he go to the crossroads."

"What are you talking about, Smokey?"

"Robert, he go missing for a year in the early 30s. Some folks say they heard him playing in a graveyard all the time. Sometimes with someone else. Now, we don't know if that be true, but at the end of that year he come back, he be playin' and singin' like no one ever before him."

"So, he did a lot of practicing."

"Or not. The story goes that he went down to the crossroads of Routes 49 and 61 in Mississippi...at midnight. There, he give his guitar to the devil. When the devil give it back, the deal was complete. He would be the greatest blues guitarist and singer ever —but the devil owned his soul."

"You know, I think I heard that legend. They were talking about it when Cream released its 'Crossroads' song last week."

"I don't know Cream, but I knowed Robert. And I knowed something else that no one in this whole world be knowin'. We be drinkin' in the bar on August 15, 1938, and he opens his shirt. Now I don't know what he's thinkin', but then he points to a tiny tattoo on his stomach. All it were was but three threes sittin' there no bigger than the nail on my pinkie."

"I don't get it."

"Well, I be a God-fearin' man who would never be goin' down

to no crossroads no matter what the devil be givin' me. But we all knew the stories about the devil-man and his price."

"What stories?"

"You see, the Lord God branded the devil with the number 666. It's right there in Revelations for all to see. It was the mark of the devil. But what would the devil mark those who is his own? Not 666. No, he have too much pride for that. But what if he gave them a mark of 333 to show they belongs to him, but was not as powerful as him?"

"You don't believe all that malarkey. Do you?"

'Girlie, you gotta learn how to cuss better if you be hangin' down here."

"Excuse me. You don't believe all that *shit*, do you?"

"Yes, I do, and I tell you one other thing that no one else in the whole world done know. Robert Johnson tell me the night before he died one more thing about his 333 mark."

"Okay, I followed the story so far, so go on."

"You see, Robert, he figure out more than anyone else about the 333. He figures out that the devil is more sneaky than we men think he is. See, the 333 was a ciphering thing. It stood for 3 time 3 time 3."

"So what's that mean?"

"Come on, your fancy white schools must of taught you ciphering. What's 3 time 3 time 3?

"It's 27. So what?"

"You know'd what year Robert was born? 1911. Do you know what year he died? 1938?

"Yeah?"

"So, he was 27 when the devil came for him—just like the mark said. Now you can believe me or call me a crazy old black man, but I know'd what Robert told me, and I know'd what happened. He died the next day of poisoning...in his stomach... just where the mark be."

"C'mon, you don't believe that crap?"

"We'll first, let me say your cussin' be gettin' better. And yes'em, I believe it, and you best be doin' so too."

"Why?"

"Because that Trio Walker got a little 333 mark on the top of his forehead. You can barely see it unless he moves his hair back. But it's there."

"Even if I believe all this, what's that got to do with me?"

"I see the way he be lookin' at you! So, you best mind what I'm sayin'." He can smell your… you know."

"Virginity? Bullshit!"

"I'm just a fool old man, but sometimes I knows what I'm talkin' about."

I loved that old man until the day he died. He told me many more stories, but the one about Robert Johnson and the crossroads always stuck in my head. At first, I didn't know why. But later events might have proven the wisdom of Smokey Joe's story.

I am writing this in 2012 with the knowledge of what happened in the ensuing years, not only to me but to…

Janis Joplin died at 27 years old. Jimi Hendrix died at 27. Jim Morrison died at 27. Brian Jones died at 27. Kurt Cobain died at 27. Amy Winehouse died at 27. Some snarky writer christened these musical greats as the "27 Club." I have to scratch my head and remember Smokey Joe's story. Had they all been down to the crossroads?

12

# "TAKE ME OUT TO THE BALLGAME"

## - ROBERT NORWOOD

$C$racker Jacks and a home run in the bottom of the ninth may have changed my life.

By April, the whole Wrigley Rockers crew had been hired as vendors. That's a big deal. Only some people make it to that prestigious level. How we handled our winter jobs with humor and camaraderie made management hire us for the season. Our job was to go out there and hawk their overpriced beer, soda, hot dogs, peanuts, Cracker Jacks, and (ugh) cotton candy.

It was an agreed-upon fact that we all hated selling cotton candy the most. At the end of the day, every single morsel of our existence was sticky. It was in our hair, our clothes, and up our nostrils. I hated my cotton candy days. The beer and soda were almost as bad as the drinks always found a way to spill. Yet, the beer days were especially good tip days, so we gladly put up with the mess. Hot dog days were okay, but Cracker Jack days were the best —no mess, no bother. On a good Cracker Jack day, you almost didn't have to shower after work. That April day was a Cracker Jack day for me.

The other good part about being a vendor at Wrigley Field was that all games were day games. This was the last place in Major League Baseball that did not have night games. Even the White Sox across town had most of their games at night. However, the neighborhood surrounding Wrigley had fought long and hard to prevent the installation of lights. At times (like that day), this could present problems.

The game was all set up to be a short and sweet Cubs' loss. Though Sara was the only diehard fan of the team, we all rooted for them. Happy fans bought more of what we were selling, and we mainly worked on commission. Longer games meant more money, but short and sweet games meant a head-start on our nighttime activities. I had already started organizing our nightly agenda when Ernie Banks hit a home run in the bottom of the ninth to tie the game. Extra innings—endless extra innings. In fact, they had to suspend the game for darkness before it could be completed.

I had decided that it wasn't worth heading back to the apartment. My plan for the evening was to go straight to the clubs. After all, I had had a Cracker Jack day. Unfortunately, the others hadn't been so lucky and were less agreeable to my plan.

"How about it, Sara? Hit the Biloxi?"

"Look at me, Maria?"

"Cotton candy?"

"Yes, Maria, and for thirteen innings!"

I understood and sympathized. Soda and beer covered Lars, Jesse, and Dax, so they also chose to go home and shower. They were not meeting any girls that night, smelling and looking like they did. They all told me that they would meet up with me later.

I needed to hear the blues that night. I needed to talk with Smokey Joe Watson. I just needed to get away from it all—and immediately. And so, it was that because of Cracker Jacks and Ernie Banks, I ended up at the Biloxi Blues Club on April 4, 1968, at 6 p.m. with Smokey Joe and no one else. That was when the world came crumbling down.

13

# "ABRAHAM, MARTIN, AND JOHN"

## - DION DIMUCI

Smokey Joe had played the blues. Smokey Joe had lived the blues—but I had never seen him cry.

He had arrived early at the club to do some warming up, and I had come straight from Wrigley. He was distraught. He said nothing but merely pointed to the TV. That moment now seems such a blur to me. So many emotions pounded in my brain.

"They killt him. They killt a good and just man. How could they do that?"

"Smokey, who? Who did they kill?"

"The reverend Martin. He be like no other man that lived, except maybe the Lord God Jesus himself."

"Oh, Smokey, I'm so sorry."

He looked at me forlornly and said nothing. He started to strum some chords and mumbled some bluesy riffs about death. I couldn't understand what he was saying and stared at him. He did this for a while. He had had a rough life, yet this seemed to be the toughest moment he had ever endured. It became so clear to me that, as a young white girl, I could never really understand his story or the story of any black person in America. Finally, he looked me in the eyes and spoke.

"What are you sorry about? You didn't shoot him. I's been around this world long enough to know that there are evil white people who will do me and mine wrong. But you is not one of them. You is a good, kind person."

I cried.

"I'll be heading home now. No blues playin' tonight. We is all livin' them."

He didn't look right. He looked more feeble and older than I had ever seen him. I worried about him.

"Let me take you home."

"You isn't trying to come on to me now?" He let the slight glimpse of a smile slip from his face. It was the only smile that I would see on him that night. I was going to say something clever to go with his joke, but it seemed the wrong time.

He didn't live far, but even the short trip seemed a burden. He took my arm for support, and I carried his guitar with my free hand. Ever so slowly, we found our way to his apartment. I helped him in, made some hot tea, and eventually tucked him in bed. While waiting for him to fall asleep, I turned on his TV. I watched in horror as scenes of rioting throughout the country were shown. Was everyone I knew in New York okay? Years later, I learned eleven people died in Chicago that night. I'm glad that I didn't know that at the time.

As I left his building, I was terrified. Jim Croce had not yet written his song "Bad, Bad Leroy Brown," which had the immortal phrase about the "South Side of Chicago" being "the baddest part of town," but we all knew that to be true even in 1968. And with the anger and riots out in the streets, I found myself walking in absolute fear. If I could only get to the train station, I would be able to make it home. I moved cautiously, sneaking a look around every corner before actually proceeding. I almost made it.

A large group of angry black men spotted me from half a block away. On an ordinary night, they would probably be curious about what a white girl was doing in this part of town. And maybe that night they *were* thinking that. As they moved closer, I stood frozen in fear, afraid to move in any direction. Though their expression did not appear friendly, they surrounded me but said nothing. It was then that I heard a voice from behind me.

"She's with me, gents, so move on."

I didn't recognize the voice and was afraid even to turn and look. The crowd seemed to move away, but it didn't seem out of fear. I didn't know what was happening until someone in the large group spoke.

"Sure, Mr. Walker, if we had known she was with you, we wouldn't have come here. Ah…you know to offer assistance."

"That was soooo nice of you. But no assistance is required."

Trio Walker was not an old man, so the deference they gave to him must have meant that they were big blues fans and were in awe of his abilities. The crowd smiled, shrugged their shoulders, and slowly departed—leaving Trio Walker and me alone.

"Thank you," was all I murmured to him.

"C'mon, let's get you to a train station."

We walked in almost silence, and my mind recalled Smokey Joe's comments about Trio. Thoughts kept rolling in my mind…*all he cares about is whiskey, women, and the blues…crossroads…333 on his forehead.* Still, he had been a gentleman to me and, yes, a savior.

"I've seen you at the club hanging out with Smokey Joe. He's such a great old man."

I didn't have the heart to tell him that Smokey didn't feel the same about him. Though the old man wasn't hateful, he was very wary of Trio. I wasn't seeing his bad side. Nonetheless, I wanted to know if he had the 333 tattooed on his hairline. I was too obvious.

"Yes, the 333 is there."

Of course, I must have looked confused—or was it terrified? Had he really been down to the crossroads?

"Getting that tattoo was one of my best ideas. It's good for my mystique," he said with an exuberant laugh. Yet he didn't give me any more information about it…ever. (Did he mean paying for the tattoo…or *getting it* as payment for his skills?)

We walked on, and we talked easily after that. Still, something was bothering me, and I couldn't place what it was. Mostly we talked about the Biloxi Blues club and the musicians who played there. Though he was undeniably the best, he deferred to his older counterparts and spoke about their styles with great reverence. I couldn't figure him out. And then it hit me.

"No offense to Smokey Joe and the others, but they all speak in a slow Southern drawl with a sort of broken English. You don't."

"Well, they all have deep Mississippi roots. They have come by their blues naturally. I didn't. They were too busy surviving to get a proper education. I admire them for how far they came from where they started."

"But not you?"

"Not me."

Our conversation was so comfortable that I could go deeper into his personal business. We had become close quickly, and we would be closer.

"What's that mean? Why aren't you like the others?"

"Berklee College of Music…class of '63—and you better not tell anybody."

"Holy shit!" was my intelligent response to that revelation.

"Yeah, sometimes I have to dumb down my speech at the club. That's why it feels good to talk to you."

With that, he left me off at the train.

14

---

# "YOU CAN'T ALWAYS GET WHAT YOU WANT"

## - ROLLING STONES

*L*ooking back after all these years, I can see things more clearly than I did while they were happening. The Rolling Stones song I quoted above seems perfect, even if they didn't write it until a year after that night—the night I lost my virginity.

It was early May when we started to feel safe enough to flock back to the blues clubs. I felt safe because the entire Wrigley Rocker crew came with me. I don't think that the others loved the blues as I did, but we had grown so close as a group that they went to make me happy. I felt safe around Lars and Jesse, who were really big guys, and even Dax, who was a bit shorter, was tough. Sara and I felt protected while in their company.

In reality, there was no need for protection while *in the club.* I had the friendship of its two biggest stars, Smokey Joe Watson and Trio Walker. Of course, like any other city in the late 1960s, getting there was more of a problem. But, once in the club, we all were welcome as regulars.

You would think there would be some romantic entanglements with a mixed group of young men and women. You would be right.

Though we had been friends for months, it was only later that I noticed that Lars and Sara were attentive to each other. In a rare show of humor, Dax would comment that *he was going to explore his dark side*. This was his way of saying that he was looking to hook up with a black girl at the club, favoring his mother's side of the family. It would have been challenging to find anyone in the entire city of Chicago who represented his father's side, Lakota Sioux.

That left Jesse and me. However, there was no Jesse and me. He was my best friend along with Sara, but there were no sparks. Besides, he knew me well enough to know where my head was.

"He'll be done after this song," shouted Jesse over the music. He was smiling at me in an all-knowing way.

"Who?" I answered, acting dumb.

"I see the way you look at Trio."

"No, No, we're just friends,"

"Not true. You're only fooling yourself if you think otherwise."

Lacy Greene, a black neighborhood girl who was a regular at the club and an acquaintance of mine, overheard us.

"You'll have a good time with that man," she interjected, "I know from experience."

I blushed, and Jesse just stared at me as Lacy continued.

"He ain't no hump-two, pump-and-dump kinda guy. He'll treat you tenderly and make sure you have a good time. But, of course, then he'll be gone and on to his next piece of ass."

Jesse and I looked at her with amazement. This was 1968, and to me, a sheltered kid growing up under the thumb of my parents, this whole concept of sex was absurd. Sex was for people in love. Sex was for having children. Sex was for after marriage. Sex wasn't a one-night stand just for recreation.

My entire life, I had planned to save myself for the man I loved and married. Sex was for the tenderness of my marriage bed. That was going to be Johnny. But I knew now that wasn't going to happen. Johnny had abandoned me and taken with him all the dreams of my lifetime. Damn you, Johnny. I decided that I needed passion, no matter how forced, phony, or short in duration.

I wanted Johnny and the promise of all he meant to me, but I knew now that dream was dead. Yeah, that night, I understood... *You can't always get what you want, but sometimes, you find you get what you need.*

I lost my virginity to Trio Walker in early May 1968.

---

I should have thought that my night with Trio was a big deal. But, looking back, I think a part of me was numb to everything—the world, my life, my feelings. I mean, that precious virginity I had held back from Johnny for so long was given easily and freely to a man I barely knew.

My cynical side thinks that somehow sex with a black man was a shot at my racist father. *If you could only see me now, Dad!* But years of reflection made me realize that it was just my need for passion at that moment...and Trio was available. This was the beginning of the age of free love. As much as Trio might have thought I was just another notch in his belt...I had used him.

# "BROKEN DREAMS"

## - JUSTIN HAYWARD

It wasn't awkward the next time I saw Trio. We both knew that it would only be a one-time thing. However, it wasn't because we had avoided each other. Just the opposite, we became very good friends. On the nights I came alone to the club, we would spend the time between his sets talking.

Interestingly, Smokey Joe was usually in on the conversations. What a weird group we made. As the spring and summer of 1968 wore on, my life fell into a pattern—days working at Wrigley Field and nights at the Biloxi Blues Club.

When the Cubs were on road trips, I explored the city of Chicago with the Wrigley Rockers. I look fondly on those carefree days—the Navy Pier, the Field Museum, and the Lakefront. We laughed a lot, and our friendship grew. However, the world around us was changing. If we couldn't see that, we could at least feel it. While we sold our beer, soda, Cracker Jacks, and cotton candy, everyone around us seemed to be getting very serious. We told our jokes to our customers, but we were the only ones laughing.

The death of Martin Luther King led to riots in the city, and even when they ended, it still seemed as if the city was ready to erupt. There was an edge to people that wasn't there before. It was leading to something; I just didn't know what. Yet I did get my first clue at work one day.

"Did you hear the news?" mumbled Jesse as we suited up for the game. Lars just lowered his head.

"What, you both got cotton candy duty today," joked Dax, not seeing how serious they were.

"RFK got shot last night. The news said he's not going to make it," responded Lars. He gave Dax a muted smile to let him off the hook for his ignorance.

"Shit," was all Dax could say.

My hand flew to my mouth, and I started to cry. Sara, who had known since the brothers had told her that morning, held and comforted me. None of us had been political, but we could not help but think that this would worsen the situation in a world already screwed up by Dr. King's death. Up until that point, we only thought in selfish terms. We only cared about how events would affect us and didn't want anything to upset the lives we had built. We had more money than we could spend at the clubs and site-seeing. At that point, we didn't look at the future. At least not until that day.

"It's going to get ugly around here…and fast," speculated Lars.

"It sure is," echoed Jesse.

"Why?" was my naïve response.

"Kennedy was a progressive. Unfortunately, there will be those who see this as a right-wing plot to silence him," explained Jesse.

"And it probably was!" howled Dax, who was the most radical of our group.

"You can't know that," objected Sara.

"It doesn't matter whether there was or wasn't; there is going to be a commotion come August," barked Lars.

"Why?" interjected the still naïve me.

"The convention?" questioned Sara.

"Oh, yeah," pronounced Lars, Jesse, and Dax almost simultaneously.

"You're going to have all kinds of people here for all kinds of reasons, and most of them won't agree with each other," sighed Lars. "I fear it's going to be a bloodbath."

It was.

1 6

---

# "LEAVIN' IN YOUR EYES"

## - LITTLE BIG TOWN

*E*verything was different from then on. We still worked our jobs and went to clubs at night. However, our Wrigley Rocker conversations became more serious. Every time we noticed something *bad* (which took in a variety of people and events), our eyes would meet, and each of us would mouth the words, "ugly's coming."

One night in early July, we were on the train on the way to the club when Sara became the first to say what we had all been thinking.

"Maybe it's time to leave. This isn't the city I knew and loved… not anymore."

"When?" I followed.

"I don't know."

"No, we can't, at least not until after the convention," shot Dax. "We need to be here."

We looked at him with dazed confusion. Each of us looked as if we were going to speak but instead stood silent.

"That meeting of minds in the convention hall will decide *my* future…maybe even yours. Maybe not so much being as you are…"

"White? Is that what you wanted to say?" I was surprised that I was the first to finish his sentence.

"And you don't have the only conscience in the group. You know Lars and I can be drafted," added Jesse.

"Not me!" boomed Dax with the first glimmer of a smile. "I'll just go and be with my people on the reservation."

"Wow, you're just a multiracial gem. You can be black at the club and Native American to hide out," speculated Lars.

"Yeah, but I can never be white!" Dax answered with a scowl on his face…which quickly turned to a smile. "Gotcha feeling guilty for being white? It's a skill I work very hard at."

We halfheartedly laughed. This was an issue that we knew was real. We could never understand what Dax's life had been like. Yet he knew we had his back.

"Don't worry about it. I'm good. I'll be better when I get back with my people at the Biloxi," hissed Dax.

"Wait a minute, just like that...you're black again? What happened to the reservation?" pointed out Jesse.

"When in Rome, brother…when in Rome."

We spent the rest of July and the early part of August trying to devise a plan to make everyone happy. Certain facts were understood by all of us. We knew we had to evolve—to change. We were split as to whether that meant moving on to some other location or doing something to join in the action that was taking place around us. Lars and Sara were for leaving the inevitable chaos of Chicago behind immediately. Jesse, Dax, and I were *for* sticking around. Dax urged us to stay and try to impact the Democratic Convention in the city. Jesse and I sympathized with him but had alternative reasons for our choice. I didn't want to leave Smokey Joe, and (I would find out later) Jesse didn't want to leave me.

Ultimately, we decided to wait until the baseball season ended to make a final decision. We were making good money for five unskilled young people. If we did decide to go, we would need money for our journey—wherever that journey would take us.

# 17

# "I CAN'T KEEP FROM CRYIN' SOMETIMES"

## - BLIND WILLIE JOHNSON

Smokey Joe died on August 8, 1968. Nobody knew how old he was at the time of his death.

He was loved like no other who frequented our little corner of the world. His funeral was attended by massive amounts of people, all of whom were black except for the five of us—the Wrigley Rockers. It seems that as good as he was at playing the blues, he had gone unnoticed by too much of the world. I guess our friendship with him was not a secret, and as the tearful crowd exited the graveyard, we were asked if we wanted to attend the "going away" party for him that was being held in the street outside the Biloxi Blues Club.

"Are you sure we won't be intruding?" I asked Trio who had offered the invitation.

"You mean because you're white?" He had a way of being blunt.

"Well, yeah," I whispered.

"These white folks want to know if they'll be welcome at Smokey's party?" Trio boomed to the entire crowd. Most of them started laughing—much to our embarrassment.

"Oh, sorry," I groaned.

"No, you don't understand. Leaving folks out because of the color of their skin is what *you do*. Well, not specifically you five, but you know what I mean. They're all laughing because you thought you weren't welcome."

"Well, thanks," I looked at the others and nodded.

"Besides, you can't believe what kind of treat you are in for—musically speaking."

"You mean we get to hear you again," Jesse laughed and slapped him on the shoulder.

"I may not even lift my guitar today. But, as I said, you are in for a real treat."

I looked at his 333 tattoo. I had seen it up close and personal, and I thought back to the first time Smokey Joe had mentioned him and the Crossroads legend. In his last days, Smokey Joe had befriended the much younger Trio, and they had become relatively close. In turn, Trio had become a warmer, humbler person. And he still played the shit out the blues. So what was he talking about?

The party went well into the night, and there would be no sleeping in this part of town. Anywhere else in Chicago, the police would have been called for this massive disturbance of the peace. However, everyone living even remotely near the ruckus was there and joined in the celebration. Plus, the police seldom came to these streets under any circumstances.

With coaxing from the crowd, Trio did play a few numbers. He played them unbelievably well but seemed uncharacteristically subdued...or humbled. Upon completing his short set, he proceeded to the microphone sans guitar. This was unusual since he never stood on the stage, minus his instrument.

"You all know me, and you know that I am not easily intimidated."

"No, you pretty much think you are hot shit," someone good-naturedly jeered from the crowd. Trio smiled but held up his right hand to calm the crowd.

"Smokey Joe was the master, and I learned great things from him in the last few months. We can only know his greatness by the company he kept."

"Like you," again the jeering was all in good fun. However, Trio responded by casually rubbing the 333 tattoo at his hairline. He loved to reinforce his legend. But as he continued to speak, he still was humble.

"Only Smokey Joe, by both his playing and personality, could get our next two performers to share the stage." He glared at the heckler, who he assumed would make another comment. He then continued.

"According to everything I've heard, these two men don't particularly like each other. However, they agreed to bury the hatchet for the sake of Smokey's memory...no, not in each other," he added, preempting the heckler's anticipated remark.

The five of us just looked on in confusion, not knowing that what we would hear would be a once-in-a-lifetime performance. From the left side of the makeshift stage walked Muddy Waters and from the opposite side walked Howlin' Wolf. The two blues legends notoriously did not get along. Perhaps it was professional rivalry, or maybe some deep-seated past slight drove them apart. No one knew. However, here they stood together because of their love of Smokey Joe. Howlin' Wolf spoke first.

"Muddy and I agreed on the song we would play for Smokey... and that ain't no easy thing."

"Because you're a stubborn son-of-a-bitch," mumbled Muddy Waters.

"And you're not?" cackled Howlin' Wolf.

Trio thought he would have to intervene, but then the two of them started to laugh. Muddy took over the intro.

"Of course, we couldn't agree on either of us doing the other guy's song, so we thought it was only fitting that we would go way back to when Smokey was young and listened to some of the best there ever was."

"We can't think of no song that more expresses how we feel about the loss of our friend Smokey Joe," added Howlin' Wolf.

"This here song is by the great Blind Willie Johnson," continued Muddy with a smirk, "and if you know this song and never heard of Blind Willie…well then you been hangin' out with too many white folks." He then looked down, saw us, and added, "no offense."

After the first note, I knew what he meant. Two years before, the all-white Blues Project band had taken the Blind Willie song and made a minor hit. This was followed by the English group Ten Years After also doing a cover of it. However, these paled compared to Muddy Waters and Howlin' Wolf's version of "Lord, I Can't Keep from Cryin' Sometimes." Unfortunately, there was no one there to record this performance, and no lost tapes will ever show up of this performance, but it will forever be memorialized in my mind.

*Soon it all would be over,*
*and I'd journey on with a smile*
*But the thought as I get older,*
*I think of what I told her*

*When my heart's full of sorrow*
*And my eyes are filled with tears*
*And I just can't keep from crying…sometimes*
*Well, I just can't keep from crying…sometimes*

# 18

# "BALL OF CONFUSION"

## - THE TEMPTATIONS

I was there for all that happened in the following weeks, but I don't know if I understood. I definitely didn't comprehend the big picture until I read it in the history books years later.

We wanted to be part of something that would change the world. Perhaps, it was because Smokey Joe had passed away and received little acknowledgment of his talent outside the black community. I don't know if that was correct, but it was what motivated the rest of the Wrigley Rockers and me. But, unfortunately, it was not what inspired most people who took to the streets in the frantic days before, during, and after the Democratic Convention held in Chicago in 1968. There were as many reasons for being there as there were people in the streets. It was chaos.

Incumbent president Lyndon Johnson had decided not to run, Robert Kennedy was assassinated, and the rest of the Democratic Party was in free fall. A struggle developed between the conservative and liberal wings of that party. It was nothing compared to the conflict that engulfed the streets of Chicago that August.

Yippies, hippies, black radicals, white radicals, and apathetic buffoons flooded the streets, and you couldn't tell the players without a scorecard—and no one had that card. People were screaming for an end to the war in Vietnam and civil rights, and it seemed like a thousand other issues that the mob thought the Democratic Convention would consider.

However, there was another player in the game. Mayor Richard Daley was the totalitarian dictator of Chicago, and he was determined to show the world that he could control the chaos. He tried but failed in his task, and his heavy-handed methods backfired. Looking back with the advantage of hindsight, Daley may have single-handedly led to the election of the other party's candidate, Richard Nixon. And we all know how that ended up.

Amid the chaos, Daley was fed a rumor that the Blackstone Rangers were planning an assassination attempt on Hubert Humphrey, his personal favorite and the Democrats' ultimate winner. The Rangers were an enigma. Some cast them as protectors of black South Chicago, while others painted them as something more violent and dangerous than the Black Panthers. The portrait Daley believed of them was somewhere between Nazis and the hordes of Genghis Khan. Thinking that he was saving the country's next president, he flooded the black sections of the city with not just the police but also the National Guard. We were there.

Unaware that anything was awry, we traveled to the Biloxi and were at its entrance when the shit hit the fan. The police were indiscriminately harassing any and all of the black residents, which led our own Wrigley Rocker, Dax, to head into the club immediately. The rest of us were curious and stayed outside.

We saw Trio Walker, in a relatively brisk walk, approaching us. He had just turned the corner and was being pursued. Just as we had ushered him into the club and told Dax to get him set up on stage as quickly as possible, we were confronted by two excited patrolmen.

"What the hell are you four doing here in this part of town? Don't you know the coons are on the rampage?" growled the older of the two men in blue.

"Oh, no, coons!" Jesse groaned sarcastically, "I thought raccoons weren't found in urban areas."

"He meant…" piped in the younger officer but was cut off by his elder.

"This wise ass knows exactly what I mean."

Jesse smiled at them both, which incited the older officer to raise his club to intimidate Jesse. Lars interrupted, hoping to diffuse the situation.

"We just came down here to listen to some great blues music. You should hear it, and he opened the door to allow the sounds of Trio Walker to escape."

"You are so full of crap that it is coming out of your ears, causing you not to hear good from the bad. That is goddam jungle music." He then turned to his young assistant and grumbled, "This is the kind of pinko hippie shit that is ruining this country. C'mon, we got better things to do besides talking to these assholes."

We breathed a sigh of relief as they left us standing there. Of course, it never occurred to those dumb shits to ask us, "If the music is so damn good, why are the four of you standing outside."

We went inside.

# 19

# "FOR WHAT IT'S WORTH"
## - BUFFALO SPRINGFIELD

*"There's something happening here…"*

Filled with pent-up rage, we made plans after we went inside. The next night, there was a free concert by the group MC5 in Lincoln Park. This meant the venue would be used as the focal point of protests. Were we shallow in wanting a little musical entertainment while conducting our civil disobedience?

During one of his breaks, we asked Trio if he wanted to join us. It seemed natural, considering the racial profiling he had been victimized by earlier in the evening.

"No, I'll leave saving the world to you white people."

"Are freaking kidding me? I only have half at stake compared to you, and I wouldn't miss it," boomed Dax. He had awkwardly stated it, but we got what he was trying to say. Only his mother was black.

"To each his own. I play the blues, but I don't have to live them."

"You bastard, don't you care ?" screamed Dax.

"I care. I don't know how holding up signs and listening to some half-assed white band will change anything?"

"Do you even understand what it means to be black? Really?" added Dax and just started to walk away.

Trio's anger was evident, but he controlled himself and whispered something that made no sense to us.

"Pumpsie Green."

"What the hell is a Pumpsie Green?" snorted Dax while the rest of us waited to hear the answer.

"Not what, but who?"

"Okay, I'll bite. Who the hell is Pumpsie Green?"

"You do know who Jackie Robinson was? Right?" smirked Trio.

"Of course, everyone knows he broke the color barrier in major league baseball by being the first black player," replied Dax.

"When?"

"Ha, I know that. The year I was born—1947. My mother told me that I could be proud of that. She said that the Dodgers got a load of crap for doing it, but eventually, all the teams came around, and the league became integrated."

"When?"

"What do you mean?"

"Well, do you think they all came around?"

"I don't know."

"Pumpsie Green was the player who integrated the very *last* team to hold out against integration—the Boston Red Sox."

"So?"

"It was twelve years later—three years after Jackie Robinson retired after a Hall-of-Fame career. Even then, the Boston fans were not very receptive to the idea. I tell you all this because that was my hometown. You don't think I know what racism is after growing up there. Do you think you had a problem being a half-breed on a reservation? You know nothing of hatred."

Trio walked away.

"But this isn't Boston, wise guy," spat Dax as he attempted to get the last word in.

Trio turned with a smile on his face. He could not have had a better setup line.

"Do you know what the *second* to last team to integrate was? No… I won't even let you guess, you ignorant bastard. Chicago! And it wasn't even the Cubs; it was the White Sox, the team that plays on the South Side of town—this part of town."

Just when we thought he was done, he turned, walked, and stood toe to toe facing Dax.

"And do you know who that player was for the White Sox? Pumpsie Green. After serving as the token house nigger in Chicago, they shipped him out to Boston so that another city could make believe they weren't racist. Do you really think you'll get any kind of break in this city?"

He walked away, picked up his guitar, and left the club.

---

I grew up that next night. Even though I had run away from home and lived in a city more than a thousand miles away from home, I had still been a child in my thoughts and actions. I never would be that naïve again in life. I left my childhood behind that night.

It started simply as a night of music, fun, and protest—in that order. Abbie Hoffman, one of the leaders of the Yippie movement, had attempted to present a "Festival of Life" during the Democratic Convention. His goal was to draw 100,000 youths into the city so that he could (in his words) "redirect the youth music and culture toward political ends" We had no idea we were political pawns. Unfortunately, we paid a steep price for our stupid naivete. Billed as "five days of peace, love, and music," it was anything but.

We should have suspected something was wrong when only

about 3,000 of us came to hear the group MC5. Possibly the same amount of police surrounded the stage. Well, that wasn't exactly true. There was no stage. The group MC5 was the only musical act to show up, and they were standing on flat ground, plugged into a hot dog stand! People sat on the floor with some standing behind them. But more than that, it was the overwhelming feeling that something terrible would happen—and it did.

Sara, Lars, and Jesse were more into the music and edged their way to a location near the front. Dax and I, not avid fans of the group, were perfectly satisfied to stand in the back. And so, unfortunately, we were in the front row for the *real* action. Just as the band upped the volume, all hell broke loose. As they performed "Kick Out the Jams," people were getting their asses kicked—and punched—and clubbed.

Who started it? I know that some agitators had been taunting the police verbally. To this day, I believe this had been their plan all along. We were merely pawns in the larger machinations of many groups trying to get their point across to the convention delegates and the world.

For quite a while, those closer to the stage were unaware of our plight. Whereas the confrontation had taken place in the back near us, those nearer to the band continued to enjoy themselves.

In the rear, protesters threw various food objects at the cops, and they responded increasingly more aggressively. Dax and I had not been involved, but we were trapped. At first, we tried to get the attention of our friends but then realized how serious the situation was and that we needed to get out—somehow. That wasn't happening. Now cut off from the larger group, we found ourselves surrounded and being pushed from all sides.

Dax blocked the first blow aimed at him by an irate officer. As the billy club made contact with his forearm, I heard the sickening sound of cracking bones. As the cop raised his arm for a second time, pure rage welled in me, and I drove my head into his stomach, or at least I tried to. He caught me by the collar and held me at a distance, his club ready to strike me.

"My, my…aren't you a feisty one? Didn't your momma teach you to respect authority? Well, I guess not…if you're hanging out with this here darkie." And there it was. I now knew why Dax had been singled out for attack despite doing nothing wrong. I looked at that piece of crap eye to eye. I won't use the word cop, officer, or policeman. He was none of these. He doesn't deserve to have any of those words written in this story. Most cops are outstanding. I should know, I married one, but that is later in my tale. No, this racist bigot and his uniform had no bearing on that.

I don't know if any or all of these thoughts came to my mind then. I thought of spitting at him as he held me in his grip, ready to lower his club upon me. But, no, spitting seemed an understatement of my feelings. Instead, I reached out with three fingers in my right hand and used my long, sharp, dirty nails to gouge three deep creases in his left cheek. He would not soon forget the bitch who permanently marked him. As blood flowed freely from the damage I had done, I waited for my punishment—satisfied that he had paid some price for his actions.

Dax tried to rise to help me, but his arm, frozen at an unnatural angle, caused his efforts to be futile. However, the look on his face soon ceased to display fear. Instead, I glimpsed an expression of confusion—just before a fist pounded the face of the asshole who held me in his grip. The bigot released me in order to break his fall to the turf.

"I changed my mind about coming," laughed Trio, "and from the looks of things, it is a good thing I did." I hugged him as tightly as I could and then immediately thought of Dax. Before I could do anything, he wrapped Dax's good arm around his shoulder and lifted him from the ground.

"I knew you would be here," Dax whispered in Trio's ear.

"Bullshit, I didn't know I would be here," replied Trio and added, "It's a good thing for your sake that I was."

Trio winked at me, and I smiled back at him. Though we had had that one night together, we had never been more than friends —very good friends. We started to walk out of the park. We needed to get Dax medical care.

"Besides, I couldn't leave my little girl alone in the park, even if I had to listen to that crappy music," he added with another huge smile. Those were the last words he would ever say to me...or to anyone.

Out of the fringes of the dark came the vengeful cop. He was upon us before we knew it. There was no doubt what he had in his mind, but Trio found himself trapped. He was unable to evade him while supporting Dax. Alone he probably could have dodged the onslaught of the madmen. However, to do so meant immediately dropping Dax, whose damaged arm would suffer from the fall. I tried to run interference, only to be roughly pushed aside. Almost simultaneously, his club came down on Trio's forehead. As blood spurted from the wound, he fell unconscious to the ground, taking Dax with him. An evil grin came upon the madman's face, and I knew that my nails were useless as a weapon without the element of surprise.

"And now you...you vicious little cunt," he snorted and inched toward me. I backed up with very little hope of escape. After Trio's punch had left him dazed, he must have followed us and waited until we were far from where any witnesses could see his revenge. However, he wasn't the only one trailing us.

It was then that I heard the welcome voice of Sara. "We were looking for you, girl. You weren't going to leave without us. She wasn't blind. She saw my situation, but her conversation oddly ignored it. Officer Bigot looked perplexed for a short time, and that was enough for Lars and Jesse to sneak up from behind and grab him. The cop was not a small person, but did I mention that Lars was 6'4" and his "smaller" brother was 6'2? They held him tight as Sara and I looked on.

"Now what?" said Lars.

"You're in big trouble, I am an officer of the law, and you have attacked me."

"From what we have seen, you didn't act much like one tonight," answered Jesse.

"I've got a feeling you don't want to go on the record about all that went down here, and we can't take the chance that anyone will believe us, so..." spoke Lars.

"You think this is going away?" replied the rogue cop with false bravado. He knew he couldn't report them. He had crushed one kid's arm and knocked another unconscious, and five witnesses could testify that it was unprovoked. He might get away with it legally, but it was not good for his career. Yet, not having the sense to understand that he was already getting away with murder, he continued to taunt them.

"So, you think we're even?" bellowed the bigot.

"No," exploded Lars, "Not by a long shot." With that, he came from behind the cop and faced him, at the same time signaling his brother to release his grip on him. As they stood facing each other, Lars took his right fist and pounded it into the cop's jaw. Two teeth flew past Jesse just as he was in the act of catching the unconscious victim of his brother's devastating punch. Jesse lowered him to the ground.

"Now we're even," spat Lars standing over the unconscious body.

With Lars's final pronunciation, we found our way out of the park and to the nearest hospital.

Unfortunately, at that hospital we would find out that we would never be even.

# "PAINT IT BLACK"

## - ROLLING STONES

As I have written before, everything changed that night. Though the five of us bonded closer as friends, we seemed to have left much of our childish behavior behind in that park. We still laughed but took the world around us much more seriously.

We even laughed at Dax trying to hawk cotton candy with a big ass cast on his arm. It was hard, and it was funny…until they fired him for his inability to balance the products and make change for the customers. That was the final factor in our decision to leave Chicago.

What had started as a plan to seek adventure together had now become an escape plan. None of us wanted to be there any longer. We had to toy with the idea of taking off to see America at the beginning of September, but I didn't know if any of us were committed to the idea. We talked about pooling our money, buying a van, and taking off before it became cold. What started as a far-fetched dream became a concrete plan after that night in the park.

Circumstances, however, delayed our departure. We had used a chunk of our money to pay Dax's medical bills. That meant we would have to stay for the rest of the season to build our funds. It was only one more month because the Cubs (as usual) were not going to the World Series.

The others might have left earlier anyway, and I told them they could go without me. Perhaps, I would catch up to them after… after I knew that Trio was better. That never happened. Bludgeoned by the rogue cop, he never regained consciousness after he arrived at the hospital. He went into a coma, and I told the whole Wrigley Rocker gang that I was staying around for him. They told me they were staying too. September turned into October and our jobs ended. It would have been a perfect time to leave, but none of us did. I went to the hospital every day, but not alone. At least one of the gang came with me.

On October 5, 1968, Trio Walker died. He had made more of an impression on the local music scene than Smokey Joe Watson. The Chicago Tribune gave him a decent size obituary. What it said, I don't know. I never got past the first line—*born in Boston, Massachusetts, on August 23, 1941…*

Trio Walker died at 27 years old!

# PART III

## "DANCING ON THE OTHER SIDE OF THE WIND"

### - CHRIS DELANEY AND THE BROTHERHOOD BLUES BAND

*"We were living lives of passion,*
*Never wanting to go slow,*
*Never thinking about tomorrow,*
*Never wanting to say no.*

*We were dancing,*
*We were dancing,*
*On the other side of the wind."*

Minnesota and Points West
(1968 – 1969)

21

# "THE WAY"

## - FASTBALL

*"Where were they going without ever knowing the way?"*

On Columbus Day, 1968, the five of us took off in search of America. I remember the date because we thought of ourselves as some kind of explorers discovering our own country. If we had headed east instead of west, we might have been in upstate New York just in time for Woodstock. However, just like Columbus, we had headed west to see lands we had never seen. We only had a vague itinerary—with our sole goal of getting out of Chicago. There were too many bad memories.

We had chipped in for an ancient VW bus. It almost sounds like a cliché from the sixties. However, it served its purpose. We bought tents and a Coleman stove and thought we were set. It never occurred to us that fall in the mid-west would get cold very quickly. It had always been our plan to ultimately make it to San Francisco for the dynamic music scene that was developing there. This had been our plan *in August*. But, delayed by the events around the convention and Trio Walker, we never recalculated the effect of the weather. What can I say? We were young and stupid.

We got about 75 miles outside Chicago when we had the first mechanical breakdown of the ancient VW bus. It gave us our first laughs.

"Okay, which of you guys can fix this?" questioned Sara.

"Don't look at me. I opted for poetry as a senior elective over auto shop. Unfortunately, that now appears to be a bad choice," Lars replied just a little too quickly.

"I always followed in my brother's footsteps. Ditto, a bad choice," Jesse echoed his brother's decision.

"It's a good thing that we didn't *all* grow up as privileged white namby-pambies," derided Dax.

"You mean you can do something?" I spoke hopefully for all of us.

"Shit, man, on the Rez, this hunk of junk would be considered a late-model luxury vehicle. I've fixed up worse crap than this with my eyes closed," laughed Dax.

Our laughs were partly because of his statement and partly out of relief. We would avail ourselves of his mechanical skills many more times on that trip.

---

A few years later, Chris Delaney and the Brotherhood Blues Band released the song with which I started this section. This tune described the next few years of our lives and probably mine more specifically.

> *We were living lives of passion,*
> *never wanting to go slow.*
> *Never thinking about tomorrow,*
> *never knowing where to go.*

. . .

Such a wild and crazy life we led. Whenever I listen to that song now, I like to romantically look back and think that was us—dancing on the other side of the wind, enjoying life and each other's company...living for the moment.

I then look at the reality of all that happened and think *we had our heads up our asses.*

---

Our first stop was Alexandria. No, not the famous one in Virginia. This one was in Minnesota and had a sign that mysteriously read "Birthplace of America." Huh? We got the whole story from Lars and Jesse, who grew up in the town.

"A Viking party made their way here before being attacked and killed by...umm...the local natives," started Lars.

"Oh, here we are again, the bad guys in the story," Dax quickly responded.

"Well, in this case, that happens to be true," stated Jesse matter-of-factly.

"Wait, when did all this happen?" I asked.

"Oh, hundreds of years before Columbus," said Lars.

"Okay, so the Vikings discovered America first. Just another shot at Columbus and us Italians," I defended, thinking how proud I would make my Romano and Longo ancestors.

"Don't take my word. Just go see the Kensington Runestone in the museum. It was dug up about a century ago. It tells the story of how a small group of Nordic Vikings made it this far into America only to be wiped out by...you know who," Lars revealed and surreptitiously pointed to Dax.

"So, the story had a happy ending," scowled Dax.

"Of course, many experts have debunked it," Jesse mumbled.

"Hey, you're killing my story," Lars rebuked his brother. "I'll take you to see the Kensington Runestone later."

"Museum fees…a big source of town income, I bet," I quipped.

"Hey, you use what you got," Lars now smirked, letting on that maybe even he didn't buy into the story."

"Hey, at least one good thing came of the myth. Where do you think the Minnesota Vikings football team got its name?'

We all laughed at that final comment and made our way to Lars and Jesse's childhood home.

<hr>

We knew that Lars and Jesse's father had suffered some medical problems, which was one of the reasons for our stopping in this town. He seemed to be on the road to recovery, and both he and his wife offered us their hospitality. Amazingly, they had enough bedrooms to put us all up, though it did lead to a very awkward moment.

"Mom, Dad, this is my girlfriend Sara," announced Lars quite unexpectedly to his parents during our introductions. Now in the close quarters of the van, we had seen something developing. However, we didn't think it had progressed to the official "girlfriend status" level so quickly.

Lars' mother quickly hugged Sara, but his father responded differently.

"That doesn't mean that you two can sleep together under our roof. That's for after she has a ring on that finger."

This was the beginning of the age of free love—but not in this traditional Minnesota home. Lars seemed as if he would react but soon thought better of it and just nodded. Sara and I slept in what had once been the guys' older sisters' bedroom, the brothers in their old bedroom, and Dax on the couch in the den.

It was a short but wonderful stay, and we ate and slept better than we had in a year. Some of the gang considered taking up permanent residence in this area. That was until the last night.

A little past midnight, I woke up to arguing from the floor below me. No one else seemed to notice. However, I was curious, so I descended the stairs and found a spot just off the kitchen and listened as Lars and his father went at it.

"You have to do what's right...and legal," ordered his father.

"No, Dad, I don't think so."

"You don't have a choice."

"I think I do."

"I'll not be part of any breaking the law."

"I won't ask you to do that."

"You weren't brought up to be a traitor."

"I am not a traitor. And if you saw the things I saw in Chicago, you'd understand."

"I'll never understand."

"I don't expect you to. But I've got to do what I've got to do."

"What will I say when they come looking for you?"

"Tell them the truth—you don't know where I am. We'll be leaving tomorrow."

"What will become of you?"

"I'll be fine. Don't worry."

I peeked in to see them hug. I was surprised that his mother had been there without saying a word. After their embrace, Lars exited the room and saw me eavesdropping. He said nothing but handed me an official-looking piece of paper—his orders for a physical in preparation for his induction into the army. Lars had been drafted...and he wasn't going to go.

## 2 2

# "ON THE ROAD AGAIN"

## - CANNED HEAT

He didn't have to tell us. We already knew that Lars had a plan… and it didn't include us ever getting to see the "infamous" Viking Runestone. He gave us the details later once we were on the road. Despite the impending cold weather, we started our journey west on a more northern route than initially planned. We would still see as many sites as possible. However, now we would end up in Seattle, where Lars and Sara would then slip across the border to Canada.

Lars continuously told us that we still needed to enjoy ourselves until we parted. We had to keep up that "Wrigley Rocker" spirit as much as possible, and I remember we tried. With my mind set on the ultimate departure of Lars and Sara, I found it hard to concentrate. The good times and laughs were immeasurable, but the details all seemed overshadowed by our destination. They come back to me now and only as brief snippets of reality.

I remember our first stop being in Bismarck, North Dakota. It was a stop that Lars and Jesse wanted, but Sara and I had no idea why. Conversely, Dax *did* know why and was not a happy camper.

Lars and Jesse were our tour guides and chief researchers in all travel matters, and Jesse, in particular, was obsessed with this area being the sunflower capital of the world. I had never cared about them one way or another. But Jesse did, so we all agreed to stop by the biggest damn crop of them I had ever seen. They stretched for miles, and it seemed in every direction. I couldn't get over the feeling that I had seen this scene somewhere before—giant (I mean taller than Lars) flowers as far as we could see. But, with the one enormous circle on top— they reminded me of something...

"The Day of the Triffids," whispered Lars in my ear.

"Damn, you're right," I answered, recalling the cheesy horror film of the 1950s about giant killer plants that unrooted themselves and threatened humanity.

Jesse brought down one of the plants behind me and laid it on my shoulder. Okay, I didn't really think it was an alien-killer plant, but it did temporarily scare the shit out of me. I went to smack Jesse on the shoulder to show my feelings. However, he quickly ran into the field of sunflowers. I followed, and for some reason, so did all the others. Okay, I won't make a corny reference to us being flower children.

We underestimated the sheer size of the field as we ran in every direction. Only Dax quickly found his way out. Then, of course, he would claim it was his native instincts that helped. Not so for the rest of us. I could hear Jesse taunting me.

"I'm over here," he screamed, but I had no idea where "here" was. I could hear Lars and Sara running and giggling for a while, but soon there was silence. I just got more lost, never knowing whether I was heading toward anyone or anything. Then, suddenly, I came upon Lars and Sara. Umm...how do I put this discreetly? They were...

"Get a room!" yelled Jesse from the opposite side of the clearing.

"With five of us in that damn van, this is as close to privacy as we get. So get lost...will you?" grumbled Lars, trying to cover up Sara as she lay on the floor on a bed of broken sunflowers.

"Sorry," snorted Jesse and ran off into the woods. I followed, still looking for revenge for his Triffid prank. I heard him breaking flowers, and I chased the sound. I began to run at full speed (well, as much as the Triffids would let me.) Then by sheer luck, Jesse and I ran right into each other—so close that we found ourselves face to face. He had a weird look on his face, and until this day, I think he thought about kissing me. How I would have reacted, I don't know. I had had my brief encounter with Trio back in Chicago. Nevertheless, I had decided that the next time I gave myself to a man, it would be someone who I cared for and who cared for me. That could be Jesse, but I wasn't ready yet. Awkwardly, we walked out of the field only after Dax yelled directions.

"Hey, palefaces, you went in there with the sun at your back. To get out, walk in the direction of the sun."

"We're coming," yelled Jesse

"Thanks, Dax," I muttered as we emerged from the field.

"How you palefaces took over this continent, I'll never know."

But we did know how that happened after our next stop in Bismarck.

---

Lars was a history buff. Eventually, he would get a Ph.D. in some obscure facet of American history. This was ironic because he got it from a British Columbia university and never returned to America even after President Carter pardoned all the draft evaders in 1976. I found this out from Sara, who did return to Chicago after their divorce. But that's later in my story.

As the de facto leader of our little group, we allowed Lars to influence our touring stops, and our next one was a Mandan Village along the Missouri River. Both Lars and Jesse had a bit of obsession with explorers Lewis and Clark and wanted to stop at the national park dedicated to their spending the winter there.

I have to admit that we were fascinated by *this* story. I believe that so was Lars because he went on to live most of his life in Madoc, Ontario. Never heard of it? Well, that was Lars' obsession.

---

"Why are we here?" grumbled Dax.

"Madoc." Lars' eyes lit up like it was Christmas morning as we entered the Mandan Village Historical Park and made a beeline to the main building at its center.

"What the hell is a Madoc?" fired back Dax seeming to grow angry at his time being wasted.

"Who. 'Who is Madoc?' should be your question. And he is the person who brings you and me together."

"More paleface riddles," responded Dax, but he still followed us into the building.

"Let him tell you the story, Dax. You'll understand," chimed Jesse.

"Is this another one where my people end the villains?"

"Quite the opposite. Watch and listen," instructed Lars, and brought us over to a painting on the museum's wall.

"What the hell am I looking at? Some kind of cultural subversion? These look like…"

"Blonde Indians? Is that what you were going to say, Dax?" questioned Lars with a look of satisfaction.

"What kind of bullshit is this? Now you're really pissing me off! Is this just another dig at my culture?"

"No, Dax, if this picture is true, it brings us closer together.

Now I just need to determine whether this painting is accurate. Still, in a way, I don't want to know if it isn't."

Lars didn't lie that day. After settling in Canada, he attained college and post-graduate degrees in the area of pre-Columbian settlement of North America. I have even seen some of his work published. Though I don't believe Madoc's story, I know that Lars did, and he would spend a lifetime researching it. I could see the look in his eyes that day and knew his fascination and dedication were authentic. To him, the story of Madoc was as real as anything he could see or touch. So I sat and listened intently as he told the tale.

*Madoc was a prince of Wales. When fighting broke out among his many siblings upon his father's death, he chose to go exploring. With about a hundred men, women, and children, he set sail in 1170 on the "western ocean." He soon returned to Wales to recruit more colonists for "an abundant western country" he had found. Madoc was never seen again. However, there were hundreds of legends about his ultimate fate, and they entail large sections of the United States.*

*The story goes that he made landfall in Mobile Bay in Alabama. Then, through the course of a millennium, it is believed that his followers and their descendants consistently moved north along the Mississippi River. Various structures along the way are said to be of European design as their millennial-long journey finally took them to this Mandan village.*

*When President Thomas Jefferson commissioned Lewis and Clark to explore the newly acquired lands of the Louisiana Purchase, he specifically mentioned that the "Welch Indians" should be investigated. The journal logs mention that the Mandan had many tribe members who seemed to have European features and spoke a language reminiscent of Welch. So the Explorers decided to investigate further on their return trip from the Pacific.*

*Based on the Lewis and Clark report, a man named George Catlin followed in their footsteps four decades later. He sent back various commentaries that insisted that a Welch dialect was being spoken. He even painted pictures of the tribe, with about twenty percent of them appearing to be blonde.*

"Wow, that's amazing," interjected a wide-eyed Sara. "And the pictures prove it."

"Well, no," responded Lars. "Catlin only wrote and painted what he *heard* about. He didn't actually see any of them."

"But Lewis and Clark must have followed up," I chimed in.

"No..." Lars started but couldn't finish what he wanted to say. He stood silent, and for some reason, all our eyes turned to Dax. Fury raged in his eyes as he looked at us and finally spoke.

"There were no Mandans when Louis and Clark returned. The entire tribe had been decimated by smallpox—smallpox brought to them by these same explorers to whom they had shown hospitality. While the American members of the expedition had immunities in their systems for the disease, the Mandan did not. It spread like wildfire among the helpless tribe members. It didn't matter whether or not they had thousand-year-old European genes somewhere in their bodies; they just had no way to deal with the plague. None survived." After he finished speaking, Dax left the museum almost in tears.

## 23

# "MAGICAL MYSTERY TOUR"

## - THE BEATLES

I wrote at the beginning of this memoir that I still had to decide if I would pass this on to my children. I am not proud of what I did on my Magical Mystery Tour of America. Nonetheless, I have decided not to hold back all that happened. Whether they see it or not is another matter. This may be just for me.

At first, I thought that my one-night stand with Trio Walker would be the most embarrassing revelation to my kids. I realize now that my kids laugh at the concept of "saving yourself for marriage." Then, of course, there is the question of an interracial affair. This bothered me, but not for the reason anyone might think.

When I wrote earlier in this memoir that I needed passion, I did. Yet, that may not have been the only reason I sought it out from Trio. I may have only been fooling myself. Interracial sex would not bother my children any more than premarital sex would. However, my motives might cause a bit of a rift.

Maybe I took Trio to bed not because of our racial differences but rather because of them. I was so angry at my racist parents that

I thought this was the best way I could hurt them—even if they had no idea what I was doing. I was thumbing my nose at my parents by giving myself to a black man. I sold my body for spite. That may be the most embarrassing thing (so far) in my story to reveal to my children. Was I the real racist for using him to strike out at my parents?

That brings me to the next revelation I don't want to give my kids. The five of us did an enormous amount of drugs during our Magical Mystery Tour across America. That is probably why we called it that—it was magical and a mystery because we could not explain or remember much of what we did. I mention this now because our drug use became significantly more severe after our trip to the Mandan Village. The more we experienced things together and felt each other's pain, the more we retreated into a drug-induced haze. As a result, much of what happened that night and every night after is lost in a fog that only lifted months later when we arrived in San Francisco.

I don't know if it's memory loss or the fact that I conveniently forget details. I know that it all started in Minnesota. Lars had a problem. He was not a heroin addict or anything like that. Before coming to Chicago, Lars used marijuana entirely too often—like every day—multiple times a day. Jesse convinced him to go with him to Chicago to change the pattern of his life. It worked for quite a while—until the convention, the beatings, and the death of Trio. Our departure from Chicago and return to the brothers' hometown was just a sneaky way for Lars to retrieve the stash that he had left behind hidden in his parents' attic. However, his other attempt to fight his demons was to immerse himself in history. I don't think they teach that at AA or Narcotics Anonymous, but eventually, it did work for Lars. Later years would find him clean and healthy.

I don't know if Sara, Dax, and I sensed this, but we agreed to all his touring decisions. All of Lars' historical stops stick so firmly in my mind. But, unfortunately, so much of the rest of our adventure does not. I now realize that our last "educational diversion" was the end of most of our sobriety—and it was cause and effect.

---

Little Big Horn. I remember the tears and the vomit. I also remember Dax's slight smirk that he tried unsuccessfully to hide as we toured the site of Custer's Last Stand. We had all seen the glorified version of the events in at least one Hollywood western that solidified Custer as a martyr and folk hero—at least to us palefaces.

We arrived a bit late for the last park ranger tour of the day, so we allowed Dax, who had taken the tour many times, to guide us through. He promised to give a fair and balanced account of the events of that infamous day. (Well, as fair as a half Lakota Sioux could be considering all that happened before, during, and after the Fifth Calvary attacked the estimated 6,000 Sioux with approximately 250 soldiers on June 25, 1876.)

Dax went through the tale doing his absolute best to give an accurate account—the same one he had heard years ago from an informed paleface park ranger. He detailed Custer's ego that first had him not wait for reinforcements from other troops in the area and then split his own forces into three. All those with Custer died.

"What the hell was he thinking? I mean, it was elementary math that should have told him he couldn't win," offered a confused Sara, and we all nodded in agreement.

"He was stupid," I added.

"No," Dax screamed vehemently. "He thought that one of his soldiers was equal to ten savages. Yes, he thought my people were so primitive that it would be no contest. In reality, Custer's enemies were hardened warriors—and they carried much better weapons.

While Custer's men had to reload after every shot, the Sioux used repeat action rifles—and they used them well."

"Gee, I never got that out of the books and movies," added Jesse.

"Books and movies written by white men," responded an annoyed Dax.

Sara and I were on the verge of tears, and we didn't understand why. It was so long ago, and it was hard to see it all as real, even standing on the very grounds where it occurred.

"The grunt soldiers weren't to blame. I hope they were at least honored by the army."

Dax laughed, and this upset the four of us.

"It's not funny," I yelled.

"I'm not laughing at what happened to them. I'm laughing at your hypocrisy. Where were the tears and the anguish for the lost Mandan?" Even you, my friends, think an Indian life is worth less than an egotistical general and his men. Do you know what the Sioux did to Custer's body?

"Do I want to know?" questioned Jesse.

"It doesn't matter what you want. I'm going to tell you."

"The squaws came onto the battlefield when it was over, and all of the seventh cavalry was dead. They sought out General Custer specifically. They carefully punctured both his eardrums."

"That's harsh," whispered Sara.

"Do you know why?" No one answered, so Dax continued.

"The squaws screamed, 'You never listened to us. You never wanted to know what we wanted or needed. Now you'll never listen to anyone.'"

We stood stunned, not knowing what to say to Dax. We should have known he wasn't done.

With a slight smirk, he continued. "Custer's corpse got off easy. All of his soldiers were stripped of all their clothes—and then castrated. Their penises were then placed in their mouths. I'm guessing you didn't see that in all your great Hollywood movies… did you?"

Sara and I puked in unison.

24

# "EIGHT MILES HIGH"

## - THE BYRDS

No one spoke from that moment on. We returned to the van and traveled back to our campsite. Still not a word. The conflict could have irrevocably torn our group apart. I know at the time, I thought the whole issue silly. Why was Dax so emotional about events that had happened a century before? I was young and naïve then and didn't realize that these issues were as current as the Vietnam War to Dax. The treatment of his people was not history because it was still going on. To the four of us, it was just things that happened so long ago that were interesting but not real.

To Dax, it was all too real. He had left the reservation because of the horror of living there. In Chicago, he saw that racists also reviled his black persona. His anger was growing daily, and he saw no way out. We thought we were losing our friend—until Jesse stepped up.

I don't know if he planned what he said or if it just came from his heart, and when it did, it spoke for all of us. He didn't force the issue. Instead, he carefully and casually started a blazing fire. We were all hungry and knew that food was long overdue. While the fire smoldered and we munched on some hot dogs, no one spoke. Instead, we all seemed to stare into the fire, collecting our thoughts. And then Jesse began.

"Do you think Maria hates you because you are Native American or black?" I was embarrassed that Jesse used me as an example, but he quickly continued. "Do you think that of Sara, or Lars...or me? Do you?" Jesse was practically screaming, and at the same time, I could almost see tears beginning to swell in his eyes.

Dax said nothing.

"Did we ever say or do anything to make you think that we ever thought of you with anything less than love and respect?"

"Well, there was the Mandan Village?" whispered Sara, and Jesse's eyes glared with fury at the attempt at humor.

"Do you remember Chicago at all? Lars is probably on a wanted poster there if the asshole cop told his story...and so probably is Maria. Didn't she leave that prick with scars he'll never rid himself of? Didn't we all get you out of the crowd and to safety after your arm was damaged? And didn't we all use our money to pay for your care in the hospital?"

"Okay, yeah, thanks," whispered Dax begrudgingly.

"No, you damn jerk, we don't want thanks. We did because you're our friend...and we love and respect you. And though it's hard at times, we may even like you."

That drew a small smile from Dax, which gave me the courage to speak.

"We can't begin to imagine your life or the pain you have felt. But we want to. You tell us if we say or do anything that offends you."

"Deal?" added Lars and offered his hand.

"Deal," answered Dax, and Lars' handshake turned into a hug.

"Wrigley Rockers forever, yahoo," screamed Sara, and we all turned to look at her.

"Your timing is completely off tonight," I growled at her but smiled.

---

For a long time, we sat and stared into the warm glow of the fire, feeling the equally warm glow of friendship. Dax spent a great deal of time poking the embers incessantly like his mind was working overtime. I thought that he was having second thoughts about us. Of course, he was, but not in the way I thought.

"You know there is one problem with friendship?"

"Yeah, Dax, what's that?" proffered Jesse.

He held back at first, but then Dax reached into his pocket and retrieved something. He held it in the palm of his hand.

"Friendship means you have to share." He showed what he had. "You're my tribe now...right?" Dax looked at us with a mischievous eye.

"Well, it's more like *our* tribe—you know, no chiefs, no followers," answered Lars.

Dax ignored that comment and went on.

"In my tribe, we have a religious experience that bonds us with nature and each other. We take it very seriously, and it is almost like a Christian sacrament in our eyes. Are you ready to make that kind of commitment to each other?

*What the hell is he talking about?* I thought.

"This is no joke. You will never be the same after this."

"What the hell are you talking about?" voiced Jesse putting a voice to my thoughts.

"Peyote," was Dax's simple answer.

Before that night, the word meant nothing to me. I knew it vaguely as a drug made from the buds of a cactus and that somehow it was tied to Native American culture. Scratch that. I may not even have known that at all, and I may be giving myself credit for more knowledge than I had at the time,

With that night's real or imagined memories haunting me, I have done my research throughout my lifetime. Peyote was like nature's LSD, and though we had been using heavy doses of marijuana, we had not ventured into anything different or more potent. This was a drug that caused vivid hallucinations. It affected all of the senses. Its effects could last as long as twelve hours.

Did we know any of this? Did we care?

We each took a bud (or more) of peyote, and reality became lost in a sea of dreams that were all too real.

Let me start by saying what I know to be a fact about the whole experience...nothing. We woke up the following day around the dying embers of our firepit...and were all naked. This was a Montana morning, and it was probably a balmy 31 degrees. That's it for facts. The rest is all blurred memories of what may or may not have been true.

We tried to compare notes about "our religious experience," but it seemed that each of us was holding back an embarrassing memory. As for me, I remember scattered tidbits of insanity. I remember seeing letters floating in the sky that *tasted* like ice cream...except for the letter "Q," which tasted like spinach (yuck!). Some trees grew from saplings to hundred feet tall oaks and then disappeared and reappeared as firewood that I could place on our blazing bonfire. People from my past talked to me in parables about what was good and evil in life, but they often made no sense.

My dad told me to make sure I put the garbage can in my bed, and my mom told him it was already there. (Was this some reference to people in my bed?)

My deceased childhood friend Diane sang "Johnny B. Goode" quite well, which was unreal because she couldn't sing a note on key in life. And continuing my musical theme, I saw my long-lost boyfriend Johnny playing bass in a band along with my long-dead lover Trio on guitar. Oh yeah, and Ringo Starr was their drummer.

And then there was the sex.

Because we all were naked, some of these hallucinations may have been true. But I guess I'll never know. The only way I could have known for sure was if either Sara or I had become pregnant, and that didn't happen. So, the who…with whom is a mystery lost forever.

I saw John F Kennedy with Marilyn Monroe (May have been accurate on some level).

I saw Richard Nixon with Howdy Dowdy (Probably not valid on any level).

I saw Mick Jagger and Lucille Ball having a good time while her husband Ricky looked on in a voyeuristic way.

I saw Abraham Lincoln trying to seduce the Brady Bunch daughters.

I saw Martin Luther King, Jr. …and my mom.

And I might have seen Sara and Dax…and Sara and Jesse…and Jesse and Dax.

I remember (or imagined) a long interval in which Sara and I became involved, and the three guys stood by, leering as we performed intimate acts.

And most of all, I remember Jesse and I were involved in something that we had both been thinking about for a long time.

Did any or all of this happen? I don't know. But, on the other hand, our nakedness and the general soreness I felt down under told me that something had happened. But what?

We all clothed ourselves, stoked the fire, had breakfast, broke camp, and were on our way. We never talked of the incident again…and we never took peyote again.

25

# "I'M A MAN"

## - BO DIDDLEY (AND LATER THE YARDBIRDS)

Our Yellowstone visit came not long afterward. We decided that, for the sake of peace and harmony, there would be no more historical stops. I know that we did other national parks… and they were beautiful. But the whole "eight miles high" thing makes them hazy. We had been stopping along the road to skinny dip in any reasonable-looking body of water. At the time, it was our only way to get clean. It was amazing that we had few inhibitions about seeing each other naked. But, of course, much of the world was not as free-spirited and our "bathing rituals" soon ended. Well, the increasingly cool temperatures may have had something to do with it too.

In Yellowstone, we stayed at a campground and used public bathhouses. Sometimes, you have to live a life of luxury. We toured the place for days and saw all the magnificent sights. Its beauty stunned us into a semi-sobriety. (This was helped by our constant contact with park rangers.)

The entire park sits upon a volcano which I imagine could erupt someday. For lack of a better word, it is covered with a crust of soil and water. The heated water often breaks through the crust, resulting in the beautiful geysers and striking multicolored heated ponds. Of course, I won't mention the forests, mountains, flowing rivers…and animals. This brings me to one of the more dangerous, or at least exciting stories of our Magical Mystery Tour.

On our third day of touring the sights, we parked in a lot and took off to see something called the Dragon's Den. It was a small cave that would periodically shoot steam from its mouth, giving the impression that a dragon was inside. It was fascinating. Yet, the events that followed made us forget how cool it was.

As we trekked back a quarter mile from the cave's location, we started to hear a commotion from the parking lot. The tenor of the crowd was loud but didn't give us any clue as to its cause. The funny thing was that we heard a mixture of laughter among the cries of distress. Then, as we approached, we started to hear words…Buffalo…in heat…battle…and…van!

Coming into the clearing, we saw three buffalo trudging through the parking lot. In front was a male and female intent upon producing some tiny buffalo babies. Following about forty feet behind lumbered another male. I don't know if he had a previous relationship with the female or was following the scent of hormone perfume. For whatever reason, he had chosen to challenge her current suitor for the rights to her virginity.

Both males eyed each other with vicious and evil intent, and it was clear that a battle would soon ensue. I knew from watching a ranger film the day before that these could be violent and destructive to the surrounding areas. Luckily, the threesome had cleared most of the parking lot, and only one vehicle lay in the path of the soon-to-be encounter—our van!

The crowd looked on with horror as the two bison bulls turned toward each other menacingly. We all held our breath, wondering how we would survive if our van became the victim of this love triangle. How would we go anywhere and do anything once stranded in one of the most underdeveloped areas of America?

We all watched the battle unfold. Well... not all of us. We soon saw Lars running into the parking lot right into the middle of the soon-to-be war zone. He was waving his hands to the two combatants. At first, Lars looked like the referee setting the ground rules for the fight. The two bulls didn't seem to be showing any deference to Lars until he threw rocks at them! Both macho males may have forgotten the lovely lady of their dreams and decided to team up against this madman who was attacking them. They grunted and hissed, pawed their hooves into the ground, always signs of an imminent escalation. They started to move toward our friend, and we were about to look away in horror when we saw Jesse streaking onto the scene. He was barely looking at his brother but instead made a beeline to the van. While Lars was only seconds away from becoming permanently sandwiched between two angry bison, Jesse started the van and drove to the opposite end of the parking lot. We looked at Lars as the two enraged bulls were now chasing him. Lars was young and athletic, but even Usain Bolt only ran 27 mph while winning all his Olympic medals—and a buffalo can hit 40 mph.

It was apparent that the crowd had lost all its joy and amusement as they realized that this was now a matter of life and death. I joined Dax, Sara, and many in the crowd and ran toward the action. We all screamed like maniacs in hopes of distracting the charging bulls from their mission. Although we perhaps did make them hesitate a split second, we couldn't tell. While Lars sprinted toward a waist-high stone wall that surrounded the lot, we knew any edge we could give him would increase his chances of survival. The crowd screeched and yelled as a diversion until we saw Lars dive over the wall just ahead of being gored by the lead attacker.

When he was out of sight, the two bison soon lost interest and returned to their pursuits. Finally, the challenger seemed to realize that his opponent was much faster than he was and that he might seek female companionship elsewhere. So, the happy couple went their way for a night of amorous pleasure, and the loser went off searching for an easier target for his urges.

***

For us humans, the reunion was joyous but brief. It occurred to us that park rangers would soon be on the scene, and they may not look kindly on Lars' stunt. Without a word, the hugs were quickly replaced by a race to the van to make our getaway. While we were all boisterous on the trip back to our campsite, Sara sat silent. That lasted until we exited the van, at which point she promptly slapped Lars in the face.

"Are you a goddamn idiot? Nothing was worth that risk," she sobbed. "I could've lost you."

I reacted differently and hugged Jesse like there was no tomorrow. I snarled, "You Johansen brothers are insane." My reaction was different because there was no bond established between us. Someday, there might be, but for now, there was not. I could not claim to be hurt by his actions because he owed me nothing but friendship. Yet the hug we shared seemed a bit more than friendship.

Dax broke up the love/friendship fest with a simple statement.

"You wouldn't see any Lakota pulling that crap. We have over two thousand years of dealing with *Tatanka* to know better. You got freakin' lucky." He walked away, shaking his head.

Jesse looked strangely, and he, too, walked away. That left me on the other side of the van from the ensuing fight between Lars and Sara. I should have minded my own business. I didn't.

"We needed our van...," started Lars before quickly getting cut off by Sara.

"More than I need you? More than you need to be alive? Are you nuts? What were you thinking?

"I...I...,"

"Come on, spit it out, asshole."

I couldn't see them, but something changed in the conversation. The anger seemed to subside, and Lars's voice broke as he spoke.

"Do you know what today is?"

"Lars, no, and I don't care."

"It's November 1, the day I was supposed to report for induction into the army. Instead, today, I am officially a fugitive."

"So what? You figure suicide by buffalo would somehow solve that problem?"

"No, I knew I needed to be able to get to Canada, and with no van, I saw no way of that happening."

"Oh," Sara's voice seemed to soften, and I could tell she was now hugging him tightly. "But the Lars, I know you would figure out how to make Canada happen with or without a van. So there's something else going on. What is it?"

"No, no, that's it."

"Lars…honey, you're fucking lying."

With that, I heard Lars start to sob, and I felt like a horrible person for listening in on this conversation. However, I now had no choice. I couldn't slip away without being seen.

"I'm feeling like a coward—just like my father told me I was. I'm running instead of fighting for my country."

"But Lars, we were together in Chicago. Is that the government you want to fight for?"

"I don't know if I really feel that way, or am I just finding it convenient to think the draft is wrong because…I am a coward?"

"Okay, if you have second thoughts and want to change your mind and stay…"

"No, I don't think so."

"Okay, then I have to ask again why suicide by buffalo?"

"I'm still a man."

"I sure hope so."

"No, listen. Let me get this out."

"Okay."

"I was raised to believe that real men are tough and brave and don't run away from fights. So I guess on some level, I think that is what I am doing to my country—running out on a fight."

"Or you could look at it like you are fighting a different war... one against the system."

"Am I?"

"Aren't you?"

"I just don't know. I know that at that very minute, I needed to show my bravery to you, to Jesse, to myself...to everyone."

"Okay, now that's stupid."

"No, it's not. It's what I felt...and feelings can't be right or wrong—they are what they are."

There were no more words, and I slipped away as they hugged each other.

# 26

# "HELLO. GOODBYE"

## - THE BEATLES

There is not much more to the story of the Wrigley Rockers. In a business-like manner, we made our way to Seattle and soon to the Canadian border. We all knew our Magical Mystery Tour through parts of America was ending. More than that, our tight-knit friendship would be torn asunder.

By the time we arrived at our journey's end, we had barely known each other for a year. We had been through so much that it seemed like a lifetime. Unfortunately, I would never see Lars again, as he permanently took up Canadian residence. Through the years, we wrote to each other, and somehow, I picked up that he still retained some guilt about abandoning America. Why? Most draft resistors who fled the country returned soon after President Jimmy Carter pardoned them. As a result, many obnoxiously took the attitude of "I told you so." This did not sit well with the war veterans, many of whom had suffered injuries or lost friends.

From Lars' later letters, I didn't get that attitude. He felt he had left the country purely for himself and the life he wanted to build with Sara. He grew even more confused when he and Sara ended their marriage in 1980. I stopped hearing from him after that.

Sara returned to Chicago and started a new life. She and I are still in contact now and then. However, our real friendship would never be the same after she walked across the border. The world of the Wrigley Rockers, in effect, ended that day.

At the time, I questioned why Jesse didn't also cross into Canada. His bond should have been stronger with his brother than with Dax and me. Or maybe, it was just me that he was staying around for. He didn't say that to anyone, instead opting for the attitude that he just needed to escape his brother's shadow and be his own man. I thought, *really?*

I'll never know what was going on in everyone's mind as we said our final goodbyes. Lars and Jesse clenched in a hug like they never had in their entire lives together. Indeed, it was probably the first time they had ever been separated since Jesse's birth. Sara and I held each other closely. She had become almost a sister to me—a confidante and ally in our constant friendly clashes with the three male members of the group. When we broke our embrace, Dax surprised us by hugging Sara and Lars. Tears were in his eyes. That rough, defensive, combative persona he constantly exuded slipped away, and we saw how deeply he did feel. Dax recovered quickly, mumbled a goodbye, walked away, and yelled, "Remember the Mandan!"

"Remember the 7th Calvary," answered Lars, to which Dax turned, smiled, and gave him the peace sign, which quickly devolved into a middle finger. He kept walking.

Jesse and I stood staring at the couple. There were no more words to say. We arranged to stay by a pay phone until Lars and Sara could safely call us with assurances that they had made it safely into Canada. It's crazy to think how easy it would have been to use cell phones. However, Lars and Sara started their new life on New Year's Day, 1969, and pay phones were still the only way for us to communicate. Eventually, when they were settled, both brothers contacted their parents and exchanged phone numbers.

And so, at the dawn of 1969, a year known for the moonwalk, Woodstock, and the summer of love, Jesse, Dax, and I set out on the next leg of our American adventure.

# PART IV

## "SAN FRANCISCO NIGHTS"

### - ERIC BURDON

The City by the Bay
(1969)

2 7

# "SAN FRANCISCO (BE SURE TO WEAR FLOWERS IN YOUR HAIR)"

## - SCOTT MCKENZIE

Our trip from the Canadian Border was long but uneventful. The three of us were feeling empty by the loss to our group. Our funds were starting to grow low. Our travels now depleted the accumulated bankroll created by our labors at Wrigley. We also agreed to give more than half of what we had left to Lars and Sara to start their new life in Canada.

The cost of gas in 1969 was only $.34 a gallon—much cheaper than the cost of motels at that time. Therefore, we drove in shifts nearly twenty-four hours a day, with the non-drivers sleeping as much as possible. We didn't know what we expected to find in San Francisco, but we had to try. In 1967, Scott McKenzie released his song, San Francisco (Be Sure to Wear Flowers in Your Hair), and I am guessing that we felt the song's aura drew us there. *If you come to San Francisco, you're gonna find some gentle people there.*

We needed gentleness after the tumultuous year we had had. Little did we know that the 100,000 people who felt the same vibe of the song and had overrun the city in the summer of 1967 were now gone. This was 1969. We were two years too late. That "summer of love" of 1967 was long gone by the time of our arrival.

I knew that we had never considered ourselves trendsetters but did not realize that we were so far behind the curve.

By October 1967, those who had come for the "Summer of Love" had vanished. Some had left disillusioned. Some had left to try something different on remote communes. Some had left to return to the real world of school, jobs, and futures. And some had no futures. Instead, as drug usage took a stronger and more deadly turn, many became trapped in a life-long sentence of addiction— and for many, that life wasn't *very* long.

We had no idea about all this as we headed into the eye of the beast. I don't know if we would have changed our destination if we did. The illusive San Francisco of 1967 is what we were seeking, and we were too blind to see it was not there anymore. Our little research showed a place rich in the one thing we all agreed on —music.

The city may have devolved from its "Summer of Love" attitude, but at least it had been replaced by a city of music, music, and more music. We didn't research the issue further. That was all we were interested in—I thought. There was an ugly side to this San Francisco, and I rationalized that we could steer clear of it. We didn't.

We quickly found jobs, a cheap apartment and settled into a new steady life. I only remember a little of the job or the apartment. We found a dump just on the outskirts of Haight-Ashbury, which became too expensive because of the faux hippies who hijacked it. These phonies lived very button-down, traditional lives. To actually live in Haight-Ashbury, or "Hasbury," as some writer dubbed it, you had to have a job in a bank or something substantial in that vein. However, at night these phonies could don their "hippie" clothes, go out on the town, and pretend they were participating in the long-gone hippie movement. Occasionally, they would write home to Tulsa, Omaha, or some other place of origin and tell everyone back there that they were living a "free spirit" lifestyle that would be the envy of their Mid-Western friends. It was all lies.

Our home sweet home had three bedrooms which was its only redeeming quality. Getting hot water was hit-or-miss, and we had to bundle up when it got cold because the heat, too, was sporadic. It was good that we had trained ourselves in our long trek across the northern states of America during the chilly autumn. Our three-story walkup did come complete with some pets—of the rodent variety. Still, we had a roof over our heads for the first time since Chicago.

Like Chicago, it was again all about the music. Excuse me while I name-drop just a bit of who we heard and saw...

- Janis Joplin and Bo Diddley at the Winterland
- Grateful Dead and Jefferson Airplane at Golden
  Gate Park
- Credence Clearwater and again Jefferson Airplane
- The Doors and Elvin Bishop at the Cow Palace
- The Who at the Fillmore West
- And then there was the Wild West Festival at Kezar
  Stadium which had Joplin, the Airplane, Country Joe,
  Santana, Sly and the Family Stone and the
  Youngbloods.

More than a decade and a half later, that same Jefferson Airplane group had morphed into the Jefferson Starship, and then just Starship. They reflected better than I ever could when they sang in 1985 "We Built This City on Rock and Roll."

We heard many more groups, but with the passage of time, I can only remember the most famous acts. In reality, if it isn't apparent already from what I have written, the three of us lived for the music. It made the drudgery of our daily lives go away. Dax had a decent job as a mechanic, while I became a waitress and Jesse a bartender (at first, with only daytime shifts). Yet we often talked to each other during our time in San Fran. We became as close as any three friends could ever be. We shared ourselves without any restrictions. I would only find out later that each of us held back one secret from the others.

2 8

# "DO YOU WANT TO KNOW A SECRET? "(REPRISE)

## - THE BEATLES

*I* had feelings for Jesse. I realized it more and more each day. But I didn't act upon those feelings for a while. It was awkward with Dax living with us, and I didn't want him to feel like a third wheel. However, my main reason for holding off was my fear of rejection. We had gotten so close on many occasions. In the sunflower field in North Dakota, we had a moment. But now? I just didn't know.

The situation stayed this way until mid-March, and then Dax mysteriously stopped hanging out with us as much. He was there living with us and being our friend, but something else was going on in his life that he would not share with us.

"Come on. What's been going on with you?" tried Jesse one night after dinner.

Dax looked at him like he wasn't even worth answering. Finally, begrudgingly, he replied, "Nothing." *A lie.*

"You do remember that I was...I *am* the good paleface in our group?"

"Hey!" I interjected.

"Maria, you know that I'm talking man to man here," scolded

Jesse...but then he smiled at me and laughed out loud. Then, he turned back to Dax and continued, "Where's that fun-loving black man-*slash*-Indian that we know and love?"

"Or this week, is it Indian-*slash*-black man?" I added, trying to be funny. But, unfortunately, my comment went over like a lead balloon. Dax scowled at me, but just as quickly, a smile started to creep across his face.

"You understand that you are the only two people in this world I would allow to talk to me like this? So yeah, I took it from Sara... and Lars—a.k.a the bad paleface you referenced." Then he did the unexpected and went to the two of us and hugged us.

"In this ugly world, you two are my rocks. But..." He let the word hang there for a bit before eventually finishing the sentence, "I wish you two would stop making believe that you don't want to screw each other's pants off. It's obvious from where I stand that that's what is happening here." He knowingly shook his head and abruptly left the room, saying only, "See you later...and I hope it's naked."

Jesse and I were speechless. What do you say after that?

"Hey, Janis Joplin's at the Winterland tonight."

"I'm in," I quickly answered Jesse.

*Well, so much for my secret.*

---

Awkward, tongue-tied, self-conscious, uncomfortable, uneasy. I didn't need a thesaurus to explain how we both felt. Dax had called us out, and to use a gross but entirely accurate metaphor, *it was time to shit or get off the pot!* Janis Joplin was an excellent stall while we both tried to figure out the next step.

And she was damn good that night. We got lost in her singing, yet somewhere in the middle of her version of "Summertime," I noticed that we were holding hands. As the song continued, we looked into each other's eyes, and I thought *this would finally happen.* He slipped his hand from mine, moved slightly behind me, and put both arms around me, and rested his head on my shoulder. Soon his lips were kissing my neck.

Music has always been an aphrodisiac to me. *Did this go back to Johnny and his obsession with music in every facet of his life?* No, I had to think, *this is Jesse, and this is the start of something extraordinary.*

Janis sang on, though I noticed her performance less and less until she started to sing my absolute favorite tune by her, "Piece of My Heart." Then, unconsciously, or maybe consciously, I sang along with her opening lyrics…

*Didn't I make you feel,*
*Like you were the only man?*

I continued to sing the words softly and thought no one, especially Jesse, could hear me. But he did because he held me tighter and tighter until Joplin's voice filled the air with the dramatic crescendo of the chorus.

*Take it,*
*Take another little piece of my heart now, baby.*

I heard no more words after that as Jesse turned me toward him and gave me the long, passionate kiss I had waited so long to receive. Not many people walked out on a performance by Janis Joplin, but we did. We made our way back to our apartment.

Dax didn't get to see us naked (that night), but he sure would have been proud of us.

1967 might have been the summer of love for most of the city. But 1969 was for me. It had none of the erotic passion of my one night with Trio in Chicago, but it was a warm, comforting feeling of being loved without the drama or roadblocks of Johnny.

# "WE BUILT THIS CITY ON ROCK AND ROLL"

## - STARSHIP

*I*t started quite accidentally. While Jesse and I were enjoying our quiet nights at home after our long hard days at work, the spring flew by in a flurry of concerts and love-making. Of course, we did other things, but I don't remember anything that was as much fun as the love-making and the concerts. Am I being repetitive?

By the start of the summer, Jesse got an offer that he couldn't pass up—to switch his bartending shifts to nights. Bartenders made immensely more money with nighttime crowds that they did during the day.

So reluctantly, we gave up a great deal of our time together. It was okay with me because our relationship was rock solid by then. Jesse was given his big break by his manager Allen Wong, and he had to take it. As the weather warmed up, I would take the streetcar to the bar and hang out. His boss didn't mind because he liked Jesse. Sometimes Dax even came—if he was in a good mood. One night Allen looked at the three of us with a smirk on his face and joked, "The Mod Squad." We didn't get it, and we stared at him blankly.

"You know, the TV show, The Mod Squad," stated Allen in disbelief.

"Allen, we don't own a TV. Maybe if you paid me more, we could afford one," replied Jesse with a smile.

"No, I don't think I've watched a single show since I left New York more than two years ago," I added.

"What's a TV?" chimed in Dax, only half serious. So much of his childhood had been spent on a reservation without TV or reception.

When Allen realized that we weren't kidding, he tried to explain.

"It's three young, I mean really young, cops who work undercover. The tagline is 'One white, one black, one blonde."

"But I'm not blonde," I answered. I understood what he was referring to, but I just wanted to bust his chops.

"I don't care. I think I'll call you three that anyway."

It was interesting that Allen, third-generation Chinese, did not seem bothered that the 'Mod Squad' was missing one particular minority.

I only mention this story because, eventually, we would warp the whole Mod Squad name to create the name of *our* band.

I remember distinctly it was July 3 when Dax and I took a trip down to the Wild Thing Club. It was a beautiful summer day, and neither Dax nor I wanted to stay cooped up in the apartment, so we jumped on a streetcar and made our way to the Embarcadero and Fisherman's Wharf. We had some ice cream as we strolled along but still found ourselves a bit early for the time that we were supposed to arrive.

Jesse had gone to the club much earlier to prep for the nightly crowd, so when we made an entrance, I expected to find him working hard. I didn't. Instead, as Dax and I walked in the door, we heard the melodic sound of two guitars accompanying some perfect harmony. We held back so as not to interrupt the impromptu performance by Jesse and Allen.

I was in awe. I had randomly heard Jesse occasionally sing while we were on the road, but I had no idea of the force and timber of his full voice. And damn, he played the guitar—he never told me that. Dax wanted to barge in, but I restrained him so that I could hear more.

They did some Credence songs and some Beatles songs, but the harmony on "Bridge of Over Troubled Water" took my breath away. But then, my trance was broken by the booming voice of Dax yelling, "How about some soul music?"

"Hey, Dax. Hey Maria," yelled Allen as if he had known we were listening. "Well, so glad to see the whole 'Mod Squad' here." I frowned at the stupid reference, but Dax, a rare show of life, grabbed a microphone.

"How about 'Knock on Wood?" offered Dax, and Allen and Jesse complied. One verse into the song, Dax dragged me up to the stage and encouraged me to sing along. I always could sing. I had just never tried it in front of others.

Before I knew it, we were performing various current songs that were tinged with two, three, and sometimes four-part harmony. It was some of the most fun I had had since coming to San Francisco. Eventually, Jesse and Allen had to return to work, and the band whose instruments they had been using arrived—none the wiser about our short "borrowing" of their equipment. They were too distracted by the fact that their lead guitar had not shown up, and the rest of the band members were fighting about some insignificant matter. That band did perform that night, but not very well, and Allen had to warn them to get their act together. The next day was July 4, and the club would be full.

On July 4, we played everything we thought we could pull off without a mistake. Yes, I did say "we." The minor squabble of the house band, weirdly named Goosedown, had escalated to the point of an actual fistfight, and they had broken up. This was not great timing for Allen and his soon-to-be arriving holiday crowd. He quickly called Dax and me and told us, "To get our asses down to the club and become rock stars."

I think they were being nice to me. I was, by no means, necessary. Without me, they had three great singers (Dax, Allen, and Jesse). However, they quickly convinced me that I would be the "Grace Slick" of the group (Yeah, right).

When Dax and I arrived, we realized that Juan Castillo sat behind the drums. He was a third-generation Mexican American who was one of the nicest guys in the world. More importantly, he was the calm in the storm of the group that had once been Goosedown. He seemed ready to play with us, but we only had an hour to get some standard songs down. Nevertheless, miracles did happen in that hour. When we started to play, I noticed that Jesse was on the bass guitar. I remembered Johnny.

Moments before we took the stage, I believe it was Juan who came to the realization that we needed to have a name. Allen looked around, mumbling, "Gee, I've got my Mod Squad here and..." He looked around, started to laugh, and then spoke out loud, "Nordic-looking white man—check, Italian-looking white girl—check, Black/Native American man—check, Latino man—check, and Chinese man—check." He then started to ruminate thoughts in his head but was interrupted by me.

"Hey, asshole, how come you're all men, and I'm a 'girl'?"

"Sorry, okay, okay, Italian American woman—check. However, that doesn't change the name I picked."

We rolled our eyes when he announced we would be the "Odd Squad."

---

There were many great groups in Frisco then, and we were not one of them. We were a decent house band in a decent little club, and we were all making a little extra money. There were no record deals pending or stadiums to be filled, but we were having fun, and that's all that mattered.

# 30

# "TIME IN A BOTTLE"

## - JIM CROCE

That summer was one of the most beautiful times of my life. We listened to music at concerts, we played music at the Wild Thing Club, and through it all, Jesse and I were inseparable. It was a time that I will never forget—a time that I never *want* to forget. I felt the true beauty of romance in a way I never had before. To be able to hold hands in public or walk with our arms around each other was a feeling that had eluded me for so long. Sometimes, a good cuddle at home was as good as…well, you know.

We didn't aspire to be anything more than the house band at the Wild Thing Club, yet we were getting invited to play at other venues. The peak was when we performed as an opening act at a three-day Wild West Festival at Kezar Stadium on August 22. It featured Janis Joplin, Jefferson Airplane, the Dead, Santana, Country Joe, and many, many more. Of course, we were already home and in bed before any of the stars even got in the same time zone as the concert venue. However, it was an experience that I will never forget. However, it was our last moment of glory. It was not that anything dramatic occurred. It's just that in this world, shit happens.

The events that followed in the autumn proved that it all was not as real as I thought. Or maybe it was real, but things do change. In September, the crowds in the club began to thin, and all of San Fran seemed to go into slumber. More and more, a full band became a luxury that the club could only afford once or twice a week. I started taking more waitressing shifts, yet Jesse did not have to return to bartending full-time. Instead, he and Allen played a scaled-down acoustic show for the audience. Sometimes, I joined him (for free), and we had fun.

However, the duo was often asked to fill in here and there at other clubs—no big paydays but some off-the-books cash which helped. I did start to miss Jesse as he was out of the house five or six nights a week, either practicing or performing.

By October, I could see that Dax was slipping away. I had seen him truly happy for a few brief months that summer. The serious side of my friend had taken a back seat to his enjoyment of being on the stage. He was the true soul of our group in both the literal and figurative senses of the word. I still can see that big smile as he sang something slow and tender by Otis Redding or Percy Sledge. Or I imagine him jumping around in unheard-of acrobatics as he sang harmony with me on Eddie Floyd's "Knock on Wood," playfully faux knocking on my head as Juan did the actual knocking on his snare drum. My rebuttal was to sing an obscure Stones' song called "Play with Fire," pointing in his direction as a warning. Such good times.

However, as summer turned to fall, he started to miss the few gigs we did have, and more often, it was just me singing with guys. I knew Dax was into something big. I didn't know how historically big until it was too late.

I was miserable most of September and October. Juan and Allen had come to share the house with Dax, Jesse, and me. When the whole gang was there, it was a great place to be, full of laughs and good times. However, more often, Dax was not around, and Jesse and Allen were off doing their acoustic thing. Some nights it was just Juan and me, and Jesse trusted me so much that he never seemed jealous that I was spending so much time with another man. Then Juan started to pick up some sporadic drumming jobs, and I was alone. I found I was by myself so many nights that I broke down, bought a TV…and even watched the Mod Squad. However, soon the events proved that the feelings of the summer were not as genuine as I thought. Or maybe they were real…but again…things do change in this world.

November arrived, and I started to rethink many of my life choices. Was this all there was? However, then Jesse would come home, and I was happy. Perhaps this would be enough—a good man in my life, a few friends, and a roof over my head. However, soon that group of friends became much smaller.

After November 20, I only saw Dax once again. I knew where he was, but that didn't matter.

# 31

# "REVOLUTION"

## - THE BEATLES

I woke up to Jesse screaming from the living room to our bedroom. He sounded insanely worried about something, and I had no idea what.

"Maria, think hard. When was the last time you saw Dax?"

"Probably two days ago. You know, sometimes he crashes at friends' houses," I answered, now starting to worry.

"But we're his friends. Why…What do they have that we don't?" ranted Jesse sounding like a jealous boyfriend.

"They're Native American…we're not…if you hadn't noticed."

"Have you ever met any of these so-called friends?"

"Yes, but now you're weirding me out, Jesse."

"Look at the TV," he ranted and pointed at the screen.

We did.

*The former prison on Alcatraz Island has been taken over by an estimated eighty Native Americans, led by Canada Means, Richard Oakes, and John Trudell. The justification for the occupation is a little-*

*known agreement from 1868 known as the Treaty of Fort Laramie. That treaty stated that all Indian lands in government possession that were abandoned should be returned to Native American hands. The leaders, calling themselves IOAT—Indians of All Tribes, have seized Alcatraz Island because it has been decommissioned as a prison by the United States government. At present, it is estimated that 89 men, women, and children are involved in the occupation.*

We knew that one of those 89 was our friend Dax. I had met him on the street one day, and he had reluctantly introduced me to his friends, Canada Means and Richard Oakes. It was a bit awkward. I felt as if Dax was ashamed of having a white friend. Means and Oakes seemed disinterested in even saying hello to me and soon continued on their way. Dax shrugged his shoulders and followed them like a puppy dog. I should have suspected that he was up to something with these two. However, I was so wrapped up in my own situation that I thought no more about it. After listening to the TV broadcast, Jesse and I went into Dax's room. On his neatly made bed was a simple note.

"I had to do it."

"So do I. So do we," I pleaded to Jesse. We had to assist Dax in his quest. With all the stealth of secret agents, we located members of Dax's organization who were not on Alcatraz. We then solicited contributions from the communities we knew agreed with the cause. Finally, on a cold and foggy night in the late fall, we took a boat out to the island with much-needed supplies and, more importantly, more volunteers seeking to be part of the action. When we arrived, Jesse and I sought out Dax.

"What the hell? Are you two crazy? This isn't your fight." That was the "warm" welcome we received from our friend.

"We may not understand the cause that well, but if you're for it, we're here for you," I pronounced proudly. Expecting gratitude, we received only Dax's wrath.

"You guys had hundreds of years to make things right with my people...and did nothing. We learned that if we want our rights, we will have to take them. Isn't that what your forefathers did in 1776?"

"Yeah, but even they had help from outsiders. We couldn't have won our independence without the French. So, Dax, Parlez-vous francais?"

I don't know if my logic got through to him, but he did smile at us. He then took us to see the island and their situation. Afterward, he walked us to the waiting boat, and we vowed to return.

"Don't," Dax again displayed anger. We argued for our right to help him. He argued that the best way we could help would be by staying away.

"I love you guys, and I'll never forget my *good* paleface friends, but...this is one case where your whiteness is a detriment. The politicians are all dancing around the situation because they don't want to be seen as the ones picking on us poor minorities. But you guys are another story. They'll throw the book at your white asses for aiding and abetting insurrection. Seriously, they'll show no mercy to you. So go with my peace and love always."

We almost found out first-hand that Dax knew what he was talking about. On the return trip to the mainland, the Coast Guard intercepted us. Faced with being captured, we realized everything that Dax had said. It all became very real. We envisioned our incarceration, our trial, and ...who knew what?

Our trip organizers made a dash for it under the Golden Gate Bridge. The dark shadows of the bridge gave us cover as we jumped overboard and swam to shore in the cold, dark waters. Only one person was on board when the Coast Guard seized the vessel. He was booked...but let out. He was Native American. The ensuing months would prove Dax's warnings prophetic as non-Native

American activists were pursued, arrested, and punished for being occupation sympathizers.

We never saw Dax again. The media dubbed it the "Occupation of Alcatraz Island." Eventually, an estimated 400 people participated. It started on November 20, 1969, and lasted until June 11, 1971, when the government, on President Nixon's orders, took back the island and made it a tourist site.

By January 1970, I was long gone from San Francisco. I went through many transformations in my life that this memoir will reveal, but I never forgot Dax. For a few years, I wondered what had happened to him.

On February 27, 1973, I turned on my TV and saw the occupation of Wounded Knee by 200 Oglala Sioux. They were part of a group called AIM (American Indian Movement) that was protesting many of the issues that the Alcatraz group had brought to the public. They had chosen the site of the 1890 infamous Massacre at Wounded Knee—the unprovoked killing of 250 mostly unarmed Lakota men, women, and children. There, front and center for the cameras was Dax Lightfeather. He had finally gone home.

# 32

# "SYMPATHY FOR THE DEVIL"

## - THE ROLLING STONES

I grieved the loss of Dax. I knew there was nothing I could do about his situation. He was where he wanted to be. That didn't dampen my sense of loss. However, I didn't know then that it was just the beginning of my life becoming a shit show. I couldn't foresee that it was just the first step in a downward spiral that would conclude in everything I knew crashing to earth less than three weeks later.

I sought out music—my go-to escape from stress. I spent a great deal of time going to the clubs where Jesse and Allen played. However, Jesse seemed to have less and less time for me as he and Allen practiced even during their breaks. I then decided to seek out other concert venues. However, traveling alone as a young female could prove dangerous even in the Age of Aquarius. Dax was gone, and Jesse and Allen could have been on Alcatraz, too, for all I saw of them. Sometimes, I drafted Juan to be my concert buddy.

Before you think this story is going in the wrong direction, Juan and I were just friends until the end. Juan was tall, dark, and handsome, and would have been a catch for any available woman. However, I was still in love with Jesse—until I wasn't. So, no, Juan was just a friend. In fact, he was the one who helped with my departure from Frisco just before Christmas of 1969. But I am getting ahead of myself.

---

Jesse and I were supposed to attend a huge concert on December 6 at San Jose State University until the powers that be at that location decided that they were not in the mood for 100,000 crazy kids trampling through their hallowed grounds. Next, they tried changing the venue to Kezar Stadium, but there was a conflict with a 49ers' football game. The site was changed again to the racetrack in Sonoma, but there was an argument between the owners and promoters, so at the last minute, they switched to another racetrack east of Livermore.

Jesse realized it was too far for Allen and him to make it there, after they performed at the opposite end of town. Therefore, it was Juan and I who went to see Santana, Crosby, Stills, Nash and Young, the Grateful Dead, and the Rolling Stones.

From the beginning, the concert vibe was just not right. It could have been because it was being held at a racetrack and the stage setup was not very conducive to the audience. Or perhaps it was the security detail...Hell's Angels. Nothing seemed right at Altamont Racetrack.

---

There was no clue what would come when Santana started the concert with a great set of songs that included "Evil Ways" and "Soul Sacrifice." However, when the Jefferson Airplane began to perform, singer Marty Balin had to jump into the crowd to break up a fight.

The problem intensified as the day went on. The Hell's Angels' "pay" for their security services had been unlimited beer, and the more they drank, the more *they* became *the* security problem. A local group, the Ace of Cups, had their lead singer hit with a beer bottle, and Stephen Stills was stabbed in the leg with a bike spoke. Seeing this, the Grateful Dead refused to perform, leaving the night's final performance to Rolling Stones. In every sense of the word, this was the climax of an event that will never be forgotten.

In an irony above all ironies, the Stones were playing the song "Sympathy for the Devil" when it all went to Hell. Someone was stabbed to death right in front of the stage by a Hell's Angel. I was there and saw it happen, yet in all the chaos, I am not sure if anyone, including me, could understand the horrific event's details.

I didn't see a gun, but according to later accounts, a man named Meredith Hunter pulled a gun and aimed at Mick Jagger. One of the Hell's Angels grabbed his gun with his left hand and then stabbed him to death with his right. Other Angels then stomped on his body.

I didn't see that last part happen because I was one of the thousands running in panic. My only thoughts were that it was all over. The Age of Aquarius, the time of peace and love, the hippie movement, and the Woodstock Nation all died that day at that racetrack called Altamont.

# 33

# "IT'S ALL OVER NOW"

## - THE ROLLING STONES

$\mathscr{I}$ wanted to see Jesse. I needed to see Jesse and have him hold me in his arms and tell me everything would be alright. First, I needed to find out where he was. He should still be at the club he was playing at that night. Yet if I went there, he might already be finished and be on his way home. Therefore, I decided to return to the apartment, even though it was early, and I knew I wouldn't have Jesse there. Juan did everything to comfort me, but he wasn't my boyfriend.

When we arrived, I first noticed the faint glimmer of light in our bedroom. Jesse could never be home this early, so I feared that we had stumbled on a robbery in progress. I wanted to rush up, but Juan wisely told me to take it slow. He would go first and carefully check out the situation. He ran to our bedroom while I kept my distance. He found it unlocked and slowly made his way. Impatient, I followed not too far behind.

Juan put his finger to his lips to alert me to be quiet. He heard noises from our bedroom and looked through the crack in the door. He ran toward me, whispering that we needed to leave. However, I was too angry, or stupid to leave. I knew there was something he did not want me to see. I pushed past him, not knowing what it would mean.

Jesse rolled over in surprise and looked at me. He had been cheating on me…with Allen.

This explained quite a few mysteries that had puzzled me for the previous few months. Why did the time spent practicing and playing not add up to very much income? Why had Jesse been distant and our love life in decline?

I remained numb and silent as their naked bodies untangled. I left and cautioned Juan not to follow me.

If you think this was a surprise twist to my story, imagine how it felt for me to live through it. I stayed away from our home for three or four days while I got my head together. That's what I told myself, but there would be no getting anything together until I spoke to Jesse. I had to know what he was thinking about all the months he had spent with me. With much trepidation, I called and asked him to meet me alone at Golden Gate Park.

"I love you, Maria," were the first words from his mouth. I thought of not answering at all and letting him proceed with an explanation. However, I was too angry to let that happen.

"You have a funny way of showing it," I screamed at him. I hadn't meant to do that, but confusion and heartbreak welled in my heart.

"No, Maria, I love you as I have never loved anyone before," was his soft-spoken reply.

"And Allen," I continued to vent my anger.

"Maria, it was the first time with…"

"A man," I finished his sentence and continued, "I don't know if that makes it better or worse than if you cheated on me with another woman. To be honest, I didn't know the answer to that question. If he loved me more than any woman in the world, but didn't want a woman at all, was that less hurtful? I decided I had to listen to him to find the answer I sought.

"I thought I could spend the rest of my life with you...to marry you...to have children...to grow old with you."

"I *did* think that's where we were heading." I couldn't hold back the tears anymore, but I listened.

"I always knew that I was different from Lars and all my friends. I faked interest when they talked about their lust for the opposite sex as young teens. My mind was already confused by my desire for many of the guys in my class. I guess I fooled everyone, including myself, about who I really was."

"And you fooled me," I barely replied…barely able to respond.

"You must understand that I love you more than I can describe, but…"

"But now you know that we could never last because you know that your heart belongs with Allen."

"God, no! Allen has always known that he was gay. Yet, somehow, I allowed my closeness with him to give me the courage…the courage to try…"

"Say it, damn it. The courage to screw a man!"

"I was going to say an *alternate lifestyle*, but yeah, you're right."

"And?"

"Maria, it's where I belong. I said that wrong. It's who I am. I had to try it."

"So was Allen the experiment…or was I?"

"It's not that simple. I thought that I could be straight, that I could fit in. I was wrong."

"So? Allen?"

"No, there were no feelings there at all. You can't understand. I wish I had the love and comfort I have with you and the desire and passion I have with Allen."

"I don't know if I should be proud or insulted by that statement."

"Proud. I will never love anyone as I love you. I hope you will stay, my friend forever."

"No," was my firm answer. In the moments of conversation, I had come to a decision—I was leaving. It wasn't just the heartbreak of Jesse but also the loss of Dax and my disillusionment with the entire San Francisco scene.

"Please, Maria, I need you to be my friend," pleaded Jesse.

I couldn't do it. I couldn't stay...and knew I couldn't be his friend. That day I couldn't find the words to explain what I felt. Then, two years later, a group named Lobo released a number-one song that explained what I should have said to him.

*"I love you too much,*
*To ever start liking you.*
*So don't expect me to be your friend."*

I related the story earlier of how I gave up on Johnny, and this had the same feel. It was a cold January day in 1970 when these very thoughts came back to my conscious mind. I hadn't heard the song again because that song had never made it to the West Coast. But I found myself humming the same tune and even softly singing the words just as I had when I left New York in 1968. I packed my bags. I gave up on Jesse.

*"Lord, he's all I've got,*
*And giving up is so hard to do."*

Perhaps if I had stayed, Jesse's life would have been different. I might have done something to change his fate. Maybe I'm giving myself too much credit.

Sara told me that he died in 1983. At the time, no one knew or understood the insidious disease that took him. Years later, it would have a name...AIDS.

# PART V

## "VIVA, LAS VEGAS"

### ELVIS PRESLEY

Las Vegas
(1970 to 1972)

# "DEVIL IN DISGUISE"

## - ELVIS PRESLEY

"Freedom's just another word for nothing left to lose." For some reason, this lyric kept rolling through my brain as I sat on the bus from San Francisco. Occasionally, I sang or hummed the tune aloud. I know this because the elderly lady sitting next to me was not a big fan of the late Janis Joplin's "Me and Bobby McGee" and was giving the evil eye as only mean old ladies can do.

It was the first time in my life I was utterly alone. From my overpowering parents to the Wrigley Rockers, there had always been someone there to talk to, to support me, and to help me. Now I had no one. But, like I said, "nothing left to lose."

After buying the bus ticket, I had about $47 in my pocket and some extra clothes in a backpack. This was all I had to show for more than two years of being away from home. I had been a pseudo-hippie long after hippies were no longer an "in-thing." I thought long and hard on that bus ride about where I would go from there, and my decision was inconsistent with who I had been.

Freedom is *more* than nothing left to lose. It is the ability to make your own choices. I decided that to make my own choices, I needed money—at least enough to be genuinely independent. Therefore, this little traveler was heading to Vegas to make money in any way possible. No more beads, fringed vests, or fingers in a "V" sign for peace. If this meant I had to tart myself up with makeup and tight clothes to make money, so be it…on to the glitz of Vegas.

Though I hid it well in my hippie persona, I knew I looked pretty good in a mirror. (False humility had no place in LV). I accentuated my physical assets in a way I never thought I would. I decided to dye my black, mid-back-length hair platinum blonde. This served as a disguise and added a higher level of sexiness. The credo of many at the time was that "gentlemen prefer blondes." In Vegas, it helped to be preferred. Gone also was the part in the middle of my hair that had been held in place by a headband that made me look more Native American than Italian. I lined my eyes with just enough mascara to make my green eyes pop. My lips displayed various shades of red, dependent upon my purpose that day. I didn't plan on being a hooker, but I knew that in "Sin City," how you looked went a long way toward getting you what you wanted. And I wanted independence, the kind that only money can buy.

I also decided that if I was going to start over, I would do it entirely incognito. Just in case my parents or Jesse wanted to come looking, I would be harder to find. I decided to hide my Italian heritage. The sound you hear is my grandfather Gennaro Speduti rolling over in his grave.

"Becky" always struck me as the ultimate WASP name. For the last name, I chose Simon, after the only person I knew in my Catholic high school who wasn't Italian or Irish.

I started my life as the blonde Becky Simon by finding a room to rent for twenty-five bucks a week. That meant I had two weeks to find a job before finding myself on the street.

With all the confidence of the sexy, new me, I walked from

restaurant to restaurant, searching for a waitressing job. However, it didn't matter how much cleavage you showed, it didn't make the customers buy more pancakes. A girl in the room next to me relayed that little fact of life.

"Now drinks…that's a whole other story. After a few drinks, guys think they stand a chance of hooking up with a beautiful girl like you."

"Really?" I wonder why this obvious fact eluded me.

"And this is Vegas, so sometimes they are right. Oh, it may cost them their wallet, but they'll get what they want."

"But I didn't come here to be a hooker," I stated a bit too emphatically.

"Good," replied the girl I would come to know as "Misty," though obviously, it was not her real name.

"Yeah, good. Because every damn one of us girls will be faced with that choice sooner or later. It's good you thought it out ahead of time…you know, it helps if you have your priorities set."

In reality, I hadn't thought out anything. This was my Catholic school upbringing speaking out of habit. Sex outside of marriage equals hell and damnation. Okay, I had already crossed that bridge, but to do it for a living? That seemed a whole other level of damnation, or, as Dante wrote, a lower ring of hell.

"I have so much to learn," I whimpered pathetically.

"Okay, lesson one: You can tell your boss is feeling you *out* for a 'promotion' when he feels you *up*. Yeah, it's standard practice to grab your boobs as a test. If you don't flinch, then you just might be auditioning for a job in the topless joint the guy owns down the street. And if you're already in the topless joint, you might be a candidate for extra-curricular fun and money."

"Misty, how do you know all this stuff?" I asked quite naively. She laughed heartily, stripped off her top, and stood before me naked from the waist up.

"Sorry, I just needed to get into my 'work clothes,'" chuckled

Misty. "Yeah, I took that first step, and I guess I'll wait for my next 'feel up' to think about what lies ahead."

Misty would be the closest thing to a girlfriend I had while living in Vegas. Eventually, her next audition came, and she took the job. After that, her financial status grew in leaps and bounds, and finally, she had enough to move out of the crappy joint we had shared. We still saw each other outside of work, but something had changed. Under the exterior of the beautiful clothes lay a sad little girl. She had made her choice, and I believe it had ripped out her soul.

# "STRANGE BREW"

## - CREAM

Giving up on the concept of working as a waitress in a food joint, I started to look into the bar scene. After failing on my own, Misty recommended me to her boss. I knew from our discussion that this meant that, at some point, I would have an "audition." I remember the Grassroots' song, "Live for Today" (and don't worry about tomorrow), continuously replaying in my head. I hoped to make enough money before my big tryout day. Then, again, maybe he wouldn't even want me. How would I feel about that if I was rejected? I didn't want to be a topless waitress, but did my pride make me want to be asked?

My first job was at a place called the Runaway. Is that irony or what? I had run away from home in January of 1968, and here I was over two years later, still running. As I have written many times in this memoir, Johnny always spoke to me about catching the wind. He said it would take us somewhere great—to a beautiful life together. But I hadn't caught any damn wind; I had become lost in that wind. I had been through so much and still didn't know which way it was blowing me.

Yet, I survived and carved out a decent life in Vegas. I started having some acquaintances I hung with in my free time. Notice I didn't say friends. I had friends in Cambria. Johnny, Gio, and the rest of the band were a part of my life, as was my best buddy Diane. But they are all gone now, mostly dead.

And then there were the Wrigley Rockers, Trio, and Smokey Joe. The latter two rested in peace, and the Rockers scattered to the four corners of the Earth. No, I didn't want friends anymore; that way, I wouldn't get hurt again. With Misty and our new gang, it was a loose tie of I'll-see-you-around-when-we're-all free.

Misty knew everyone I worked with at the Runaway because it was where she had started. It was a good thing. When I was hired as a bartender, I unequivocally lied about my knowledge as a mixologist. My boss, Denny, or "Dirtbag Denny," as I called him behind his back, knew how to make money off the misogynic men in his joint. Therefore, I don't know if he ever noticed that I knew nothing about making mixed drinks. I also think he hadn't looked beyond my sexy blonde hair and pushed-up boobs.

The main bartenders, Tom and Jerry (real names—you can't make this stuff up), took me under their wing and helped me to survive until I knew what I was doing. It was Tom who laid down the game plan.

- Reading the labels goes a long way toward making simple drinks.
- Ask the patron how they like their drink made—very often, they will give you a clue about what's in it.
- I should serve mainly the drunk patrons so they wouldn't notice if I made a mistake.
- I would serve the ones more interested in looking at my breasts than paying attention to what I gave them.

Tom and Jerry both laughed when I screwed up—which was quite often. When I did make a mistake, Jerry would shake his head and sing a verse from a famous Cream song, "Strange Brew...girl, what's inside of you?"

My social life consisted of all of us going to the diner when our shifts ended at 4 am or so. It was usually Tom, Jerry, Misty, me, and a rotating cast of people that one of us vaguely knew. We laughed a great deal...ate some pancakes...and then laughed some more. Months passed. I won't say I was gloriously happy, but I was content to go with the flow. My philosophy was much like Scarlett O'Hara's in *Gone with the Wind*—"Tomorrow's another day."

I was starting to spend some money and splurged and bought a car. Okay, not a new car. I don't even think my car was new when it was new. However, when it worked, the 1961 Mercury Comet was my pride and joy. It spent as much time with the mechanic as it did with me. If I were the jealous type, I would have thought my car was cheating on me with my mechanic. "Joey, the Stache" (because of the ever-present Fu Manchu on his face) was excellent at his job. His Brooklyn accent was telling, and there was a rumor that the mob had brought him to Vegas to work on their cars. Maybe he even emptied the contents of a trunk occasionally in the desert...if you catch my drift.

However, he was always honest with me. Every time I had the Comet repaired, he would caution me, "The next time this clunker breaks down, leave it where it sits and walk away...and take off the plates so that they can't be traced back to you. Those cops will find you and make you pay to have it towed to the junkyard."

Yet that 1961 Mercury Comet was the final piece of my freedom. On its good days, it took me to the solitude of the desert. I particularly liked walking in the Red Rock area, just outside town. It was so peaceful. Occasionally, I brought a folding beach chair. Sometimes, I would sit for hours, taking in the sun and sand.

Now and then, this could bring on depression. Lounging in the sun and sand raised the question...what's missing? Answer: The ocean or, for that matter, any body of water! I had grown up at

Rockaway Beach and Jones Beach. With this much sun and sand, I was supposed to be hearing waves crashing in the background.

I have to laugh at what I just wrote. Cambria Heights always seems to pop up in my thoughts. Johnny and his band had wanted to be musical stars, much like the one group that did make it out of our area through their music. The Shangri-Las were different because they were four women who didn't play instruments. But they were singers, and they were from Cambria, so they were role models. What does this have to do with the trajectory of my writing? The hit that propelled them to stardom was "Remember, Walking in the Sand."

There I sat, relaxing in my little getaway in the desert. Still, I was haunted by memories of my past…in the sand…at the beach… with Johnny. I remembered walking in the sand. At those times, I felt lonely and homesick for a life that no longer existed.

My malaise was evident at work. It was Tom who noticed. Eventually, we would grow to be friends, and before you get the wrong idea, there was absolutely, positively no sexual tension. Tom was one of the most decent men I have ever met, and he was extremely happily married. I guess he saw my incipient depression and invited me to dinner at his house. His wife Nancy was wonderful and self-confident enough not to be jealous of the sexy version of me at twenty.

I went there frequently and even volunteered to babysit occasionally so they could go out for a "date night." I enjoyed playing with Amy and Molly, their young daughters. It made me realize that this was a path my life could take.

Often after the girls were in bed, the three of us would sit and talk about life and other things. I couldn't understand why these thirty-somethings had taken me into their lives. Indeed, I had become so jaded that I expected at any moment for them to suggest ménage à trois. I thought that their interest was too pure for it to be real. I was wrong. They were as good as they seemed. I think they suspected my skepticism because the talk got serious one night.

"You know, Becky (that's me, in case you forgot), what my whole goal in life is?

"I don't know, Tom…maybe to win the super jackpot at the Mirage?"

Nancy laughed at my answer, but Tom just stared at me.

"No, I've seen people win big time in this town, and their life did not always change for the better.

"Try me," I glibly responded. "Okay, then, what is your ultimate goal?"

"To keep those two little girls, Amy and Molly, off the pole," Tom announced passionately.

I started to laugh, knowing that his reference was to the pole that strippers used in their acts. But then, I noticed he and Nancy were dead serious.

"This town will chew you up and spit you out…and not even blink while it does. I don't want that for my girls. If I could find a job somewhere else making the kind of money I do here, I'd be gone in a second."

I realized then that I was an extension of that belief. They were friends because they liked me… but also, they hoped to show me another choice in life…one not on a pole.

Tom left the room and came back later with something strange in his hand. He looked at me seriously as he handed me a little glass vial.

"What's this?" I asked, looking at him strangely.

"For an extreme emergency. But use it wisely—this hard-core stuff—tough to come by."

"Use it how?

"If you are ever being harassed or find yourself in a dangerous or awkward position while waitressing, pour this in the aggressor's drink. It works almost instantly to knock them out cold. Some waitresses and bartenders call it "the last resort cocktail."

"I can handle myself," I replied, both offended that Tom thought I was weak, but also touched that he cared enough to worry about me.

"Becky, you never know in this town," interrupted Nancy. "You can never have enough weapons against the sleazebags."

I smiled and stuffed it in my pocket, never thinking I would need it and not knowing how much I would.

Time flew by and I developed what could best be described as contentment. I had my late-night pancake breakfasts with the rotating group of people I worked alongside. I had my "family dinners" with Tom, Nancy, and the girls, I had my quiet visits to the solitude of the desert, and I had money for the first time in my life. However, I knew it was just a matter of time before I had my "audition" with "Dirtbag Denny," my pervert boss.

36

## "FOXY LADY"

### - JIMI HENDRIX

will always wonder if my family visits with Tom's family influenced my decision. I don't know if I ever considered following the path "to the pole," and beyond. However, my relationship with Tom and Nancy solidified my confidence and self-pride. There were just certain things I would not do for any amount of money.

I had come to expect that my audition would be coming soon. Misty had mentioned that hers had happened about six months into her stay. I was rapidly approaching that timeframe.

I considered various tactics to turn down his implied offer. Yet I had to face the fact that this was a training ground for bigger things. I had seen that it was either move up or move out. I wanted to stay right where I was, but that was not an option. Therefore, I was going out with a bang. I was going to slap him or kick him in the balls! That was it. I would go down in the annals of Vegas history as "Ballbuster Becky, the woman who gave Dirtbag Denny his due."

It never happened the way I expected. My audition came at an inopportune time for either slapping or kicking. The pervert waited for one of those rare times when I took the drinks I had prepared to a table. Loaded with a tray of eight Johnny Walker Blacks, for which I expected an extra-large tip, I found myself face-to-face with my boss.

"Maybe I could help you with those," Denny awkwardly mumbled. However, he firmly planted his greasy paws on my boobs instead of reaching for the tray. In my mind, the scenario would always involve only one boob and leaving me a free hand to slap the sonofabitch in his face. It never occurred to me that I would be balancing some very expensive scotch on a tray when the action happened. I improvised.

I took the entire tray of high-end drinks, raised it above his head, and then dumped it all over him. I could have worried about him taking the cost of the booze out of my pay, but I knew I now had no job, or pay, to take it out of. I enjoyed watching him bathe in the most expensive shower he'd ever taken. If he had ever taken a shower at all.

I didn't wait for him to get the satisfaction of throwing me out of the place. I shimmied across the floor to the door, shaking my ass as I had never done before. As I reached the exit, I turned to see Tom and Jerry laughing hysterically…and the dirtbag standing in the middle of the floor—wet and mortified. I couldn't resist one last dig. I walked behind the bar and grabbed the knife I had used to slice lemons only minutes before. I held it up for Denny to see.

"And that was no accident. Keep your hands to yourself. You're lucky I didn't cut off your balls."

# "PEACEFUL, EASY FEELING"

## - THE EAGLES

There had been a great deal of tension building in me waiting for that moment. It was all I had thought and worried about. It was all I had prepared for. That's probably why I felt such great relief when it was all over.

Would I have used the knife? No, I'm not crazy, and I didn't intend to spend years behind bars for the sake of one moment of pleasure. But Dirtbag Denny didn't know that, so maybe he'll think twice before auditioning anyone else. I doubt it. Guys like that get their kicks out of having power over women. I put him out of my mind the minute I walked out the door. I went home, put on jeans and a black sleeveless blouse, and took my trusty Mercury Comet out to the desert. This was a typical game plan for me. However, I usually did not do it at 3 am.

As I write in 2012, I think of the lyrics to the Eagles song that came out in the early 1970s— "Peaceful, Easy Feeling." I was thinking that I was finally at peace and felt at ease. But another line of the song was also true "I want to sleep in the desert tonight with a million stars all around." Okay, I know that the actual song lyrics say I want to sleep *with you* in the desert, but there was no "you" to sleep with, just me and the million stars. But that was okay. I liked myself; it was all I needed.

I mostly had mindless dreams while sitting in my well-worn beach chair. Then, I realized that with my black Comet pulled off the road in this out-of-way place, I was invisible to the world—an outsider. However, the world was not hidden from me.

At first, it was just a muffled rumbling in the distance. Then, as the vehicle grew closer and took shape, I knew it looked familiar. Yet something was different. The logo that should have announced the famed casino's name was covered by a hastily attached cloth cover disguising the less informed than me who owned this vehicle. Why someone had done this remained a mystery, as much as why this van was even on the road out of Vegas at 3 am. That moment I remember not caring. However, in the months to come, it would become a mystery I would solve, and it would change everything.

However, my immediate reaction was to have an ah-ha moment. The poorly masked van from the Flamingo Hotel and Casino guided me to my next move in life. With my experience as a bartender and waitress at the Runaway, I was ready to apply to one of the big boys in town, and why not the Flamingo Hotel and Casino?

I thought back to my last night in Cambria Heights and all those flamingos implanted on my lawn by my boyfriend as an insult to my obnoxious father. After that, I knew I would apply for a position at the Flamingo. Thanks, Johnny, for the inspiration.

My peaceful, easy feeling was now disrupted by the excitement I felt for my new game plan. I drove the Merc immediately to Tom and Nancy's to tell them.

"Damn, that was some exit," Tom smiled and hugged me. "You should have heard him bitching and moaning after you left. I don't think anyone ever stood up to him like that."

"You doing okay?" was Nancy's more downplayed response.

"Yeah, I'm good. In fact, I want to run something by you."

"Shoot."

"I'm thinking of applying to the Flamingo. I don't think they'll let me bartend, but I make a pretty good waitress."

Nancy looked at me with an I-know-something-you-don't-know look in her eyes.

"What made you pick that place?" quickly asked Tom.

"Oh, just some inspiration…some visions of a lawn filled with flamingos—plastic ones."

"Huh," reacted Tom and Nancy simultaneously.

"You think I shouldn't do it?"

"On the contrary, it's such a good idea that I think I'll do it too!" chuckled Tom.

"Yeah, maybe me too," added Nancy.

"Now, you know we discussed this, Nan. What about Amy and Molly?" Tom questioned without any negative judgment.

"What are you guys talking about?" I was really confused. It was Nancy who made the situation clear.

"The Flamingo has been recruiting Tom to work at one of their casino bars for years. However, it would mean a pay cut until he can build up a regular clientele of big tippers. He would go from the big fish in the little pond to vice-versa.

"We couldn't make it on less money." Tom took over from there. "However, you sticking up to Dirtbag Denny made me realize that I couldn't be a part of what he was doing anymore."

"We were just discussing how to financially do the moral thing and still survive," interrupted Nancy. "I think it's a great move for you, and Tom can even put in a word for you with the bosses. But we still have to decide if we can make money to get out of here and still do the right thing—and, you know, set a good example for our girls."

An interesting idea occurred to me. I just didn't know if Tom and Nan would buy into it.

"What if all three of us worked there, and we worked shifts that allowed one of us to always be here for the kids?"

"You'd do that for us?" asked Nan.

"I'd be doing that for all of us. We'd all be making money to get to where we want to go. Isn't that the point? Besides, I get to spend more time with those two adorable little girls."

"And you could move in with us here so you can save on rent money," offered Tom, and Nancy nodded in agreement.

"To the escape from Sin City," yelled Tom just a bit too loud and put his hand out, and both Nancy and I put ours on top of his, much like the Three Musketeers.

Our celebration was interrupted by the two blonde four-year-old twins.

"What's going on here?" croaked Molly, barely awake.

"Yeah," repeated Amy.

"Come over here, girls," encouraged Nan. When they joined our circle, she put their little hands on top of ours.

"To escape," repeated Tom, conveniently leaving out the "Sin City" part of our pledge for the girls' sake. Molly and Amy smiled at this game.

# 38

# "PRETTY FLAMINGO" (REPRISE)

## - MANFRED MANN

My life was again filled with flamingos, albeit gaudy gross ones. I realized the plastic ones on my lawn weren't works of art. However, they weren't all shades of neon like the ones at the Flamingo Hotel and Casino, often flashing in nauseating and hypnotic ways. This is not to mention the one that adorned my uniform. Its head was sewn into the fabric wrapped around one of my breasts, and the rest of the pink monster proceeded down my body. If Johnny could only see me now. Or better yet, Fred, the original flamingo on my lawn. *Oh, Fred, forgive me.*

Other than that, the whole situation was working out well. Surprise, surprise, something I planned actually came together. Nan and I often worked days, and Tom took the lucrative night shift. This was to be expected, being he was the one they recruited, and we were just the players to be named later.

The money was rolling in, and it looked like we would all be leaving Las Vegas soon. Not paying rent helped make up for my pay cut going from a bartender to a waitress. I did contribute to our little compound by helping out with the food. Our little arrangement was almost perfect for about six months—and then the mob came to town.

***

Their arrival was to be expected since the mobster Bugsy Siegal made Vegas both a mob cash cow and a recreational getaway. It was like they were taking a vacation in their own personal bank. Everyone knew what was happening, but too many cops and other government officials were profiting from the situation for it to change…and so it didn't.

I saw it first-hand in the winter, spring, and summer of 1971. And the money just didn't come from gambling but also from drugs and prostitution. Dirtbag Denny was small peanuts compared to the operations that were run out of places like the Flamingo. Naively, I ignored the morality of it and, in my mind, wrote it off as victimless crimes. Besides, soon I would be out of there, to parts unknown but definitely better.

It was understood that the bartenders and waitresses with the most seniority would be placed at the beck and call of the big shots, the capos of each crime family. However, there was money to be made with the minor leaguers like Nan, Tom, and I would be serving. The second tier of wanna-be capos was all ours. In fact, during peak mob activity, Tom was called in every day to service the underlings. Their nights were otherwise occupied, and I soon found out how.

# 39

# "BAD TO THE BONE"

## - GEORGE THOROGOOD AND THE DELAWARE DESTROYERS

Nan and I had been serving the second team for a few days when I saw him. He looked familiar, so I started a conversation and served him his first round of drinks at noon. Why would he talk to me? To state the obvious, I was twenty years old with a nice body and face… and I was tarted out to the utmost allowed by the directives of Max Factor. This was all you needed with a late forty-something guy with a gut on him that revealed he had a wife at home—a wife who fed him plenty of pasta while offering very few services to use up those calories.

It was not like any of them were going to get anywhere with us. We were under strict orders to direct any sexual offerings to the administrator in charge of such things. In the real world, we would have called him a pimp. But here in Vegas…

"So, where are you from, big boy?" This type of guy liked that kind of talk.

"Queens, New York. You ever been there?"

*A-ha, I thought so. However, I wasn't going to let him know I grew up there. So instead, I assumed the role of a dumb blonde.*

"No, is that part of Brooklyn?"

"No, it's a lot classier. I'm from southeast Queens. They call me the 'King of Cambria Heights.' Dominick Provenzano is my name, but most of my guys call me "Don" Provenzano—if you understand my meaning."

Bingo! He was from the area where I grew up. I then realized why I knew the name and who he was. However, I stayed in character.

"I'm sorry, I don't speak Italian. My name is Becky, and I'm just an Irish girl from San Francisco." I did have my hair dyed blonde, but I still looked every bit of the 100% Italian I was born as. He was too stupid to notice.

"Too bad, Italian is the thing to be," he boasted.

"I-tal-yun," I purposely mispronounced. I then added, "What's a don?"

"A boss, a big shot," he proudly croaked.

If I were my usual sharp-tongued self, I would have responded, *If you're such a big shot, why aren't you upstairs with the real bosses?* But, instead, continuing in dumb blonde status, I merely cooed, "Oh, that is so impressive."

Then everything changed. Two much younger men joined Dominick Provenzano. One was in his early twenties, and "The Don" introduced him as his son Guy. The other was in his early thirties and he was introduced as his nephew...holy shit...Richie Shea.

I had met Richie Shea four years before in my parents' living room. He was the detective on the case to find Gio DeAngelis and my boyfriend, Johnny Cipp. However, being here with his uncle and cousin meant that despite being on the police force, he was still in the mob. This also told me that he hadn't been looking for Johnny in an official capacity but in a mob capacity.

I remembered Johnny being coy about how his problems had begun, but in a moment of weakness, he had mentioned Guy Provenzano, or as he called him, "Mad Guy" Provenzano. Now this "Mad Guy" and his cousin, the pseudo-cop Richie Shea, were sitting before me.

"You look familiar to me. Do I know you?" questioned Richie Shea.

"Yeah, vaguely familiar to me too. You come from Queens?" added Mad Guy.

Before I had a chance to blush or stutter, Dominick cut in. Thank goodness I had given him a phony backstory before the other two even sat down.

"No, this, here is Becky from San Francisco."

"The only I-tal-yun I know from San Fran is the Yankee Clipper, Joe Dimaggio," I offered quickly in my best non-New York accent. I was curious to know if I had fooled Shea. It had been four years, and my long blonde hair and heavy makeup made me look quite different from the Maria Romano he had seen. I hoped that I had deceived him but couldn't be sure.

"How about some drinks on the house?" I offered. I needed to get away from their prying eyes and get them sufficiently drunk to forget about me. However, I would not be gone long. I needed to hear what they talked about. Maybe then, I could get a clue about Johnny.

When was I going to give up? It had been four years—longer than I had even known Johnny. Yet I needed some closure—even if it was not a happy ending.

# 40

# "HIGHWAY TO HELL"

## - AC/DC

Even though Shea kept looking at me with doubt, I continued to serve him all that afternoon. I was hoping to hear something relevant. *Don* Provenzano had enough juice to convince my boss that I should be exclusive to his party that afternoon. My boss listened to his request. Who says crime doesn't pay?

Nan had to take extra tables that would ordinarily have been mine. During a moment when we intersected at the bar, I explained what I was trying to do without giving too many details.

"Go for it," was all she whispered to me. But later in the day, she had quite a bit to reveal.

"Don't stare, but sleazebags at table number 6 are talking about the sleazebags at your table," Nan whispered.

"What did they say?" I responded.

"Something like 'They're not such hot stuff now that Guy got made a fool of.'"

The other guy is from Jersey and needs to know what the first guy is talking about. So, he asks for info Nan reveals.

"And?"

Nan told me what she heard.

---

*I heard the word "band," but that was all. One of the other guys chips in, "Yeah, but Mad Guy took care of those kids."*

*"What do you mean?" the Jersey guy questions. They laughed at him.*

*"I don't know how you guys in Jersey do things, but 'took care of them' only means one thing in Queens.*

*They all laughed (even the Jersey guy).*

*"Yeah, but it wasn't looked at too kindly by the guys upstairs," says Sleazebag #1. "That's why Dominick, Guy, and his cousin are still sitting at the little kids' table."*

*"Aren't we at 'the little kids' table?" asks the Jersey guy.*

*"Yeah, but there's hope we can move up someday. The bosses have made it clear that Mad Guy is going nowhere for his screw-up."*

*"What a shame," reflected the Jersey guy.*

*"If you knew Mad Guy, you'd say, 'It couldn't have happened to a nicer guy.'"*

*They laughed and sent Nan for more drinks.*

---

"I gotta know what they meant about 'taking care of it.' I have to know for sure what that meant."

"Sorry, Becky, that's all I got. Maybe you can get something from the horse's mouth?" Nan pointed at my sleazebags, then added, "Becky, what's this all about?"

"Trust me…you don't want to know," I answered and stayed close to 'my sleazebags' all afternoon.

The afternoon was uneventful until the very end.

"Richie, are you joining us at The Veal Ranch tonight?" asked Guy.

"No, you know that's not my thing, but you have a good time."

"C'mon, my dad isn't coming. We have room for one more in the van."

*Van? The Veal Ranch?* My ears perked up—*what a weird name.*

"Well, we leave about eleven if you change your mind."

"No, I think I'll just hit the poker table."

I thought, *how can I get on that van so I could have a whole night of listening to the drunken conversation?* Maybe I could learn more about *those* (band) *kids from Queens* that Guy took care of.

This would also answer my curiosity about where the cloaked vans were going…the Veal Ranch?

I didn't have to work hard to be assigned the Veal Ranch gig. Guy asked that "the babe from the Bay" be given to them on their visit. I thought it was great—a whole bus ride out and then an entire evening eavesdropping on their conversations. It never happened that way.

My boss called me at about five. I liked my boss Wes, but I could never quite get a handle on him. He was always nice to the other girls and me. He treated us with respect—like people rather than sex objects. Yet, he was friendly with the mob and was doing things that I didn't know or understand. He was a very plain man of average height and weight. His thinning black hair did not detract from his clean, bland good looks. I try hard to remember what he looked like all these years later, but he was that average.

"Becky, go home and freshen up and be back by eleven…Prompt."

"I thought the bus left at midnight?"

He laughed at my comment but not really in a condescending tone.

"No, no, no, I think you misunderstand your job. First, you go ahead of them and ensure everything is just right. Then, you set up the booze and serve their every desire when they come."

"Doug, I didn't sign up for that."

"Oh, no. You're not there for that…though I am sure, they may want you. No, the Veal Ranch is a special kind of place. One of my men, Little Nicky Glue, is there to take care of…setting up… hmm…the entertainment. You are just a wallflower…a very pretty one…however, they will have other things on their mind at the Veal Ranch."

"Little Nicky Glue?"

"You know these Italians all have nicknames. I don't know where the "Glue" moniker came from, but you'll understand the "Little" part once you see him.

"Why is it called the Veal Ranch?"

He just smirked and revealed nothing. However, his look of amusement seemed to say to me…*You are a dumber blonde than I thought.*

"Okay, now take off, and I'll see you at 11 o'clock on the dot."

I was disappointed that I would not be riding out to the Veal Ranch in the Flamingo bus… a weird statement if ever I wrote one.

I arrived on time as instructed, and Wes pointed to a dolly containing top-shelf booze and assorted food trays. I purposely played up my "Becky from the Bay" persona to pull his leg and protect my false identity.

"Hey, Wes, what's this Paste-a Fage-e-o-lee? I knew, of course, that Italians pronounce Pasta Fagioli as Pasta Fa-zul. They laughed at me and corrected me. That was one point for my WASP false identity. But, of course, I couldn't resist another one.

"And this Bracky-ole?"

"That's Braciole," which he pronounced Bra-zole giving me a look—but never saying the words *"dumb shit."* Two points.

I supervised the loading of the van by two waiters, and soon we were on our way.

---

I have told my story so far with a lighthearted sense of humor. However, what happened next still gives me nightmares..., and I would not be joking about anything for a long time. The ride to the Veal Ranch took me as expected, past my little retreat hideaway in Red Rock, then continued on Route 95 for probably twenty more miles out past Indian Springs. A lot of bad things happened in Vegas, so for this place to be thirty miles in the middle of nowhere, this must be the topper.

I now had trepidation about what I would find out there. The van turned sharply onto a dirt road and traveled west for about five miles. We were heading toward Death Valley but suddenly came upon an up-scale Ranch house in the middle of nowhere. The driver stopped at a gate, the only entrance to the compound that was surrounded by a ten-foot-high brick wall. The driver signaled with his headlights and the gates electronically opened, allowing our entry. We pulled up to the front door of what I can only describe as a mansion. It was styled in the common Southwest motif with wood, stucco, and red clay tile roof. I could tell from the number of windows visible that it easily had at least ten bedrooms. The entire place was both clean and new. But why was it 40 miles outside Vegas? Very little was not allowed in Vegas, especially if enough palms were greased. I assumed that the men of Provenzano's group were coming here for prostitutes, but even that was legal and could be easily procured on the strip itself. So why the seclusion?

The door opened, and out came *Little* Nicky Glue—barely. I

say barely because he took up the entire entrance with his head skimming the top of the door frame. He had to be at least six-foot-six and well over 300 pounds. To look "stylish," this 30-something had his long black hair in a ponytail, bell-bottom jeans, and an out-of-style blue *Nehru* shirt.

"Can you send someone out to help me unload the stuff," I asked nicely.

"I'm the only one here." He then added gruffly, "Do I look ten shades darker than you?" This told me that not only was he obnoxious but racist…and from New York. The "ten shades darker" comment was a common refrain in New York to equate helping someone with slave labor. Little did I know that this concept came from Little Nicky as first-hand knowledge.

I emptied the van by myself. On the last trip in, he grabbed my ass, causing me almost to drop all of the Pasta Fagioli on the floor. He then dared to say, "There's time for a quicky before the van with the guys gets here.

Okay, so I let the ass-grabbing go because he was huge, and frankly, I didn't have a death wish. My principles are mainly limited to guys I can take, like Dirtbag Denny at the Runaway Club. However, his comment quickly made me understand that I was in the middle of nowhere with a Bigfoot relative who could force me to do anything and get away with it. I picked up one of the steak knives meant for the braciole and brandished it in front of me.

"Sure, we can have a quicky, but it will cost you your left testicle." Of course, I was bluffing because he was so big, and I had no idea how to use a knife as a weapon. Fortunately, he didn't know that. After that, we developed an uncommon truce in which I sat on one side of the room and he on the other.

At about 11:30 pm, he suddenly stood up and announced, "Showtime! The bus will be here in twenty minutes. Time for me to prepare the entertainment."

I was finally going to meet the hookers that were somehow

worth a trip way out here in the country. They must be really special. And then I realized why...

Las Vegas was not called "Sin City" for nothing. Almost every product or commodity, or person had a price. But not this. This was something that even the most corrupt system of law and order would not accept. No bribe would permit this. I watched as sexily dressed, fully made-up young girls walked down the stairs—the oldest of the five might be twelve! What kind of perverted man would so desecrate these young girls? And it got worse.

"It's Cherry-picking time at the Veal Ranch," chuckled Little Nicky, with a laugh that was evil incarnate. I understood exactly what was going on. "Veal Ranch" was a reference to the fact that veal is a cut of meat gotten from very young cows. And to make matters worse, his cherry-picking comment meant that these girls were all virgins!

Those sick, demented assholes were going to amuse themselves by defiling these young girls. I looked at their faces and realized that every one of them had been heavily drugged, and they were unaware of their circumstances. I guessed they had recently been kidnapped either from their homes, a playground, or somewhere. In twenty minutes, these bastards would ruin their lives. Their bodies and minds might never recover from what was going to happen to them. What could I do?

I agonized before finally coming up with a plan. However, it meant risking my life...and going on the run immediately. I would never see Tom, Nancy, and the twins again. I would never get information about the disappearance of Johnny. I would have to start over...again. Yet, one look at the five painted but innocent faces told me it would be worth it.

"Hey, Nicky, how do we amuse ourselves while the big boys are busy?" He looked at me, confused; in reality, he was too stupid to see any motive for my mood change and sudden interest in him.

"We get paid very well to be attentive to their every need. Now, after they're gone, is another question."

"Oh, come on. Can't we even enjoy some of this top-shelf booze to make the night go by…until we…"

I purposely left him hanging. I could really be a real cockteaser when I wanted to be.

"No, they're strict about us being on duty."

I gave him my sexiest "come hither" look and turned to the bar I had set up. I poured a finger of Chivas and turned to him. I licked the tumbler's edge with my tongue, glancing up at him with a pout.

"Are you sure you won't join me? I don't get going without a bit of lubrication. I could see his manhood growing even as he tried to resist. It was no contest.

"Okay, just one…for now."

"For now…and later." I smiled and turned to pour his drink, two fingers of Chivas…with the additive Tom had given me—the last resort cocktail.

---

The bigger they are, the harder they fall, a concept that was scientifically proven to me only minutes later. Little Nicky crashed to the floor, landing flat on his face. From the looks of things, He was not only out cold but would require a tremendous dental reconstruction for the damage to his mouth. I wish I could have caused more damage, but I was too busy ushering the five zombie-like girls into the van.

# PART VI

## "BORN TO RUN"

### - BRUCE SPRINGSTEEN

Arizona
(1972)

# 41

# "LEAVIN' LAS VEGAS"

## - SHERYL CROW

Though I had left home more than three years ago, there never was a time when I didn't know what I was going to do next...or where I was headed. So often, with the Wrigley Rockers, the decision was not made until the night before we hit the road. However, there was comfort in knowing that we had a destination or at least a direction. However, for the first time in my life, I was winging it...and it was damn scary.

I knew I needed to head back to Vegas, but I also knew that the second van, the one with the lecherous perverts, would be coming down the same road. I had to get to the side road entrance of Red Rock Canyon before we passed each other. If I didn't, it would be impossible to miss the size and color of the Flamingo Hotel van I was driving.

I sweated out the ride as my five passengers remained semi-comatose. Then, finally, I saw the turnoff almost simultaneously with seeing headlights in the distance. This circuitous route through Red Rock would add time to my trip but would be much safer. However, time was critical. I knew it would not be long before the mob van reached the Veal Ranch and realized what had happened…even if Little Nicky Glue had not regained consciousness. Because I had the foresight to rip out the phone wires leading to the house, they would then have to drive back to the Flamingo to report my treachery. Still, I did not have much of a head start if I was to escape.

My mind was flooded with thoughts about what to do next. I knew that I couldn't take these girls to the police. Though I was pretty sure that the Veal Ranch was not an activity condoned by the authorities, I couldn't be sure of that, and it only took one rotten cop, and these girls would disappear again.

And so, I went to church. Though my visits were infrequent, I had started to attend Holy Redeemer Catholic Church during my time in Vegas. (Now, isn't that a great name for a church in Sin City.) Even though I didn't think I was doing anything sinful with my lifestyle, I sometimes felt dirty inside. Sometimes I just needed to hear a good sermon to cleanse my soul. It was not unusual for Father Barnabas to strike up a conversation with anyone and everyone who attended mass. I realized that he could never know who needed to be saved and who didn't.

We often talked casually before the ceremony. However, it was hard to have an honest conversation while I was living with the disguised identity of Becky Simon. On one occasion, he shared with me that he was born and raised in New York City and had gone to Cathedral High School. This was a school that everyone thought was for weird kids who wanted to be priests. Going there meant you intended to be celibate for the rest of your life. The rest of us were thinking of nothing but the opposite sex.

I wanted to scream out to him, "I'm from New York too," or "Hey, what do you think about those Yankees or Mets?" I couldn't do that. However, I knew him well enough to know he was a good man, so I brought the five girls to him.

We worked out a plan together. The priest would bring in some doctors and nurses he trusted to check out the girls' physical and mental health while keeping them secluded in a local convent. He then would contact the FBI on the premise that these girls may have been brought over state lines, making it their jurisdiction. Finally, he would discern their identities and contact their families to see the next step to ensure their privacy. I didn't get into too many details, I had to leave quickly. I would be a person of interest to the mob, and I didn't want to spend my life looking over my shoulder.

I made one last stop. Some people knew that Tom and Nancy were my friends. However, we had never really mentioned that I lived there. Just in case, I removed every bit of evidence of my presence. Tom was still at work, but Nancy helped me, and then she took off for Los Angeles. She had family there. I knew Tom and Nancy could fake ignorance, but it wouldn't be hard for the twins to slip about their "Aunt Becky" living with them. Meanwhile, they would claim that Nancy needed to care for a sick aunt. Eventually, Tom would join her there, and they would be out of the picture.

And so, I filled up the Mercury Comet and hit the road. I never looked back. I never again contacted my friends because I didn't want to put them in danger. Instead, I planned to drive down to Arizona, return to my old name and my old look, and hoped that I would be able to get lost in America.

## 42

---

## "FREE FALLIN'"

### - TOM PETTY AND THE HEARTBREAKERS

It was sunrise after my very eventful night when I woke up in a tourist parking area. Exhaustion had suddenly overtaken me in the early morning hours, and I stopped at the first available lot. All that had happened seemed as if it had been a dream.

I then realized that I was at the Hoover Dam. I had taken little time to do sightseeing while in Vegas. However, now I stood near one of the greatest engineering marvels of modern times. Did I have time to relax and take it all in—at least for a few minutes? I hoped I had put enough miles between Vegas and me to be safe, but after a short while, I panicked, seeing imaginary villains in every corner. In reality, I saw no one. At this time in the morning, only an occasional car drove on the road atop the dam.

Impulsively I decided to purge most of the remnants of my past life. I had to take all I owned from Tom and Nancy's house to avoid proof of my stay there. However, I had no further use for the accouterments of my former lifestyle. There would be no use for high heels, makeup, or slinky dresses. So, I condensed all my belongings into one large backpack with extra jeans, tank tops, sneakers—and of course, the $1,636 I had saved up from my work at the Flamingo.

I decided to chuck my excess belongings down into the Colorado River, which could result in trouble with the authorities. However, I wanted to do it anyway as an act of absolution—a declaration of change. The sight of my former possessions plummeting almost a thousand feet was exhilarating, almost religiously so. I got in the car and left very quickly after my purge—laughing at my crime of the century. I didn't laugh long.

43

---

# "TAKE IT EASY"

## - JACKSON BROWNE AND THE EAGLES

By the time I reached Williams, Arizona, I was feeling pretty confident that no one was on my tail. I even thought of taking the fifty-mile detour up to the Grand Canyon. However, my common sense told me I might be risking too much. I would place myself at a dead end with no way out if I were being followed. So I continued toward Winslow, Arizona.

I never made it. Well, I did—the 1961 Mercury Comet did not. Somewhere about 30 miles east of Williams, it died a slow and painful death. Smoke and noises I had never heard before started occurring suddenly. I tried to beg the old car to at least get me to Winslow, hoping that a miracle would happen there. No such luck.

This breakdown was final as my Vegas mechanic, Joey the Stache, had predicted. Rest in Peace. Hopefully, the car was at peace because I wasn't. I was in the middle of nowhere. The last sign I had seen had read Winslow – 33 miles! The only good luck I had was that I dumped everything but my backpack at the Hoover Dam.

I remembered that I had to remove the plates as I bid my car a fond farewell and started to hoof it. I got about five miles and realized that I was not in shape for a 30 miles trek and decided to do the unthinkable—to hitch. I met a nice guy who offered to take me to Winslow. We talked.

"So, what's your name, young lady?" This caught me by surprise. I had been Becky Simon for almost a year but realized she was now dead to the world. I could have said anything, but I instantly decided that Maria Romano was now back in the game. Any fear I had of Jesse or my parents finding me was long overshadowed by the sheer terror of who was chasing "Becky."

"Maria," I whispered.

"Sorry, I didn't hear you. A little hard of hearing, especially in the right ear—the one facing you."

"Maria Theresa Romano," I erupted, perhaps a little too loud.

"Now I heard that loud and clear. So, I'm guessing you are I-tal-yun?"

Doesn't anyone outside of New York know how to pronounce Italian?

"Yeah, I am." If he hadn't seemed like such a nice guy, I would have added something like, *"What's it to ya!"* That would have been the New York in me coming back with the reclaiming of my name.

"Yeah, born and raised. I have just been on a sort of road trip for over three years."

"Oh, you from Brooklyn? I pick up quite a few hitchers from there on my New York to Carolina run."

"No, I'm from Queens, the borough, eh, county right next to it."

"Hey, I once gave a hitch a few years ago to a kid named Jack, who was from Queens. I took him from Jersey to North Carolina— near my home in Enfield. Real nice kid. Hey, maybe you knew him."

"There are almost two million people in Queens. I don't think so, sir," I chuckled.

"Oh, you don't have to call me 'sir,' everyone calls me Carolina Charlie."

Carolina Charlie took me as far as Winslow, and we laughed all the way. After I bid Charlie farewell in Winslow, I *almost* got a ride all the way to New Mexico from one extremely nice man. He saw me get out of Charlie's truck and asked where I was heading. Not having a destination, I mentioned New Mexico.

"You're in luck, I'm heading there as soon as I make one last phone call. So have a seat in that flatbed Ford over there, and I'll be right out."

As I sat, I watched this small town's slow and steady daily routine and wondered what it would be like to live here. To slow down and smell the roses. Lately, I had started to miss the neighborhood of my youth. I missed all my friends that I grew up with in Cambria. I missed that feeling of it being my home. But the hometown that I had loved was no longer there. It had died when many of my friends moved away...or died. What is that old saying, "You can never go home again?" I know that, but it didn't stop me from missing it. I was in the middle of these thoughts when I was interrupted by a cute-looking guy approaching the truck.

"Do you know where I can find a mechanic around here? I'm having some car trouble."

"Sorry, I'm not a local. Just passing through myself," I answered, and for some reason, I pointed to the backpack holding all my worldly possessions.

"Oh, I'm sorry. I just saw you sitting so comfortably in this flatbed that I assumed you were from here...umm...I didn't catch your name."

"Maria...Maria Theresa Romano."

"You're traveling light...loosening your load—I like that. And as long as we are using full formal names. "I'm Clyde Jackson Browne...though my friends call me Jackson.""

"Pleased to meet you, Jackson." With that, the guy who was giving me the ride came out.

"I'm sorry to disappoint you. Unfortunately, I got a minor emergency at home. I won't be heading out."

As I got out of the truck, Jackson offered to drive me once his car was repaired.

"I'm going to Flagstaff...whenever," he sadly looked over at his disabled car.

I would have loved to have joined him for more reasons than one, but I knew that I could never head back in the direction from which I came.

"Thanks, but I gotta keep heading that way," I said, pointing east.

"Okay, Maria Theresa Romano...you take it easy."

I walked away but turned once more to look at this cute guy. I could swear he was writing something down on a pad.

# 44

# "DON'T YOU GO TALKIN' TO STRANGERS"

## - BEAU BRUMMELS

arefully, I removed enough money from my backpack to get a good meal at a truck stop. It was part of my old New York City training that you never revealed where your stash was in front of anyone. I threw a twenty in my pocket and decided I would have a delicious meal, never knowing it would be my last for many days.

The diner was exceptionally crowded. It seemed that almost every trucker heading in either direction on Route 66 was taking their dinner break at the same time. Then, finally, a waitress greeted me at the door and laughed.

"I hope you like truckers because this time of day, you will have to cozy up and eat at the table with them." She pointed to mostly full tables that seemed full of nothing but all shapes and sizes of men who drove for a living.

"Yeah, I'm good. A girl's gotta eat."

She led me to a table in the back, which was occupied by three of the biggest guys I had been in the presence of...ever.

"So, what have we here?" questioned the man directly across from where I seated myself. Though I couldn't tell for sure because he was sitting down, I guessed him to be 6'4" with a large face highlighted by blue eyes and a beard so long it disappeared under the table.

"They call me 'Monster Mash, and this here is 'Runaway Rider' next to me," he said, pointing to a dirty looking dark-haired man in the seat next to him in the booth.

"Huh?" was all I could manage.

"All of us truckers use our CB handles when we meet in person. We talk all day while driving, and it would be hard to remember who was who if we used real names in person."

"Call me Travelin' Tammy," I replied, making up a fictitious "handle" just in case some of these truckers were heading toward Vegas and might be questioned. Besides, I thought it was fun.

"This here is...," Monster Mash stopped, realizing he didn't know what to call the guy sitting next to me. He had said nothing as he sat at the booth.

"Midnight Talker," he whispered, barely audible.

"Midnight Stalker? That's a creepy handle." I laughed as Runaway Rider purposely misspoke the name.

"Talker, I said Talker," growled the guy beside me, sounding really annoyed. Monster and Runaway just gave him weird looks.

The conversation went on for the good part of an hour. I found the stories of their travels fascinating. I tried to hold up my part of the give-and-take without *giving* up too much information about the real me. Then, abruptly, all three of them got up to leave.

"Time to earn my keep," chuckled Monster. "Those shoes aren't going to get to the ladies of Vegas by themselves."

"You're lucky, I got bathing suits that need to go to Frisco," added Runaway. Then, I realized that the two of them, ironically, were heading to the two places I could never put on my destination list.

"How about you, Midnight Talker?" asked Monster. "Maybe you can give the little lady a hitch?"

"I'm heading to Atlanta."

"Perfect," said Monster.

As we all stood, I got my first good look at Midnight Talker (Stalker?). He stood at least a head over me, possibly more. His shoulder-length, greasy hair framed a face full of pimples and a mouth that was missing quite a few teeth. His flannel shirt was missing its two top buttons revealing a chest full of hair that would have been more accurately situated on a gorilla.

"Let's go," were the only words he whispered to me as we left the diner.

As we approached his rig, I noticed in sharp contrast that it was immaculate, probably because it got a good professional cleaning that its owner might have thought about getting for himself.

I thought I understood why when I hopped in the passenger side of the extremely large eighteen-wheeler. He probably lived here while on the road. Behind the front seats was a large bed. On the sides, the walls held a TV and a small refrigerator.

"Looks comfy," I offered.

"It is," was his short response. He then proceeded to say more than he had said in our entire time in the diner.

"I usually drive straight through the night. I make much better time when no one else is on the road. Plus, I like the solitude."

"Okay," was all I could think to answer his "long" speech.

"If you get tired, you feel free to go back and sleep. I don't need you to talk to me to keep me awake."

"I don't want to be rude or…"

"I don't worry about rude. People take one look at me and usually don't talk at all. So you go back and enjoy yourself."

"You sure?"

"I'm sure."

I slipped between the seats and found myself sound asleep within minutes.

My nightmare began…and it was real.

I will try to recount what happened next, but it won't be easy. I had tried for so very long to forget that night. I failed. Instead, after years of suffering (and not a small amount of therapy), I decided to take that night and own it—to be proud of it. And not worry about what could have been.

*He was all over me. How had I not noticed him stopping the truck and climbing into the bed with me? I then realized that in the diner, there had been a time when I saw his hand near my glass of water. At the time I thought nothing of it. Now I realized that he had slipped something into my drink. I was lucky to be conscious—or was I unlucky because I would now feel the pure horror of what was about to happen?*

*He had taken off his pants in anticipation of pleasuring himself. My first conscious thoughts were, "screw you," and I meant that figuratively and never was it going to be literally...not if I could help it. However, his flabby body crushed me under his weight, and his two hands pinned my arms.*

*It became apparent what he expected. I was angry with myself for being such a fool. How could I not see this coming? I thought that I had to try something but found myself immobilized by his pure size and my semi-conscious state.*

*He grabbed my breasts, and I made a murmur of protest. However, he thought that I was moaning in ecstasy. He obviously had an ego about his sex skills. Yet this gave me an idea. I played up the moaning and gave him the impression that this was the best damn sexual experience he would ever have. As he stroked my breasts, my pinned hands stroked his inner thigh. This seemed to go on for an eternity as I looked for some kind of opening. Eventually, his elation caused him to loosen his grip just enough for my right hand to be released. He attempted to take off my jeans in the tight quarters. To do this, he had to distance himself from my body to be able to unzip me. As his hands released my shoulders, I didn't attempt to escape...yet. My hands* continued to tickle his inner thigh, and I could feel his excitement, which led him to let down his guard. He thought I would use this hand to bring him further joy. He was wrong.

Given some space to move my balled fist, I pounded his testicles not once but as many times as I could as he rolled off me. I thought of nothing but escape. I attempted to scurry out of the back of the truck. However, his hand clasped my left ankle even as he writhed in pain.

"You bitch…you goddamn bitch," he screamed as he remained in a fetal position but now brought his other hand to clench my ankle. He started to pull me towards him. I resisted, but it was futile. I was slowly edging toward him. Finally, I changed tactics and answered his rant.

"That's right…and this bitch is going to kick your ass," But I didn't kick his ass—I kicked his face. I coiled my right leg toward my body and then uncoiled and struck him in the face with all my strength. I heard the crack of cartilage in his nose and saw a gush of blood sprinkle his intended love bed.

"Oops. The wrong end, but I couldn't tell the difference between your ass and your face," I taunted as he released my left leg and I slipped out of his grasp.

I didn't wait to see anymore. I scrambled over the front seat and out the door. I ran as fast as I could and put distance between us. I expected him to charge out of the truck angrily. He didn't. Had I hurt him that badly?

I soon got my answer as he bellowed in laughter. Finally, he started the truck and slowly drove away, stopping briefly to give me the middle finger. I rejoiced in the fact that he knew he could never catch me and had given up…until I realized why he was laughing.

He honked his loud horn in the distance, signaling that I might keep my virginity, but he now had my backpack with all my worldly possessions and over $1600 in cash.

4 5

---

# "HORSE WITH NO NAME"

## - AMERICA

ock Bottom…and I mean that both literally and figuratively. I can think of no point in my life when I felt more hopeless. I had no money, no extra clothes, no food, no water, no identification…nothing at all. That includes no hope.

On top of all that, I looked into the dark night and saw nothing but sand and rocks. As I rambled aimlessly, I even lost track of which direction I needed to go. Back to Winslow? I didn't even know how far we had traveled while I was unconscious. Travel east…I didn't even know what the next town was, or how far I would have to walk.

As the sun rose the next morning, I could at least discern which way was east and west on Route 66. Not knowing what lay east, I made the determination to go back to where I had come from. I walked that whole first day without water or food. I shied away from traffic, now terrified that Midnight (S)talker or someone like him lurked behind every wheel. At the slightest sound, I jumped off the road and found a hiding place.

I was irrational. I could've died of thirst or hunger while refusing to attempt to get help from passing motorists. I was in a desert, and in my delirium, I reverted back to Johnny's tradition of singing songs that somehow fit the occasion. I hummed and then actually sang a song that had only come out recently—"A Horse with No Name." Over and over, I sang the nonsensical verse about being in the desert on a horse with no name. Eventually, I gave him a name…Stupid. Yeah, how stupid had I been to get myself into this situation? In reality, I would have given anything to have a horse, no matter what it was named.

At the end of the first day, I was weak and knew that the body could only go so long without water. This was especially true as I baked in the heat of the Arizona desert. In the middle of the second day, I saw a sign that read "Winslow – 25 miles." At least I had a direction. However, without water, I might not make it.

During the hottest part of the day, I decided to take a break. Actually, it wasn't that much of a conscious effort. I just couldn't go on. I started to veer off the road, finally finding some shade behind a decent size boulder. As I went to sit, I felt something in my back pocket that I hadn't noticed before. I put my sweaty fingers in and came out with a picture of Johnny and me.

Actually, it was four pictures, the kind taken in a booth at an amusement park. These were the only pictures of Johnny and I together ever taken. We had actually gone into the booth to, eh, make out. Therefore the pictures follow a progression of us getting closer and closer together until the big kiss. Oh, those were such simple times, and this was all I had to remember them. I was looking at this picture in Vegas and stuck it in my pants without realizing it. Not only did the picture seem a lifetime ago, but so did Vegas.

Suddenly, a soft breeze blew across my hand—a wind. Johnny always talked about the wind as a metaphor for our escape. Ha, I had escaped…to a desert with no food, no water…nothing at all. Another warm gust blew by me and caught me by surprise. The strip of pictures flew from my hand.

At first, I thought about letting them go, but they were my only worldly possession. I got up to chase them, using what little energy I had. It seemed that every time I got close, they blew away farther. It was like they were taunting me. I finally caught up to them about thirty feet from where I started and just a few feet off the road. I picked up the picture, and at the last minute, I saw something too good to be true—an illusion…a mirage. There lay a bottle of water that I hoped had been discarded from a passing car with some residue of liquid in it.

Yes, it was half full. I smelled first to make sure it was the result of wasteful littering and not used as an emergency urinal. It was water, water that tasted like the purest mountain spring had created it. That was probably not true, but when you are racked with dehydration, any water is the elixir of the gods. I drank half of it, saving the other half for my journey.

I looked at the pictures of Johnny and me. Johnny, did you do that? I smiled but then caught myself. If indeed he had intervened, that would mean…that he was dead. I shook my head—too much strain to worry about my own imminent demise to think of Johnny. But I looked up in the sky…waved… put my hand over my heart and patted it.

Five miles later, I used up the last of the water in a celebratory toast to the sign that I stood before that read Homolovi State Campground—one mile. As I approached the campground, I realized that in every sense of the word, I resembled a homeless vagabond. It did not take me long to realize that I, indeed, was exactly that. My sweat-soaked and filthy clothes gave off an ungodly odor, and tangled hair and dirty face were no better. Perhaps, I could sneak into the public showers and make myself more presentable before making human contact.

No luck. There was a keypad code to unlock the door, and I didn't know it. Frustrated, I tried to make believe that I was a camper who had forgotten the code. I knocked on the door of a beautiful luxury fifth-wheel trailer.

"I'm sorry, I don't have the code, and my trailer is all the way on the other side of the campground," I begged with the most pitiful look I could muster.

"Then why don't you use the bathhouse on that side?" was the woman's skeptical response.

*Oops, I didn't think of that. Starvation and thirst will do that to you.*

The next two trailers wouldn't even answer the door, and the third yelled out the window something to the effect of, "Get lost. We don't want your kind around here!"

*What was my kind? What had I become?*

# "TURN THE PAGE"

## - BOB SEGER AND THE SILVER BULLET BAND

As all this was happening, I noticed that I was being watched by an elderly couple sitting by a campfire in front of a fairly large motorhome. Were they going to tell the office? It was a good thing that this was in the days before the invention of the cell phone, or one of the other campers would have already called the local police. However, as the man and woman approached me, they did not display a look of disgust or rejection —but rather kindness.

"When's the last time you ate or drank anything?" I heard the man say as I felt my eyes start to flutter. The world turned white, and I felt on the verge of unconsciousness.

"Grab that water and those cheese and crackers from the table, Will. This will have to do until I can get a proper meal into her." After a few minutes of eating an entire sleeve of saltines and a log of cheddar cheese, I seemed like a new person and tried to stand.

"I'm Sam, short for Samantha, and this fine gentleman is my husband, Will." They were in their sixties. Sam was about my height with long shoulder length straight silver hair and eyes as blue as a Caribbean bay. Will stood maybe 5'10" with a Yankees' baseball cap that I soon found out covered his thinning hair. He had a smile that lit up the great outdoors. His deep-set green eyes framed his well-tanned skin. They both looked very concerned for me.

"Okay, shower or dinner first?" asked Sam in a matter-of-fact tone. Will playfully held his nose, displaying his preference. I knew he was joking, but I was feeling strong enough from the cheese, crackers, and water that I decided to clean up first. Samantha selected some comfortable clothes from her wardrobe and begged me not to be put off by the "old-lady" clothes. I was thrilled to have something clean to wear. I did not have any trepidation about trusting this couple. They just seemed real and so damn nice.

Dinner was some delicious hamburgers whose meat had been enhanced by Samantha's recipe of ingredients from her traveling spice rack. The fries and homemade coleslaw would have been enough food for the three of us, but Will insisted on throwing on two hot dogs just for good measure. I was so hungry that I would have eaten the entire cow that the meal had come from, yet I deferred from taking a hot dog.

"Don't like the dogs? They're all beef," injected Samantha knowing that they could have been all horsemeat, and I still would have devoured them if something were not holding me back.

"There's only two. I don't want to take your portion."

To this response, Will and Samantha both laughed heartily.

"We weren't laughing at you. It's just that Sammie here won't eat hot dogs unless there's sauerkraut to put on them. And you don't find that condiment very often west of the Mississippi." Though I took the hot dog, sadness overtook me.

"What is it, girl?" questioned Samantha.

"My mom is the same way."

"Ah, I knew you were a New Yorker," Will laughed, almost choking on a fry.

"Sauerkraut had nothing to do with that . . . I recognized the accent the first time you spoke," added Samantha. "We're from Brooklyn, originally."

"Queens," I answered and reached for the ketchup and proceeded to cover my hot dog with it.

"Now that there is a downright mortal sin . . . ketchup on a dog? Are you kidding me?" scolded Will.

We finished the meal quietly, and I couldn't get up fast enough to help clean up after the feast. As I threw out the soiled paper plates and napkins, Samantha put away the condiments. Will restoked the fading campfire, and we were soon sitting around it and enjoying the peaceful feeling of pastel-colored sunset.

"You haven't asked me anything about myself."

"If you want us to know, you'll tell us. If you don't, well then, it's none of our damn business." I changed the subject.

"What about you two? What do you do?"

"This," answered Sam with a smile on her face. "Since we retired from teaching, we travel about in the Winnebago.

"All the time?"

"No," continued Will. "We take off for a few months at a time and travel around the country. In the last ten years, we have been in every state that our motorhome can reach, I won't drive to Alaska, and I can't drive to Hawaii. But we've seen the rest of them."

This harmless comment took the smile off my face.

"I've seen more of them than I wanted to . . . but no matter how far I travel, I can't escape my thoughts and some of the things I've done." I could see Will wanted to say something in answer to my cry for help. Samantha gave him a gentle poke that silently told him *to let me speak.*

"Johnny's gone, and I don't know where or why." I suddenly couldn't control myself. The floodgates opened. I started to cry uncontrollably. Samantha put her arm around me, and I immediately clung to her. I had to gasp for air in between my sobs.

After a few minutes, I seemed to gain control and looked into the faces of my two new friends.

"Feelin' a little better?" asked Will softly.

"That's the first time in over three years that I have said that out loud. It's really the first time since I left home that I had anyone to say it to." I almost felt guilty that I had not opened up to Tom and Nancy. They had opened up their home and their lives to me, and I had held everything inside. But my entire life in Vegas had been based on a lie. It was easy to continue a fictional life.

"Don't you have people back home that you could have talked to?"

"No, my parents are part of the problem . . . and my friends are all dead."

"Dead? You can't be more than . . . what? Nineteen?"

"I'm twenty-two."

"Seems awfully young to have friends die?"

"It's a long story."

"Well, we've got nothing but time if you want to tell it . . . or I can get out my guitar, and we can sing around the campfire," quipped Will, offering me a choice for the direction of the rest of the night.

"Oh God, I don't care if you murdered ten people. Talk to us. Please, anything to stop him from taking out the guitar and singing!"

"Oh, c'mon, I'm not that bad," declared Will, defending himself. He had a huge smile on his face that let me know that Samantha was probably telling the truth. My dour mood seemed to be broken. However, I didn't feel I was ready to talk yet.

"I like music. I'd like to hear you play."

"I don't know if it qualifies as music—so don't be so sure that you want to hear Will play until you have sampled a bit of it," chuckled Sam. However, there was a smile on her face as she tenderly handed the guitar to her husband. "Sorry, Hon, I just had to warn her."

I was struck by the feeling of how nice it was to be with good people and enjoy music again. The night passed in mellow relaxation that I had not felt in years. Late in the evening, Samantha's soft voice had taken over the singing duties, and I even joined in with her a few times on tunes that I remembered.

"Do you know this one?" quizzed Will as he hit a familiar chord combination that I recognized all too well—"Catch the Wind."

A gentle wind blew across the Arizona desert. Immediately, I was transported back to all the beauty and heartache of my former life. I remembered Johnny talking in song titles and likening them to philosophical statements. I again found myself my recurrent memory of our life together—and our final moments.

*"Me and you, Maria, we're going to catch that wind right out of this place," Over and over I have re-lived that moment in this memoir. Why? Was it the defining moment of our relationship? And here it was again being played by my new friends.*

*"...to catch that wind right out of this place. Always remember that."*

*But I had always been a skeptic. There was no getting out. Sure, my parents had moved to a neighborhood they thought was the promised land. The move, however, had not changed their way of life, their closed minds, or their economic outlook. Johnny always thought beyond that.*

*"When the band makes it big, we'll get married right away."*

*"Johnny, you're such a dreamer," I would reply. Sure, things were looking great for the band that spring of 1967. However, that kind of success might be temporary. He never denied that. Yet he dreamed for both of us. On rare occasions, he would get serious.*

*"We will get out of here—no matter what it takes." It was then that he surprised her with the fact that Queens College had accepted him. I had already sent in my deposit for the same school.*

*"If it ever looks like the band is not going to make it, and I do*

*mean if, I'll be right there beside you at school, and we'll make that future together, one way or another."*

*"Do you mean it, Johnny?" I had asked. "What about the music?"*

*"I love music more than anything in this world—except you." With that, he took out a little silver band and placed it on my finger. I gave it back to him.*

*"I promise you the future with me. I'll do whatever it takes."*

---

"You okay?" Sam looked at me.

"No." was my only reply. Samantha leaned over and again held me tight. I continued.

I told them the story of Johnny and me...every little detail. They listened.

---

My life changed that night in the Arizona desert. I had gotten my thoughts and feelings together. I had no more tears left in me, but my forlorn look of loss was obvious to both Will and Sam.

"As you sang that song, all I could think was how Johnny always said that we would catch the wind and find our way."

"Maybe, you just weren't meant to do it together," answered Will.

"But he didn't even tell me he was leaving."

"Maybe he couldn't," responded Samantha softly.

"You mean like he was dead?"

"There are other choices . . .but yeah, that is one of them."

"Let's just say he wasn't a creep, and leaving was not meant to hurt you."

"He wasn't a creep."

"So there's your answer. Let's say he couldn't tell you . . . or his leaving was better for you . . . or him . . . or both of you."

"Do you think that's true?"

"The question you have to ask yourself is a hard one. If he did it to save *your* life, then what have you done with that life?"

I had to stop and think about that statement. I understood so much now, and I chastised myself for time spent in self-pity.

We talked long into the night as the campfire burned brightly. We talked about my parents, my choices, and conflicts... Trio... and Jesse...and what I had done in Vegas...and after.

We laughed and cried as the night wore on. My soul seemed to clear itself of all the clutter and distraction that had made me lost for so long. As the morning light broke the horizon and the fire had been reduced to a few dying embers, silence took over. Exhausted, I asked a light-hearted question to the couple.

"And what about you two? What are you running from? Wandering out here in the wilderness?" Will and Sam laughed heartily.

"There is a phrase people like us use. Maybe someday, it will catch on. You know, like on tee shirts and bumper stickers. We always say . . . 'Not all those who wander are lost.'"

"I like that."

"Oh, It's not original. It's from *The Hobbit*."

"I still like it even if you are guilty of plagiarism," I joked.

Will looked me in the eye and spoke to me more seriously than I expected.

"You see, we always find our way home to our kids and grandkids. Yeah, we wander with no plan or purpose, but we are not lost. You, my dear girl, are lost."

"I guess I am . . . or was," I barely whispered.

"In fact, in a few days, we are heading home to New York. We wouldn't want to miss the twins . . . that's Bella and Ava . . . we wouldn't miss their birthday."

"How old?"

"Two," replied Samantha. She then looked over at her husband, and he nodded his approval to a question she had not even asked out loud.

"Do you want to come with us?"

"Yeah . . . I'd like that."

It would take us ten days to slowly *wander* across the country on our way home. We talked about many topics. Will and Sam shared their stories of teaching and retirement travels, and I filled in every little detail of my life. I talked a great deal about Johnny and his band. They listened though I worried that my droning would bore them. I even talked extensively about my parents and my conflict with them. On the seventh day, I called home and told my parents I was on my way.

Whether Johnny was dead or whether he had merely abandoned me did not matter. I was ashamed of what I had done with *my* life. Johnny would not have wanted me to throw away everything because of him.

Will and Sam remained a comfort in my life even after we returned home. We spoke on the phone often and occasionally I would go and visit them, though they were very often away. They are gone now and I miss them. I never forgot them and how they had been there for me in my darkest hour.

Slowly, I put the pieces of my existence back together. I asked for forgiveness from my parents for the way I had hurt them. We still argued constantly about many views they still held. This time, however, I dealt with them with considerably more patience and understanding. They loved me even if they were pigheaded. Much like the prodigal son in the Bible, we reconciled. We would always disagree, but we all could live with it.

Almost a decade later, I was married, and I had my first child.

As much as I was pressured by my parents to give the baby a "family name" and recognize a grandfather or even my father, I resisted. I named the boy Will after the man I respected most in this world. I also decided that the next child would be Sam whether a male or female. Two years after the birth of Will, my Samantha came into my life.

# PART VII

## "OB-LA-DI, OB-LA-DA"

### THE BEATLES

(Life Goes On)

Long Island
(1972 – 1990)

4 7

# "IN MY LIFE"

## - THE BEATLES

I could think of no better song with which to continue this memoir. Most of the next twenty years were beautiful. Thankfully, the sheer drama of my life on the road was never duplicated. And that's a good thing. My life became something not much different than millions of other people's lives, and again—not a bad thing.

The drama was now all in the past. There was no more assaulting a rogue cop in Chicago or skirting the law in eight states for drug possession. Furthermore, though Jimmy Carter eventually instituted amnesty, I had still "aided and abetted" the draft dodging Lars. I won't mention stealing the Flamingo van in Vegas because "Becky Simon" did that, not me. My life could have ended in disaster so many times.

If I am truly writing this memoir for my children, Will and Sam, I do not have to go into much detail. This is because they were there for much of *this* part of the story. First, however, I must tell a tale of my *almost* happiness in order to move on.

It was 1972 when I found my way back to college. I saw the irony in that it was the year I would have graduated if I had stayed home. Not being a city resident and having blown my acceptance to Queens College (and its very low tuition), I enrolled in Hofstra University. I honestly was a Long Islander now, having left behind my city roots forever.

I followed the dream inspired by my traveling buddies, the original Will and Sam, and took education courses with my eyes set on being an English teacher. Of course, as I am writing this entire memoir, I have to keep checking that it is grammatically correct. Just one little mistake, and I would hear it from someone reading it (probably one of my kids). However, while writing, I found myself lost in the past. In that past, I was a city kid, and none of us spoke well in those days. (I had to catch myself from writing "good" instead of "well.")

Those five years of college (including graduate work) are a lost memory. I dated a little, but nothing serious. Instead, I concentrated on my work, unconsciously avoiding any behavior that was even the slightest bit crazy. I reasoned that I had had more than a lifetime of adventure in my four years on the road.

It had been wild, from the blues clubs, riots, and affair with Trio in Chicago to the drug-fueled trip across the Northern plains with the Wrigley Rockers. My time as a minor rock star and commitment to Jesse was embedded in my San Francisco story. My fast times in Vegas and near rape in the Arizona desert had shocked me into reality.

While on my way home with Will and Sam, a song had just come out. It was always playing on the radio then and seemed like it had been written just for me. Of course, Johnny would have liked me thinking that.

It was by a group called Chris Delaney and the Brotherhood

Band and was called "Dancing on the Other Side of the Wind." I mentioned it earlier in this story. But looking back on the times we had, the words became even more real to me.

> *We were living lives of passion,*
> *Never wanting to go slow.*
> *Never thinking about tomorrow,*
> *Never Choosing to say no.*
> *We were dancing*
> *We were dancing*
> *On the other side of the wind.*

I had danced too long on the other side of that wind, and I understand now that it could have devoured me. It was time to get on with my life.

On my way to pick up my final paperwork necessary to participate in the graduation ceremony, I was broadsided by a car that had blown a light on Hempstead Turnpike. An off-duty New York City police officer was the first on the scene and helped me cope with my physical and mental distress while waiting for an ambulance. To my surprise, he showed up at the hospital the next day with flowers in hand, and I realized that this was not just part of doing his job.

Jason Carlson was handsome. He stood six feet tall and had jet-black hair highlighting his sparkling blue eyes and pale but healthy skin. He obviously took pride in his body and often worked out at the gym. I fell for him immediately.

Of course, my parents took issue with the fact that he was not Italian. I did not argue with them. I knew that those days were long gone. My parents' generation would be the last in which Italians married Italians, Irish married Irish, etc. Of course, I was laughing on the inside because I had shared almost nothing with them about my time on the road. I didn't want my father to die of a heart attack, which would have happened if I had told him I had lost my virginity to a black man in Chicago.

Jason and I married in 1980. I had just turned 31. In the culture of the times, I bordered on being dubbed an "old maid." I never felt that I had settled. I loved Jason Carlson.

With Trio, I had felt passion—dare I say lust. I had felt a warm, deep love with Jesse but no passion. I had passion and love for Johnny, but we had never consummated our relationship, which is a fancy way of saying we never actually screwed around. With Jason, I had everything—I thought. I'll get to that later.

William, or Will, was born in 1982, and Samantha in 1984. My life was complete. It was challenging with Jason working around the clock and me having a full-time teaching job. But we made it work.

I look back at those years with a sigh of contentment. Who could ask for more? I never did summer school, and Jason took most of his vacation in July and August. So, we bought a trailer and camped up and down the east coast in the summers. The kids' activities like soccer, baseball, dance, and karate during the school year filled our calendars. We were a happy family bonded to each other by love and shared experiences.

It was a good thing because, in 1990, my commitment would be tested.

4 8

---

# "SHOT THROUGH THE HEART"

## - BON JOVI

*I*t was a June morning in 1990, the *first* time my life was turned upside down. In that singular moment, every part of my mental and emotional state was shattered. My calm, well-organized and sedate life went off track—at least in my mind. After that, I never let *those* thoughts creep into my actual existence. However, I was never the same after those few weeks in June.

It started as a typical morning for a tenth-grade English teacher. I had put Will and Sam on the bus for their final days of third and first grade, respectively, and settled in for my last cup of coffee before heading to New Hyde Park High School. While there, I would begin correcting over a hundred essays my students had completed toward their final grades. I remember thinking, when will they understand the difference between an adjective and an adverb? That's when I heard the knock.

Upon answering the door, I spied a uniformed driver standing in his blue summer shorts and matching top, and I didn't know what to make of it. I had never received an overnight express package in my life. Because of this, my first reaction was hesitation in ripping open the red, white, and blue box. I remember standing transfixed by the actual package. What did it all mean? Should I wait until after school to open this unexpected arrival? In the end, the word *urgent* helped me to make a decision. Not noticing the tab that allowed easy access to the contents, I instead lifted a pair of scissors that lay beside me as I walked into the kitchen with the box. Neatly cutting the box open, I pulled out most of the contents.

On the table lay a handwritten note with my name on top and a black marble notebook that I had inadvertently laid face down on the table. The first thought that came to my mind was that this was a last-ditch effort by a failing student to get into my good graces by proffering a notebook full of writing. Only whoever had sent the note had written "Maria" rather than "Mrs. Carlson."

*What the hell? Why am I playing Sherlock Holmes?* I recall thinking as I turned the book over. Then, I saw the words "Journal of Johnny Cipp." Was this real? How could it be? Who was even still around who knew of our love of so long ago? I gently placed the book down and lifted the note. How could I ever forget the unique script that had written so many letters of love during our brief but real time together?

Dear Maria,

I am so sorry for all the hurt that I have caused you. Yes, I am alive and well. Finally, I am well. This journal will explain that statement and answer all the questions that I should have answered in 1967. I cannot express how I felt for you so long ago better than I have in this book. Those feelings have never died. I know I have missed out on what would have been a wonderful life with you, which is entirely my fault. I know that you did find happiness with someone else and that your life is good. Because of that, this will be the only contact that I will have with you. Staying away is the best course for me to take. You should know that I never found someone like you, which is my punishment for the horrible way I treated you. Once you have read this journal, you will understand that you must pass it on to the person listed below. This is a matter of life and death. The journal will explain.

You will always be in my heart.

Johnny

I found a second note in the box and placed it aside in the confusion. It was not addressed to me. I hoped that reading the journal would make clear who the recipient would be. Before I even picked up the book to read, I walked over to the phone on the kitchen wall and dialed my mother-in-law's number. I explained that an emergency at work would keep me busy all day and asked if she could take the kids off the bus later in the day and bring them back to her house. Jason was working overtime and would not be home until late. With this taken care of, I then called my school and explained that I had a family emergency and that I would not be in that day.

With all these details taken care of, I began reading the journal at approximately 9:45 a.m. By 9:46, the tears had started falling and would not stop until 1:16 p.m., when I finished the final page. The sadness and happiness invoked by Johnny's tale soon gave way to a sense of urgency when I realized what was at stake. I needed to act right now. I knew that at some point, I would have to explain the whole situation to my husband. However, I decided to hide the evidence until that discussion was at a time and place of my choosing. The note and book were coming with me to Cambria Heights to see a person I had never met—and never knew existed. Right now, I had to dispose of the box.

I lifted it and headed toward the back door to deposit it in the outside garbage can. It was then that I realized that the box was not empty. Turning the box upside down on my table, I watched as one final object encased in crumpled paper rolled out onto the table. I opened the wrapping, and its contents fell to the flat surface, creating the soft pinging sound of metal on Formica. My hand went to my mouth as I stared at the silver band.

The last time I had ever seen Johnny, he had placed that ring on my finger as a commitment to our feelings toward each other. I had rejected it because of a foolish sense of unselfishness. Johnny's life was in chaos. His musical career had been destroyed, and many of his friends were dead. My parents were doing everything to keep us apart, and our futures were uncertain. I didn't want to burden him with any sort of ties to me. I know now that I was wrong. I gave him back the ring, and I will never forget the look of hurt on his face when I spoke.

"Johnny, I will always love you, but I want you to come to me when you know where you're going...when you are in a good place...and when your journey is over." I should have told him I would make that journey with him no matter what. I thought I was doing the right thing. I thought it would clear his mind...free his soul. I couldn't have known that I would never see him again. I lifted the crumpled paper that had held the ring. Its message was short and sweet...a reply twenty-three years in the making.

I am in a good place in my life. I am where I am going. My journey is over.
Johnny

I put the ring on.

# "STRANGERS WHEN WE MEET"

## - THE SMITHEREENS

If I were to relate the entire contents of Johnny's journal, this little memoir would triple in length. Indeed, it would become the Journal of Johnny Cipp instead of the Memoir of Maria Romano. However, for one brief moment in 1990, the stories of Maria and Johnny again intertwined, and I still remain confused about what happened to this day.

I learned from the journal that Johnny had run away in 1967. His parents felt that he and Gio had left together. However, I understood so much more when I read that Johnny had witnessed his best friend's murder and immediately hit the road. The villain of the story, Mad Guy Provenzano, had lived up to his nickname and was carrying out a vendetta that he had against Johnny and his bandmates. However, more than just taking it out on the band itself, many of the friends and relatives of the band had died. Johnny saw the pattern and left. He never told me because he felt any contact with me might make me a target...and so he left without a word.

However, he couldn't escape the guilt. He believed his actions had led to his bandmates' deaths, so even in his new life, he was not free. He descended into decades of self-abuse from which he had only recently recovered. However, there was another reason for his guilt that no one in this world had ever known about until he sent his letter and journal to me.

Even as he lay dying at the hands of the truly "Mad Guy," Gio had refused to reveal that Johnny was hidden only a few feet away in a place we used to call "The Garden of Eden." Instead, with his last breaths, he asked Johnny to tell his secret love, Riet Carver, that he had loved her to the end.

Stricken with fear, Johnny never fulfilled his friend's dying wish. Instead, he just ran—intensifying the guilt he already felt.

———

The door opened, and I met Riet—decades too late. If things had not gone wrong, perhaps we would have been friends, maybe great friends…the wives of best friends. Possibly, our families would have had barbecues together, and our husbands, Johnny and Gio, would have played and sung while our kids played happily together. Perhaps. As it was, we were just strangers when we met.

"You'll want to…. No, you *need* to read this. It is about many things and some of them you must know. I hope it helps you the way it did me." With those words, I relinquished the worn and tear-stained black and white marble composition notebook. Having read the contents, I knew this was the right thing to do, but giving up my last link to Johnny was still hard. I also handed Riet another note that had been included in the package.

*Riet,*
*This book was always meant for you. I just*

*didn't know it. Now your lives depend on you reading and understanding its contents.*
*~ Johnny Cipp*

Riet recognized the name immediately and tried hard to place it. *Oh God,* she thought. I know who this is. He was the friend who . . . a flood of memories washed over her brain.

"There are answers in here . . . and if you need me to fill in any of the blanks, I'll leave my phone number and you can . . ." Before I could finish my sentence, the woman took my hand and said, "Come in. Please, come in." She asked me to sit as we entered the clean but ancient kitchen.

"I've waited a long time for answers, and my guess is, so did you. So why don't we go through this together?"

Riet read the journal and seemed to understand even more than I did. In a sense, we bonded over boyfriends who were best friends but were now gone. I was hesitant to leave. It crossed my mind that I did not want to leave behind the journal and all that it meant to me. However, in the end, we hugged and said goodbye. I gave her my phone number, never expecting to hear from her. To this day, I only know part of the story. Riet told me it was for my own good and because she did not know what would happen next. Both Johnny and Riet had figured out that Mad Guy had found out about her and Gio…and now, decades later, she was a target.

*Two days later, I would get a call—a desperate call to pick her up at a secluded location. There I found her covered in blood.*

5 0

---

# "SUNDAY BLOODY SUNDAY"

## - U2

I think of that night often. Sometimes, the U2 song "Sunday, Bloody Sunday" reminds me that it was a Sunday night in June of 1990 when I, without reason or understanding, rushed out into the night to help a person I had only known for two days. Indeed, I believe I understand more about the meaning of that song than my own actual "Sunday Bloody Sunday." I found her covered in blood, hiding in the woods in the ritzy north shore neighborhood of Manhasset. She would not say anything that night other than, "Thank you."

I called the next day, and the most I ever got out of her was, "There are people out there who still would do us harm."

What the hell did that mean? I put together some of the details the next day when the news announced that the body of Mad Guy Provenzano had been found. Did she…? Still nothing.

Two days later again, Riet Carver called me.

"You have to get here right now."

I remember answering something about the kids having dentist appointments and maybe coming tomorrow.

"I mean right now. A few hours might be too late."

"Too late for what?" I whispered into the phone, not wanting anyone in my house to hear.

"To see Johnny."

---

It is a moment I will never forget. Riet threw open her bedroom door, and there lay Johnny…unconscious, with three wounds bandaged on his naked body. If I had ever dreamed of a reunion with Johnny, it would not have been anything like this. I moved a bit closer and pointed at the dressings but not asking.

"Bullets."

"We have to get him to a hospital. They have to get them out," I screamed, half-crying, half-screaming.

"He's been to a hospital…the bullets removed…medication administered," countered Riet.

"But how did he get here?"

Riet shrugged her shoulders, signifying she had no idea.

"Bullshit! I bring you the journal. I pick you up bloody, and you tell me nothing. This crap ends now. Tell me what's going on."

"I don't know. I really don't. He appeared at my doorstep as you see him now—complete with a medical report and note stating not to tell anyone."

"You don't expect me to believe you…do you?"

"You must. It's the truth."

"And I suppose you don't know how he got those wounds?"

*Silence.*

"Or how Mad Guy Provenzano died?"

*More silence.*

I came to realize she did know but would never tell.

# "I LOVE YOU MORE THAN YOU'LL EVER KNOW"

## - BLUES PROJECT

Johnny lay in bed at Riet's house. At first, he was only semi-conscious. Riet struggled to get food and water into him. After seeing Johnny lying there, I told her I would help when I could. I will always suspect my motives for not telling Jason any of this. I went almost every day to Johnny's side. Well, every day that the kids were in summer camp and Jason worked.

Riet and I worked hard to feed and bathe him. We learned to dress his wounds by trial and error. We even laughed together. Riet became a friend of mine before Johnny ever had a fully conscious moment.

I try to understand my feelings after all these years. I had loved him, and he had abandoned me. Yet now I knew why. What did that mean? I loved my children...and my husband. There was no room in my life for Johnny. Yet there he was, lying before me.

I did still love him.

On the fourth day, he began to regain an understanding of the world around him. The first thing he saw was me. We both cried. I hugged him and held him tight, but we said nothing for what seemed like an eternity. Finally, he looked me in the eyes. His mouth was parched and seemed incapable of speaking. He whispered something I didn't hear, and so I leaned closer. His rasping voice continued to try and attain volume and clarity. I put my ear to his mouth, and his words were barely audible, but I heard them.

"I love you."

I was motionless, and he kissed me on the cheek. I turned in shock toward him. Our lips met… and I didn't immediately pull away. For that brief moment, it was 1967, and there were no complications to our love. It was Johnny and me trying to catch the wind. Johnny and me trying to find our way in the world. Johnny and me in love.

I pulled away and ran from the house giving garbled goodbyes to Riet. I went home. I sat in my kitchen crying. When I heard the joyous cries of my family coming through the door an hour later, I quickly went into the bathroom to freshen up—to wash away whatever I was feeling.

"Mommy, I scored a goal," screamed Will, for the whole world to hear. Jason nodded his head and beamed with a proud smile.

"Mommy, I made a dream-catcher in crafts today," pouted Samantha, not wanting to be forgotten and outshone by her brother. I held out my arms, and they both came to me for a group hug.

"What am I? Chopped liver?" Jason joked with a look of false anger.

"Get in here, you big lug," I laughed, and the kids and Jason and I joined in the most wonderful family hug ever.

This was also love, real love.

I didn't return for three days to Johnny. I only went after I had rehearsed a speech telling him about my life and family.

I never got to use it. When I walked into his room, he was sitting up and was more alert than ever. I had barely begun to speak when he cut me off.

"I'm sorry for…well you know…the…uh…"

He couldn't even say "the kiss." I could tell he was embarrassed. Was it because he had done it? Or was it because of my reaction?

"It must have been the heavy-duty painkillers that Riet gave me. I hardly remember you being here. But it's good to see you now."

I knew that Riet didn't have anything stronger than aspirin to give him.

We talked for hours about the old days, both of us keeping away from words of feeling.

"Do you remember when we won that audition, and you and Diane came up on the stage to celebrate with us?

I cried.

"Oh, shit," was all he said.

Diane had been my best friend in the world. That night at the audition, she had met Jimmy Mac, the drummer in Johnny's band. They had become a thing. Diane had died in Jimmy Mac's arms when Mad Guy Provenzano had sent thugs to kill him.

We both were silent.

"Johnny, you didn't…you know…kill Mad Guy?"

He said nothing.

We talked a few hours more before I returned to my loving family.

The next day I came to Riet's house. Johnny was in the midst of his many, many hours of restorative sleep. I knew that. I wanted it that way.

I left the silver ring on the night table next to him.

I never saw Johnny again.

# PART VIII

# "THE EVE OF DESTRUCTION"

## - BARRY MAGUIRE

New York
(2001)

5 2

---

# "MY CITY OF RUINS"

## - BRUCE SPRINGSTEEN

ill started college in 1999, and Sam followed two years later. Jason and I found ourselves "empty-nesters." I thought that it would be a beautiful new phase of our life. We would travel to exotic places and explore new opportunities. But a week after Samantha left for college, my world came crashing down. Events destroyed everything in my family...and the world. My life changed forever.

---

I was finishing my third-period class when a good friend, Haley, stuck her head in my room as the students exited.

"There's a second plane...it's not an accident," she sobbed, trying hard not to show her emotion in front of the twenty-four 15-year-olds leaving the room.

"What are you talking about? What second plane? For that matter, what first plane?"

"They want you in the principal's office...now!" Her sobbing made any further conversation impossible. I took a short walk through the eerily quiet halls to the main office. Before I got there, I ran into two of my fellow teachers who also were weeping, and I picked up the conversation midstream. Now frantic to understand, I broke into their conversation.

"What's going on? Why…?"

"A terrorist attack…two planes flew into the World Trade Center towers."

*Shit, shit, shit,* I remember thinking as I ran to the office.

Jason left at 6:45 a.m. to get to his precinct by 8 a.m. His shift was at the 1st precinct—the one serving the World Trade Center. I knew my husband well after twenty-one years of marriage. I knew all his strengths and his weaknesses. Bravery was a strength… common sense was a weakness. He would be in the center of the action, even if it meant risking his life.

I continued to the office, hoping against hope that they would have some detail to calm me. Unfortunately, all cell phone towers were down, so I knew Jason could not call me. But, perhaps, he had found a way to get through to my school. As I entered the huddled mass of teachers, I noticed that these were my regular group of friends. We all shared the same break period. *Strange*, I thought… until the principal spoke.

"I've summoned you here to give the details of the tragedy." He then proceeded to give a blow-by-blow account of what was known. However, the next words out of his mouth shocked the shit out of me.

"The superintendent, in all his wisdom, has decided that the students are not to know about this. You are to go about your day as if nothing has happened. Not a word."

"Are fucking kidding me?" ranted Joe Tringali, a social studies teacher using very unprofessional but spot-on language to state what we were all thinking.

"You know that this is 2001, and quite a few students have cell phones?" Gail Watson offered.

"Most cell towers are down," answered Gus Valakis, our principal. He continued, "I didn't make this decision, and I certainly don't agree. However, the super's attitude is compassionate in its motive. We are only one mile outside New York City. Many of these kids' parents work in that city, and these kids cannot contact them. We could have a wide-scale panic on our hands."

I wasn't listening. I was already in wide-scale panic mode.

"Those faculty that have a personal involvement may get counseling…or if need be…leave."

No sooner had he finished his sentence, I was on my way to the exit. As I made my way through the halls, it was evident that the "superintendent's plan" would not work. One class had had on a TV and news of the unfolding events spread like wildfire. I felt a tinge of guilt as I left the chaos of my high school. However, I needed to know that my husband was safe.

# "REASON TO BELIEVE"

## - ROD STEWART

nyone alive at the time and who lived anywhere near the metropolitan area knows that complete and total insanity was the basic rule of life on that day. Yet despite that, I decided to head into a city in the throes of a mass exodus. I thought of using the 59th Street Bridge to enter Manhattan but knew that the Brooklyn Bridge would take me closer to where I believed Jason to be…by the World Trade Towers. I arrived in Brooklyn just in time to see the first tower crumble. I cried—not just for my suspected loss but for the actual loss of thousands of strangers whose lives had been cut short. Still, I crossed the Brooklyn Bridge, one of the few going *into* Manhattan. What I found there was a living hell.

Plumes of smoke and debris particles filled the air and made it difficult to see or breathe. Yet I plodded onward. Professional and makeshift rescue centers permeated the streets. People with medical training were offering it in the chaos. Though they were all earnest in their treatment methods, some did with a light-hearted attitude to try to ease the anxiety of the thousands of fleeing residents and workers of the area. I looked at one couple with their makeshift gurneys and beds on soot-covered sidewalks. I could barely make out the facial features through the ash and dust that covered their faces. Yet they treated each person who stopped by them with a smile. One of the patients had written in the dust on the wall behind him, "Shylo's Sanctuary," obviously a reference to one of the dedicated workers.

But I didn't need medical help, I needed information. I knew this would not be easy. If Jason's precinct even existed as a physical facility, none of its officers would be in it. Instead, they would be on the streets helping people…or dead.

I pushed on. It was now hours after both towers had collapsed. The latent fatigue could be seen in any surviving service workers. Police, Fire, and transit workers combed through the wreckage in a vain attempt to find life. At a certain point, I could go no further—physical restrictions, both man-made and disaster-related, barred me from moving forward. I sat on a park bench that, in happier times, had been the home of hand-holding lovers and a variety of pigeon feeders. There were no lovers around here now…and certainly no pigeons.

"Maria? Maria Carlson? Is that you?" I heard a voice calling me through the dust and debris.

"Yes," I responded, not recognizing the gray-skinned speaker.

"Bill…Bill McNeely, I work with Jason. We met at a party last year at Ned Oakes' house."

I was stunned, but I did remember both him and Ned. He came and sat next to me.

"What are you doing here?" He looked baffled.

"Looking for Jason."

"Why? Why would you look for Jason here?"

Now I was the confused one.

"Because he went to work this morning as usual, and I know his squad was one of the first who would have been called to go in the towers. He's always telling me that they get called in for one or another kind of emergency. So, I'm sure he went in there."

"His squad did go into the North Tower…they never came out." He said this with sadness but with no particular empathy toward me. "Jason was lucky he wasn't there. I guess that cold or flu thing he got saved his life. He called in sick today. We lost a lot of good men. Ned, and Bob O'Flaherty, you remember Bob…"

I didn't hear another word he spoke. I was lost and confused—my emotions were a chaotic mixture of joy that my husband had never made it into the building but stunned at why.

I just drifted away from McNeely—no polite goodbye. I was numbed with indecision. Ned called out to me again as I stumbled away.

"Maybe he's at your condo? You know, the one in Astoria. I left him off one day after work last month when he had car trouble."

I knew the place he was talking about. It had been Jason's bachelor pad in Astoria, Queens, before meeting me. We lived there until our first child arrived, and we moved to the suburbs. But Jason had told me that the renters who had been there for years were moving out, and we had to decide whether to sell it or find new renters. But that had been months ago. Therefore, no one was living there now—I thought.

Had Jason felt ill on the way to work and gone there to recuperate? Or had Jason seen what was happening downtown and gone there to hide? That didn't sound like my husband, but I had to know.

It was late by the time I trekked back over the Brooklyn Bridge and arrived at my car. I then had to find my way up to Queens. Traffic varied in intensity depending upon whether I was on a thoroughfare being used by masses of people to evacuate Manhattan. I lost all track of time but was aware that the sun was going down as I entered the lobby and was greeted by Harry, whose tenure as doorman preceded even our moving there more than two decades before. He remembered me, though he seemed surprised that I was there.

"Mrs. Carlson…er…it is still Mrs. Carlson, right?"

*What the hell did that mean?*

"Yes, it is," I blurted, perhaps a bit too aggressively. "Have you seen my husband today?"

"Yes," Harry replied curtly with no details.

"Recently? I mean, is he here now?"

"Came in about fifteen, twenty minutes ago…covered in so much soot that I barely recognized him as the same man who left here this morning."

"This morning?"

"Yeah, came in about eight, like he usually does when he stays here for the day."

"This is not the first time he's stayed here since the tenants moved out?"

"No," again the short, clipped answer that told me nothing.

"I'm going up." I could see some emotion on Harry's face. Fear? Whatever it was, he tried to change the subject.

"That man is a hero. As soon as he heard what was happening, he ran down there to help with the search recovery. What a brave man."

*Brave or guilt-ridden? He was supposed to be there with his friends and brothers-in-arms. Not that I wanted him to be dead, but I know his sense of duty would never allow him to excuse not being there.*

"Must have spent twelve hours at his post trying to save others."

*Yup. Guilt. I shit-sure knew his mind and heart.*

I said no more and headed toward the elevators. I know that Harry wanted to say more. He tried to stop me. He couldn't.

I approached the door of the sixth floor room with my key card out. However, I stopped when I heard voices from within.

"I bet you feel better now, hon." (female voice)

"I don't know if I'll ever feel right." (Jason!!!)

"Come right over here and let me give you a back rub." (female voice)

"I've had a rough day." (Jason)

I used my key card and threw open the door.

"It just got a whole lot rougher," I screeched at an octave higher than I usually speak.

"Maria," was all that Jason could muster.

"Who's this Jason?" demanded the stunning (and young) blonde standing half-naked across from my husband (who was also half-naked).

"This prick is mine," I uttered, a bit calmer and actually smirking at my double entendre. Yes, the person named Jason Carlson was mine since we had been married for over two decades. His actual *prick* was mine too. It had given me numerous orgasms as well as two children that, thankfully, were away at college and would not see the spectacle of our breakup first-hand.

"What does she mean, Jason?"

"It means," I co-opted any chance of Jason answering, "is that I am his wife...correct that soon-to-be ex-wife...and you, my dear little bitch, are the other woman."

"It isn't what it seems," whined Jason.

"It's exactly like it seems. While you were supposed to be serving the city, you were busy servicing this slut. Meanwhile, I spent the day searching for you, all the while praying that you had been spared."

"He was lucky that he didn't go in today," proudly announced little Miss Bitch Slut.

"Yeah, tell that to Ned Oakes, Bob O'Flaherty...and the rest of his squad who won't be coming home tonight. Better yet, tell their wives who will cry in empty beds tonight...and for a very long time."

"Oh yeah," started the slut. I cut her off.

"Jason knows what I mean." I then looked him right in the eyes and spoke again. "You know *exactly* what I mean. You may forget what you did to me today...but I know you, and you will never forget what you did to them."

He never did forget.

# "GOODNIGHT SAIGON"

## - BILLY JOEL

*I*'ve tried to put song titles to each of my memoir entries. I became enamored with that idea when I read Johnny's journal in 1990. He did it so well, and I remembered how he used to do that all the time before he even wrote in his journal. He called it the "Soundtrack of My Life." Considering that, I am really stretching the concept with "Goodnight Saigon."

In that song, there is a line that is often repeated. It was written about soldiers in Vietnam but could well have been about first responders on 9/11.

"We said we'd all go down together."

The song was meant to demonstrate the attitude of the brothers in arms during the war. However, the spirit put forth was similarly felt by those who gave their lives at Ground Zero...except Jason wasn't there for them. He didn't go down with his brothers for no reason other than lust. A logical person might think, *what could he have done to make their deaths not inevitable?* How could his presence have changed anything? What would it have meant besides just one more death? But logic had no place in Jason Carlson's thoughts—and if it did find purchase, guilt suffocated it quickly out of existence.

Jason spent eight to ten hours daily after his regular eight-hour shift breathing the toxic fumes at ground zero. He and so many others had given up the idea of rescuing anyone—though it took most of them a long time to admit this fact. Their dedication to their colleagues would prove fatal. In a sense, Jason's guilt did kill him. I know because I was there at the very end.

# PART IX

# "THE END OF THE LINE"

## - TRAVELING WILBURYS

New York City and Long Island
(2008 -2013)

55

---

# "IF THE SUN COMES UP WITHOUT ME TOMORROW (YOU'LL BE FINE)"

## - TRACE ADKINS

Jason died last December—December 11, 2012, to be exact. He suffered greatly, and I had overcome my animosity toward him enough that I felt every bit of his pain. Indeed, I was the only person by his bedside until the very end. Well, not exactly...there was also one new friend of his—an old "friend" of mine. And this is where my story gets insane.

From 2001 to 2008, I had no contact with Jason after our divorce became final. Of course, we shared two children. However, they were already adults by then, so there was no question of sharing custody or any other drama that goes along with divorce.

Though I never went into details, Will and Sam understood what happened. Jason, to his credit, was honest with them. They interacted with him when their schedules allowed, though our children were now quite busy with careers and families of their own. Sam was following in my footsteps and teaching. Will was in the final year of his residency in pediatrics when Jason was diagnosed with Leukemia and a variety of mysterious diseases associated with time spent at Ground Zero.

Jason was working on "Slut Bitch #3" when this all went down, and she rapidly dropped him like a lead balloon. At first, this was not a problem since Jason was still relatively independent. Though in ill health, he was self-sufficient for the first two years. However, by the beginning of 2012, he was increasingly incapacitated. Driving to treatments became extremely difficult, and Will and Sam stepped up for their dad. They had long ago forgiven him for what he had done to me. They created an intricate schedule that wove together their three lives and allowed for Jason's care and their careers. I was very proud of my two children for all they did for their father. Despite our differences, I had to admit that Jason had been an excellent father before and after our breakup. Both he and I were rewarded with two wonderful, caring children who were now there for him for whatever he needed.

"Mom…er…Dad would like to see you," remarked Samantha hesitantly one afternoon after visiting him.

"Why?" I was abrupt. It had been over ten years since I had had contact.

"Mom," she started, but tears overcame all her attempts to speak.

"What is it, Hon?"

"Mom, he's never going to recover. He's known that for a long time, but the doctors brought Will and me in to make sure we understood."

I held her tight as convulsions of tears kept her from catching her breath. I thought back to all the times that Jason held her and comforted her when some tragic event had upset her. Sometimes the words and caresses of a loving mother were not enough. Sometimes she just needed to be Daddy's little girl. I thought back to all the good times we had had as a family—all the joy and laughter of those twenty-one years. I tried to imagine what our lives would have been like if I had never uncovered Jason's infidelity.

How long would my ignorance have protected my happiness? On that tragic day, when terrorists destroyed so many lives with their acts of violence, they also destroyed my family.

"Okay, I'll go," I whispered in my daughter's ear.

# 56

# "TOMORROW NEVER COMES"

## - ZAC BROWN

Jason did not leave the condo in Astoria very much. In reality, he was having difficulty getting to his doctor's appointments. Twice a week, he had group rehab treatments. I kept thinking, *what the hell were they supposed to accomplish?* I mean, these guys were not getting any better. I would eventually realize that it was their mental well-being that was being rehabbed. Being with a group of guys going through the same hell was supportive and lifted their spirits.

When I walked into the condo, so many memories flashed through my brain. Our first home—the place where he carried me over the threshold on our wedding night...our first Christmas...the Thanksgiving when I burnt the turkey, and we had to go out for Chinese food. The place where I brought our newborn son for his first night with us. But it was also the place where our marriage ended on that long ago night in 2001.

Samantha answered the door at his apartment. She gave me a big hug, stayed a few minutes, and then left to do some errands for Jason. I don't think she wanted to be there.

I was awkward. What could I say, "Hey, you're looking good?"

Because both he and I would have known it was a lie. He looked like death warmed over. We both knew he did not have long.

"Why did you want to see me after all these years?" I asked cautiously.

"I thought you'd take me back, and we'd shack up while no one's here."

Before I could answer, a warm smile came across his face, and he started to laugh. However, his outburst was interrupted by a deep and persistent cough which I thought would take away his breath permanently. When he finally stopped, and the involuntary tears ran down his cheeks, he again looked at me. I had even forgotten where the conversation had been halted, so I almost needed help understanding his first words.

"Hey, you can't blame a guy for trying, can you?"

Seeing him in this shape also brought tears to my eyes. I remembered the tall, handsome, macho man I met at my traffic accident almost four decades ago. His weight was now reduced by the chemo treatments which also took away his beautiful thick hair. I softened and sat on the bed next to him. I held his hand. He smiled before going into a brief cough.

"She doesn't know that I know," Jason barely was audible.

"Who doesn't know what?"

"Samantha. She doesn't know that I know she got offered a principal job up around Syracuse."

"What are you talking about?" I was totally confused.

"Her husband let it slip when he was here one day. You know he actually likes me. However, that might have something to do with him being a state trooper and all. You know, respect for the fellow blue."

"Go on."

"Well, she's got the job if she wants it for next September. She has to answer soon. As a trooper, Scott can transfer anywhere in the state, so that's no problem."

"What's holding her back?"

"Me."

"Oh."

"I also know that our son Will has been holding off his application for Doctors Without Borders because of me."

I was starting to get the picture, but it was not perfectly clear until I saw…his gun.

"Jason, what are you thinking?"

"I think you know what I am thinking because you know me too well. I need to know that you will make sure the kids follow their dreams when I'm gone… and…and that they don't feel guilty at all. I need you to do that, and this will all end for the best."

"You're still an idiot. What if you just wound yourself? Or, if you are successful, do you want your memory to be tinged with thoughts that you were a coward at the end? This idea is stupid."

"You got a better one?"

I didn't answer right then but held his hand tighter. Samantha soon returned to the condo, and we all waited for Will, who was finishing his shift at Montefiore Hospital. He lived there in the spare room of his father's condo.

I jokingly told the three of them that I was cooking a family dinner…and promptly ordered a pizza. There still was nothing like Casio Pizza even thirty years after we used to enjoy it as newlyweds. We argued over whether it was correct to fold your pizza in the middle or hold it flat. The question of using a knife and fork was never even considered by the full-blooded Italian mother of this family.

We laughed and it felt good.

"Remember when we went camping at Wildwood Park in Wading River, and Will climbed a thirty-foot tree and couldn't get down?" Samantha never let Will forget it.

. . .

"And your father refused to let anyone help get him out of that tree. After your dad thought Will had learned his lesson, he climbed up and retrieved him. However, he wrenched his back carrying him down and had to take two weeks of sick leave."

"Hey, Dad, remember when you and I ran the Great South Bay half marathon together when I was ten?

"Will, how could I forget? I had trained four months to run it, and you asked me the week before to try and do it."

"Yeah, and you insisted I had to prove I could make it so you wouldn't have to stop and take care of me," laughed Will. "So, you said to me, 'our block is exactly a half mile around…prove it. You sat in a lawn chair while I ran around the block twenty-six times."

"Do you remember what happened then?"

"Of course."

"I don't. I was only eight and it was a long time ago," added Samantha.

"Well, we're at the 9-mile mark of the 13.1 mile race, and Will starts to tire. I slowed down to encourage him, and then an amazing thing happened."

"Yeah, it was pretty amazing," interrupted Will.

"The crowd realized that it was a ten-year-old doing a half marathon. Suddenly, everyone is chanting, 'Will, Will, Will.' This kept up for the next four miles."

"And how did it end?" questioned Samantha.

I laughed. I knew how it ended.

"Well. I look down at Will to encourage him that only a tenth of a mile is left. He looks up at me, with what I can only describe as a sinister smile, and he speeds up. He is now determined to beat me to the finish line."

"And I would have had you too."

"I broke every rule of physical training to beat him. After I held back for him all race, there was no way I would let him finish ahead of me."

"Your father won by a nose…but paid the price," I butted in.

"I tore every muscle in my right leg and couldn't run for a month. It was worth it not to give Will the satisfaction of victory over his dad."

"How macho of you," laughed my daughter.

"Yeah, but it didn't last. Will looked at me as I was writhing in pain on the floor and said to me, 'You're still going to be able to take me to my hockey game this afternoon…right…Dad? "

Sam and I smiled and shook our heads.

"I'm going to be laid up for a month, and he's going to play two hours of hockey that very afternoon. Youth is wasted on the young."

"I always wanted a rematch," added Will looking at his father, who was at this point having trouble walking to the kitchen. He stopped mid-sentence. I could see he was trying hard to hold back a tear.

"I'll tell you what, son. In my file cabinet is my certificate from that day. Look at my time of completion. You beat that any time in your life, and I will consider you the winner."

Jason was a great father to the end. He knew how to build up both kids when they needed it and sometimes how to put them in their place when they occasionally needed that too. Will was putting in 12 to 16 hours days in his residency but was still in great shape. The day before Jason died, he bested his time by three seconds.

# "LEAN ON ME"

## - BILL WITHERS

Three days later, I made sure that we were all together again.

"Samantha, you are taking that job near Syracuse."

"Mom, how did you even know?" I smirked.

"Will, you send in that acceptance for Doctors Without Borders."

They both had the same question on the tips of their tongues, and I cut them off at the pass.

"I put in my retirement papers yesterday. I should have done it years ago. I didn't know what to do with my time, so I held off. Now I know. I'll help my family—all three of you. "

"Maria, you don't have…"

I cut Jason off.

"Slut bitches, numbers one, two, or three wouldn't do it…so here I am." However, I smiled. I had to tell him that he had hurt me and that I was the better person. No more words were spoken… just a big group hug like we used to do in happier times.

By early July, Samantha and her husband had sold their home and moved to Syracuse and a new life. This was particularly emotional for me because she had just discovered that she was pregnant with her first child.

Will left in late August for a small hospital in Kenya, though he also hinted that one of the doctors going with him was someone he had met in their training sessions and thought was the real thing. Jason and I had an empty nest. I had mixed emotions. If children are truly confident, successful people, they will find their own path to happiness. As a parent, I was very, very proud of them. However, I was very lonely. I had plenty of friends, but no one to share my life with. I was with Jason for now. But I knew that wasn't for long. It hurt to see him wasting away. I knew he wouldn't be around when Will came home. He wasn't going to be around for Christmas.

By September, I had gotten into taking Jason to therapy three times a week. I lived in the spare bedroom of the condo that had once been our love nest. A few days a week, I got a nice old lady to look in on him while I went back to my home in Floral Park and took care of the mundane jobs that remain a part of home ownership.

When I brought him to rehab one day in late September, he told me I didn't have to stay.

"How are you getting home?"

"Oh, I think I'll just die here?" He smiled widely. "Lou says I need to work on my gallows humor. How was that?"

"Jason, that was morbid, and not in the slightest bit funny."

"Come on, you always had a sense of humor. Could you give me some material? I need to sound witty for these guys here at rehab."

"Jason, how would insulting you be a good thing?"

"Well, if it comes from me, they think this guy is laughing at death. He must be cool or brave…or crazy."

"Jason, is there a Bitch-Slut #4 here that you are trying to impress?"

"No, there's only guys…besides, I got you…Babe."

"That was a poor imitation of Sonny and Cher."

"See, you already are showing that quick wit of yours."

"Okay, let me think a minute. Here you go. Try these out." I rattled off a few one-liners.

*"I'm so thin I model for a stick figure drawing class."*

*"I have to run around in the shower to get wet."*

*"I put the die in diet."*

*"I can count using my fingers, toes, and ribs."*

"How is that?"

"You've got to write these down."

However, as I started to write, he started to cough uncontrollably. I couldn't leave him this way, but he kept waving me away. I found a nurse and asked about this Lou guy.

"Oh yeah, Lou comes here almost every day."

"He's in that bad shape?"

"No, he's much better off than most of these guys. He walks fine. He even drives himself here. I think he likes being with the gang. You know, the whole "blue line" thing.

"So, if Jason says he's got a ride home, he means it?"

"Lou is one of the most dependable men you'll ever want to meet."

I waved to Jason and was on the way out when he yelled to me. I thought maybe it was something important until I realized he was trying out his insult schtick.

"I'd insult you back, but I don't think you'd get it." He started laughing hysterically…followed, of course, by extreme coughing.

I was grateful for the break that Lou gave me. I could drive Jason and then be free the rest of the afternoon to meet friends or see a show. The situation was working out well. Lou never came into the condo but rather helped Jason to the door, called out to me, and then left. I should have been suspicious. I'd find out why he never came in after Jason died.

When I found out who Lou was.

By the end of November, the end was near. Jason could not even get out of bed, and a catheter had to be inserted. He had almost stopped eating completely. There would be no jokes. Instead, he held my hand and occasionally smiled.

Will couldn't make it back from Kenya, but luckily, we both had iPhones, and he would Facetime Jason and wish him happy Thanksgiving. Jason wasn't seeing too well, and the screen was small, but I could see that my son was crying. He knew that he would never see his father again.

Sam and her husband Scott came down to share the long holiday weekend, and it was tough for her to leave on Sunday. She wanted to stay, but her school district would not have been so agreeable because she would soon be taking a maternity leave from her job.

On December 13, 2012, Jason looked up at me and whispered, "I'm sorry for all I put you through."

I was unable to speak, even as he struggled to say more.

"You know… for the three slut-bitches and…and all this…I love you."

He smiled and died. If only all the years had been like our beginning and our end.

# "TIME TO SAY GOODBYE"

## - ANDREA BOCELLI AND SARA BRIGHTMAN

Jason's funeral was a somber spectacle that would be recreated far too many times as the death toll of workers from the Ground Zero site grew. We couldn't know then that the numbers would eventually overshadow the number of victims on 9/11 itself.

The police escort was magnificent as we passed thousands of men in blue lining the streets around Our Lady of Victory Church. As we worked our way to the National Cemetery, enormous flags hung from fire truck ladders, and police cars lined the route. They were not just New York City or New York State Police, but rather from dozens of forces across the country.

At first, I believed that Jason worked in the rubble because of an extreme sense of guilt for not going down with his friends. However, I knew deep down that he might have been there just the same if he had been sleeping on his day off when the planes took their toll. I knew Jason, and I knew this was something he would feel he had to do.

Much of that day is a blur. Some big shot in the police union arranged a flight for Will to come back for the funeral. As much as

I appreciated the gesture, I couldn't help feeling angry. Why couldn't they have done this while Jason was alive so that Will could have seen his father and spoken to him one more time?

Of course, the pregnant Samantha was there with her husband. And so, the four of them, Samantha, Scott, Will, and his newly ordained fiancé, Heather, took turns comforting each other and me all day. I felt their love. However, more surprisingly, I felt the loss of Jason more than I ever expected.

At the gravesite, there was one final eulogy. As I listened, I grew increasingly uncomfortable as I felt I knew the speaker. When it was over, I asked Joe Smolinski, a fellow rehab partner of Jason's, about the person giving the eulogy.

"Oh, that's Lou. He's great. He's always there for us, even when he's not feeling well himself. Can you believe he retired from the force in 1988 and still volunteered to work at Ground Zero endlessly in the months following the disaster?"

"Yeah, Jason always talked about how Lou took care of him… and everyone…but especially him. He never understood it, but he appreciated it. Hell, I appreciated it. His help gave me some semblance of a life."

"Well, once again, Mrs. Carlson, you have my sincerest sympathies."

"Please call me Maria…and would you do me a favor. Could you ask Lou to come and see me after everyone leaves? I want to thank him."

"Will do…Maria."

"Hey, Joe, what is Lou's last name anyway?"

"Oh, Lou isn't actually his name. We all call him that in reference to his rank when he was on the force. 'Lou' is short for lieutenant. He was a lieutenant of detectives. So, 'Lou' was a sign of respect. His real name is Lieutenant Richie Shea."

5 9

---

# "AND SO IT GOES"

## - BILLY JOEL

*I* had not seen him since Las Vegas in 1971, and had to stretch my imagination to recognize him. His head, once ablaze with bright red hair, now showed only a glimpse of that color. Hell, his head only showed glimpses of hair of any color. The dreaded disease that took my ex-husband had also ravaged this man before me. I remembered him as tall and fairly good-looking, but now what stood before me was a stooped-over, withered old man.

"My condolences, Mrs. Carlson," was all he said. I assumed he was feeling me out, trying to see if I remembered him at all.

"And I am pleased to meet you finally...Lou. You were a great comfort to Jason in his final months...and also a great help to me."

I needed to know if he remembered me from his visits to my house after Johnny disappeared. I needed to know if he knew where Johnny was now and what it meant to him. I needed to know about Johnny's shooting in 1990. But he gave no clue about anything and merely answered my statement politely.

"It was my duty to help Jason. No, that's wrong. It was my pleasure. We were brothers in blue. If you need anything, please call me."

He started to walk away, and two fairly gigantic men came to his side to aid him. It was now or never.

"I do need something. I need answers!" I screamed to him though he looked around to see if I had caused a disturbance at the gravesite. However, most visitors were long gone, and my family stood at a far distance to afford me privacy.

"Shea…Richie Shea… right?"

He turned back toward me, a sinister smile covering his face. He walked slowly toward me, leaving behind his bodyguards, ensuring that our conversation would be private.

"What would you like to know, Mrs. Carlson, or have you returned to the name Romano with your divorce."

*Oh shit! He remembers me from the Heights and his search for Johnny.*

"Or maybe I should call you Becky…wasn't it Becky Simon in Vegas. You know…ah…when you liberated some working girls from their…um…jobs."

*Oh, shit, shit, why didn't I think to leave things well enough alone? But if he knew all along, why hadn't he done anything? He may have retired from the police force in 1988, but I knew that he was part of the Provenzano gang while on that force and after.*

Just when I thought I had infuriated him with my recognition, a smile came across his face.

"And I thought you didn't know who I was all this time. Silly me."

"I didn't until Joe told me," I then realized I might have caused Joe problems but was soon dissuaded by Shea.

"Yeah, I like Joe," he whispered as if I wasn't there. He then turned back to me, full of renewed purpose. "So, what do you want to know?"

There was so much. Where to start?

"Tell your family you'll meet them later. Let me take you out to lunch."

I don't know why I trusted him, except something in his demeanor told me that he would not harm me. I assured my family I would meet them at the condo later. I needed to see Jason's friends. They didn't seem to understand but complied with my wishes. Shea led me to a large limo—which I could tell was not rented for the occasion, but his regular means of transportation.

He took me to a little Italian restaurant where it seemed he was well known and received like royalty—or to be exact, like the "Don" of the mob…which he was. This was a scene right out of the "Godfather" movies. The closed sign was placed on the door, and his twin tower bodyguards took position outside the door. We were alone.

"I can bring a chef in if you want something to eat." Was this an act of generosity? Or was it to display his power and wealth to me? I declined, and he started to speak.

# 60

# "THE STORY IN YOUR EYES"

## - MOODY BLUES

"My fuckin' cousin was nuts! Excuse my French. I knew that from the beginning. However, my Uncle Dom, his father, was not. It was he who lured me into the family business even though I loved being a cop. Most of the time, I was a good cop though I would guess that some of my promotions came from my uncle's paid connections inside the force. So, for many years I led a double life—good cop by day and good mob connection by night. I was able to justify it for two reasons. First, I never did any of the violence toward anyone…and, second, I was getting fuckin' rich."

"What changed? What happened to your idyllic life?" I interrupted quite sarcastically.

"Johnny Cipp and that damn *Those Born Free* band of his… that's what," Shea screamed at me in one of the few times he lost his cool. He saw me in tears and knew he had hit a raw nerve, and he played into it.

"You're showing more emotion than you did at your husband's funeral."

"Ex-husband," I interjected.

"So that's it. You still have feelings for this Johnny "Fuckin'" Cipp, as my cousin always referred to him."

I revealed nothing. Indeed, I didn't understand the emotions I was going through myself.

"Finish the story. Though I know much of it from Johnny's journal." Mistake! He knew nothing of the journal that Johnny had written and that I had given Riet, Gio's lover. I don't know how that would help Shea, but I needed to hold my cards close to my chest.

"A journal? So, you have had contact with Johnny since 1967… sonofabitch. It must have happened in 1990. Now things are beginning to make sense."

"They don't, not to me…and isn't that why we're here…to get answers to *my* questions?"

Shea thought for a while before speaking. However, before he started, a deep and all-consuming cough shook him to his very core. It seemed to change his expression, indeed his whole attitude."

"Maria, I don't have to tell you, of all people, that I am dying. It won't be long before I follow Jason's path." He paused and looked at me with a sensitive, almost emphatic expression.

"Go on," I encouraged. I was finally going to get answers.

"Maria, I was a good cop," Shea started, but I interrupted him.

"Ya-da, ya-da, ya-da. I know, you were wonderful. You said that already."

He held up a hand for me to stop, but I didn't. I had waited long enough.

"No, if this is all about you, I should get back to my family," I barked.

His look was one of surrender.

"I will tell you everything I know. You may also fill in some blanks for me.

I didn't agree to the deal but urged him to speak.

"I am doing my own sort of twelve-step program, not for alcohol or drugs, but for all the evil I have done in this world. I have nothing to lose. What can anyone on this Earth do to me that the disease can't top?"

I looked into his eyes and knew I would finally get the truth.

"My cousin, Guy Provenanzo, earned his nickname 'Mad' Guy. He had so much ambition, but he was a cruel and vicious man at heart. Those close to him knew this from when he was a little boy. When his father started to give him a bit of power, the results were devastating to those in his way. Johnny Cipp and *Those Born Free* got in his way."

I did everything I could to hold in the emotions I was feeling. I knew much of the story from reading Johnny's journal but hearing it from the other side was illuminating…and sad. I thought that he would start at the beginning and tell the story in some chronological order. But…

"Mad Guy ordered the deaths of all of Those Born Free…and anyone associated with them! Friends and family were all targets. I politely advised him that he was crazy, and he almost added me to the list. He was just so angry at the band for ruining all his plans. He kept screaming the word 'vendetta, vendetta, vendetta.' I think he envisioned that this is what the mob was all about. However, the capos above him were not pleased with his behavior and almost eliminated him for bringing attention to the organization."

"But all the guys did was play at his club." I interrupted.

"All! That's all they did? That's what you think? When the police raided the club because the band guys were all underage, it destroyed all Guy's hopes and dreams. They took away Guy's liquor license and his wide-reaching plan to set up a string of clubs that could serve not only booze but a wide variety of illegal products and services. It all ended that one night. He now had the law and his bosses on his back. In his mind, the blame for all his problems lay on the band. And so, the bloodshed began."

I looked at him in awe. By my estimation, at least a dozen people had died.

"And where did you fit in?"

He bowed his head and was silent for a very long time.

"I never killed anyone...but I also didn't stop it from happening. For that, I will answer to a Higher Power very soon. I have tried to do what I could to make amends though I know I could live a thousand years, and that would never be enough time to make things right."

"Are you expecting sympathy from me...or forgiveness?"

"It's too much to expect...but not too much to ask," he mumbled.

"Oh, now you are quoting a Mary Chapin Carpenter song to me. At least get your own lines."

"You're right. Do you want me to go on?"

"Please do," I barked, seething with disdain.

"At first, Guy didn't know that Johnny was in the band. When the raid occurred, Johnny had slipped into the crowd and so was never listed on the police report. By the time the other four band members were...um...gone, he..."

"Not gone, you bastard! Dead! Say it, 'By the time the other four band members were murdered'...and then continue."

To his credit, he did say it just like I asked.

"By the time the other four band members were murdered, Johnny was gone."

But I had read Johnny's journal and knew that Johnny wasn't gone. He was hidden only a few feet away in the Garden of Eden while Mad Guy executed his best friend Gio. It was only then that Johnny ran. Johnny left the Heights, his family, and me without a word. After reading what he wrote, I realized that he made the right decision.

When the police, in the form of Richie Shea himself, came to question Johnny's parents about their missing son, they gave away nothing because they knew nothing. Richie Shea then came to my house.

"When you came to me in Valley Stream that afternoon months later, what did you expect?"

"Oh, I was pretty sure you and Johnny were still a thing when he left. I hoped by staking you out, I would catch Johnny coming to you, but he didn't. I guess maybe he didn't really love you."

Then, I let my anger get the best of me, and I revealed something Shea didn't know.

"You're a goddamned idiot. Johnny hadn't run yet. He was there for Gio's death. He heard the torture of his best friend without being able to do anything. It messed with his mind for decades. And if that wasn't enough, with his dying breaths, Gio had asked Johnny to tell his girlfriend, Riet Carver, that he loved her to the end. Johnny was so traumatized by witnessing Gio's death that he didn't honor that wish …he just took off to…"

"To where?"

Had this all been a trick? Was this whole conversation a ruse to determine Johnny's whereabouts for some final revenge?

"I don't know," was all I spoke, never acknowledging Johnny's flight to Key West."

"So, he had promised Gio to care for Riet…now that explains Johnny's visit here in 1990. Guilt for abandoning her."

Now he had me. He knew more than I did. In 1990, I had read his journal, brought it to Riet, and then left. Three days later, Johnny shows up at Riet's house with three bullets in him. I helped her care for him, but neither Riet nor Johnny would reveal anything to me. Furthermore, I suspected that Riet knew how Johnny got shot—but not how he ended up at her doorstep.

"Yeah, but Johnny came here because Mad Guy had found out about Riet and was going to kill her and her family."

"And Mad Guy almost did," Shea revealed with great remorse in his tone.

"What happened?"

"Maria, I swear to the God who will soon be judging me, I

don't know. Yet the results had an everlasting effect on my life. I know Guy tricked Riet into getting on his boat. I know this because I was the one who set up the scam. There were others there, probably Johnny, but I don't know for sure."

"You're lying," I insisted.

"Would I admit to setting up the trap if I was lying?"

He had a point.

"The next morning, Guy and his brother Tony are missing, soon to be found floating in the Long Island Sound. Riet is home, and Johnny is in the hospital with three bullet holes in him.

More than that, in the hospital, nobody seems to know who Johnny is. He has no ID, and he has no medical records. However, I had all my cop friends scanning everywhere for anything suspicious after my two cousins turned up dead. They found this mysterious guy in a hospital with bullet holes in him that were a match to the gun Guy always carried."

"You mean all your *dirty* cop friends…don't you," I couldn't resist the quip.

"Well, that goes without saying." He smiled knowingly. "I was no longer on the force myself but rather Guy's consigliere.

"Oh, of course," the venom had returned to my voice.

"So, I find Johnny in the hospital…and there is no Mad Guy around anymore to report it to. In fact, I am now given his job. The head bosses assumed that it was a rival gang that made the hit. So, not to leave a void in leadership, they quickly appoint me boss."

"How convenient," I smirk.

"Yeah, but I assume that it was probably Johnny who did Mad Guy in, but I'm not telling the bosses that. However, the proof of what really happened is lying in front of me in a hospital bed. What should I do?"

"Well, I know you didn't kill him. Why not?"

"First of all, I'm not a killer. However, because I know you would be skeptical of that statement, I will tell you my other reason."

"Go on."

"Dead bodies tend to show up all too often. If Johnny's body ever, and I do mean ever, surfaced, they would test his blood and find it a match for the blood found on Guy's boat. The mob bosses would know I lied and...."

"No more Richie Shea?"

"Precisely."

"So, what did you do? Wait, I know. You took Johnny from the hospital and…"

"…took him to Riet's." He finished my supposition.

"Okay, that mystery is solved. But did Riet know?"

"No, and she still doesn't," he said confidently.

"Shea, she never will. She is dying of breast cancer and is hooked up with a painkiller drip that has her barely conscious."

"So, where did Johnny end up?" His question again alarmed me.

Honestly, I had no idea where Johnny had gone after the affair. What I did know was where he *had been*—Key West. But Riet and I agreed that the fewer people who knew where she had taken him, the better. That included me. I guessed that he was back in Key West, but there was no way I was telling Shea that.

"I have protected you, Maria. I never told Mad Guy I suspected you were Johnny's girlfriend in 1967. He might have just killed you just for spite. Likewise, I never told Mad Guy that you and Becky Simon were one and the same in 1972. Without blinking, they would have killed you for messing up their underage prostitute ring."

"Bravo…you didn't side with the perverts—those goddamn pedophiles. Please don't use the euphemism "underage prostitute ring."

"Still, I was always looking out for you."

"You think that all those actions…and taking Jason to rehab… What? Makes us all even?"

"I was hoping."

"You're still a goddamn idiot. Let's say for a minute that you and I are even, and that God above says, 'Wow, he did right by Maria Romano. He's a decent guy. Let's allow him through the pearly gates. He is so wonderful."

He didn't say anything, but his expression told me this might have been his dream. I crushed it.

"No, you fuckin' asshole, what about Johnny? You are here making amends to me very sincerely, but what about Johnny? You know, the guy who spent decades in a living hell of drugs and alcohol because of everything that happened in 1967? Does your redemption program include him?"

"Yes, and that's why I am trying to find him. To make things right."

I might have believed him, but not enough to give him any clues about Johnny's whereabouts.

"I will find him, Maria. I will do as much as possible for him… with or without your help."

I hoped he meant it. I thanked him for all his help with Jason, and then his henchmen drove me home.

# 61

# "MIDNIGHT CONFESSION"

## - THE GRASSROOTS

January 2013

It has been a few months since I have written in this book. I realize how alone I am. My children truly love me, but they are gone. Will's term in Doctors Without Borders will end at some point, but who knows where he and his future wife, Heather, will settle down.

There will be joy in my life very soon when Samantha gives birth to my first grandchild. But even then, it is heart-wrenching because they live three hundred miles away. So, perhaps, I'll move up there. I know she will tell me it is a great idea, but is it? Do I want to be that clinging old fart who infringes on the excitement of their youthful lives? I need to take stock of things. I need to find new and exciting adventures.

So, what did I learn writing this memoir? I had a passionate affair with Trio in Chicago, and he died. I truly cared for Jesse, but he couldn't return my love fully. It was not in his nature.

I spent most of my adult life with Jason and thought I had it all, only to find out I was not enough for him. I started this whole writing adventure with an idea, "I only cared about four men in my life, one of them went missing, two of them cheated on me, and three of them died."

Do you see where I am going with this? Only Johnny's love never had closure. Only Johnny's love was pure and passionate. It was the only one that I knew that would have lasted forever if given a chance. But that should be no surprise to anyone reading this. Didn't I also start this journey by writing *that I had a secret? In the 46 years since he left me behind, there has never been a day that I have not thought of Johnny.*

Am I foolish thinking of him in such idyllic terms, or is it the failures of all the others that make Johnny seem so wonderful? Perhaps he is not. Perhaps, the years have destroyed the Johnny I knew…and loved.

And did Shea ever find Johnny and what did he do?

Because of Johnny's obsession with song lyrics, I think that I will finish this memoir with one. He observed that all our emotions, thoughts, and actions could be best summarized in something written about people millions of times removed from our reality. However, if the words fit, we could take possession of them and make them ours. We could use it to make us feel deeply.

There is a song I cannot get off my mind lately, which does just that. It plays repeatedly in my head, at times driving me to near insanity. It was an obscure hit by an equally obscure group called the Grassroots, and I don't know why I even remember it. I know it is just a dream…just a fantasy. But still, the song plays in my head.

*In my midnight confessions*
*When I tell all the world that I love you*
*In my midnight confessions*
*When I say all the things that I want to*
*…I love you.*

# EPILOGUE

**"I Know You're Out There Somewhere"**

*"'Cause the promise that we made each other,*
*Haunts me to the end.*
*I know you're out there somewhere,*
*Somewhere, somewhere"*

- Justin Hayward and the Moody Blues

# EPILOGUE SCENE 1

**February 2013**

Johnny Cipp stood ankle-deep in the warm waters adjacent to Fort Zachary Taylor Beach. He did this quite often after performing at his Key West club. The night spot, appropriately named the Those Born Free Club, did not serve alcohol. After decades of abusing his body with every substance known to man, he had gotten straight in 1990. He had opened a unique night spot in the world's per capita drunk capital. It was strictly a place to hear good music. He cornered the market on those music-loving yet sober occupants of Key West. He was happy…or as happy as he could be after a tough life.

After closing his club, he frequently found his way to this secluded beach to relax. Often, he would play some guitar or have a late snack. But mostly, he just peered out into the moonlit sky.

There he envisioned his long-dead friends from his band. They were playing and singing…and having a generally good time. So much so that in one of his darker moments of the past, he had tried to join them by drowning himself in these very waters.

With help from friends, he had gotten better. He might still be a bit crazy, but he knew these illusions were just ways of remembering the good times. The times with the band…and Maria. He still thought about her often. He missed her, but he realized it was all his fault that they had never gotten together. Now she was married, at least she was the last time he saw her in 1990. Yes, if only he had made better choices back in 1967.

As usual, Johnny walked barefoot into the water up to his knees. He did this to remind himself that no matter how tough life got, he would never resort to *that* solution again. He gave his ceremonial wave and whispered, "See you again soon, my band in the wind." With sadness, he thought, *no one remembers us, but as long as I am alive, you will live on in my memories.*

His thoughts were interrupted by a distant voice.

"Hey, Johnny."

For a split second, he was reliving the illusion of the band talking to him—a fantasy that had driven him to insanity two decades prior. It then became clear that this voice was real.

"Hey, Johnny 'Fuckin' Cipp, as my cousin always called you."

When he was lamenting that no one remembered him, Karma kicked him in the ass. He knew immediately who was hidden in the darkness near the dunes, and it was someone he had hoped against hope had forgotten him. Yet as the figure moved forward into Johnny's moonlit view, it was not what he expected.

Richie Shea was bent over, and only a cane allowed him to move over the hard-packed sand. Far in the distance, he could make out two large figures that he assumed were Shea's bodyguards The man he had despised for decades hobbled toward him.

"You thinking of going for a one-way swim?"

Johnny wouldn't give him the satisfaction of knowing he had once done that.

"Perhaps, you would have enjoyed that...you know, me doing your job," answered Johnny.

"Johnny "Fuckin'" Cipp, I never tried to kill you. Now my cousin, Mad Guy, that's another story altogether."

Shea started to cough uncontrollably and lowered himself into a sitting position on the sand. Johnny sat down next to him, but said nothing. Shea found it hard to breathe.

"Little known secret...just between you and me...I have never killed anyone in my life. Sure, I covered many of them up for my cousin, but I never did it myself."

"So...when you threatened me with death in 1990 if I ever returned to New York?"

"I would love to play poker with you. It was a bluff. If I killed you, I would have had to kill Riet and her whole family because they all knew what had happened."

"You mean that I almost missed Riet's funeral up in New York for no reason."

"Well, not exactly. There is still a good chance that you are going to die because you went to that funeral."

"What the hell are you talking about? I thought you said..."

"Not from me, you idiot." Shea's voice grew in volume in frustration. He then went into a prolonged coughing spasm that seemed to tear out his insides. When he got his composure back, he continued.

"When you killed my cousin, his son Dominick was little. But now..."

"I didn't kill Guy."

"Yeah, sure, and I made my money moonlighting as the tooth fairy," responded Shea, ignoring Johnny's comment of innocence.

"I didn't," Johnny reaffirmed.

"You got to understand; I don't give a damn. You actually helped me. All the power fell to me...and I can't say I haven't enjoyed it."

Shea then began another devastating hacking session. This time blood flew gratuitously from his mouth.

"You, okay?" asked Johnny.

"Of course, I'm not okay, Johnny… I'm dying. The doctor gave me eight months…nine months ago." Johnny heard the comment but also realized that for the first time ever, he had just called him "Johnny" without the expletive following it.

"I'm not here for your pity. I'm here to warn you. When I die, Mad Guy's son gets the power, and he wants you fuckin' dead for taking his father from him."

"But I didn't…"

"Okay, someone killed Mad Guy, who wasn't named John Cippitelli…right?"

"Right."

"No, wrong. As far as Dominick is concerned, you did it…and by the way, his nickname in the mob is 'D-Mon. Does that give you an idea of what you are up against?"

"He has to find me."

"Hey, Asshole, how do you think I'm standing…well… sitting here? I had you followed from Riet's funeral. He's got all the resources I have, so it's just a matter of time."

"So, what do you want from me?"

"You *are* dense. I am warning you to fuckin' leave."

"I can't. I have a life here."

"And I'm telling you that you will have a death here too."

Shea suffered another coughing fit, and Johnny stared at his long-time pursuer.

"Why are you doing this? Why do you care what happens to me?"

"Perhaps, the fear of what lies on the other side. I don't know… maybe remorse… regret…or restitution. You see, Mad Guy gave me the job of tracking you down. For years I carried a picture of Those Born Free in order to identify you. But as time passed, I saw the picture for what it really was…a bunch of young guys trying to make it out of the Heights…the right way. Guys who were loyal to each other to the end. I had to think, who was I being loyal to…a maniac."

Johnny had so much more to say, but Shea waved him off. He started to rise, and his bodyguards tried to get to his side, but Johnny caught him under the arm and helped him.

Now they were face to face, inches apart.

"Besides, I'm doing this for Maria."

"What are you talking about?"

"Maria Carlson…or should I say Romano. I had her picture with me for years too. Mad Guy wanted me to keep an eye on her in case you ever came back to her. You didn't. In one way, that was a smart move. You stayed alive. However, how did you ever leave her?"

"What the hell do you know about her?" Shea again had Johnny's attention.

"Hey, Dumbshit, the rest of the world went on while you were hidden down here in Key West. I know she ran away from home and had some…um…for lack of a better word, let me call them adventures. I know she pissed off the *whole* mob with her actions in Vegas. Of course, that's compared to you, who just pissed off one crazy guy. Luckily she was living under a fictitious name, so they never put two and two together."

"And you never said anything? You want me to believe that you took her side over your cousin…and the entire mob."

"I love that woman…oh, not in a romantic or lustful way, but rather like a big brother. I've come to admire all she has done—the person she is. She's the reason I am here trying to help you…and you're being an asshole doesn't make it easy."

Johnny thought long and hard about this final statement and looked upon Shea as vaguely human for the first time. He couldn't resist the next question.

"Have you seen her lately?"

"In fact, quite a bit. You see, my impending demise is the result of spending time at Ground Zero. Believe it or not, I was a good cop and loyal to the men in blue."

"Huh?"

"And I wasn't the only one. A few months ago, Maria's husband died of the same thing that will kill me. I got to know Jason, and through him, I got to know Maria. She deserves some good times."

Shea stopped speaking as if a sudden thought had come to his mind.

"Hmm... I may find a way to help Maria again."

"Maria…"

"Ah, look at those dough eyes. You still love her. Don't you?"

Johnny didn't answer. He didn't have to.

"Well, if you're going to die down here waiting for D-mon, you should think about calling or visiting Maria. I can't be sure, but I think she still has feelings for you."

Shea now had the help of his two bodyguards as he climbed the dunes.

Johnny couldn't be sure, but he thought he heard Shea mumble, "It may cost me my immortal soul, but…."

# EPILOGUE SCENE 2

**March 2013**

Though she couldn't explain her motives, Maria had often visited Richie Shea following her husband's death. Perhaps, it was to repay him for the kindness he had shown toward Jason. Perhaps, it was just her empathy for someone who she saw as someone surrounded by many, but cared about by none. No, Maria herself could not explain her actions. Despite all the horror Richie Shea had inflicted on so many people, she knew it was the right thing to do.

Maria realized that it would end soon when Shea asked her to come up to visit him in the hospital. The twin tower bodyguards smiled at her as she entered the room. They had come to like Maria and her generous spirit. Maria noticed that Shea's condition had visibly deteriorated since her last visit two weeks ago.

"You don't look so good," Maria unconsciously uttered.

"I know. However, you, on the other hand, look wonderful,"

answered Shea with a glint in his eye. "Being a widow suits you well…no disrespect to Jason."

"I'll make believe you never said that."

"Maria, please close the door. Tweedle-Dee and Tweedle-Dum are nice enough and very loyal to me, but I don't want them hearing what I have to say to you."

Maria, looking at him skeptically, closed the door.

"Do you still care for Johnny?"

"That's a stupid question. I haven't seen him in more than two decades. So why do you ask?"

"Because I have."

"Have what?"

"Have seen him in less than two decades. I saw him last week."

"What the hell are you talking about?"

"I had him followed from Riet's funeral. I needed to talk to him. I needed to see if he was worth the price I am going to pay to save him."

"I'm still not understanding what you are talking about."

"Mad Guy's son is just waiting for me to die, to go down to Key West and kill him."

Maria wanted to say so many things about all that Shea had revealed, but all that came out was, "He's in Key West?"

"You *do* care," smirked Shea. "I knew it."

"No, no, just curious what happened to him."

"I call bullshit on you, Maria."

"Okay, I care what happens to him. I always did…always will. I always dreamed about us eventually getting together. But Richie, it was just a childhood fantasy. That ship has sailed."

"Has it? Think long and hard before you answer. There is a lot at stake here."

"I don't know what you mean."

"Maria, I've led a horrible life. I've done awful things to people. Yet the one act I never performed, or ordered others to perform, was a hit on another human being. Still, I've spent quite a bit of time and energy trying to make up for my other sins of the past…you know, with the Big Guy upstairs.

"Wait a minute, you Richie Shea, head of the crime syndicate in Southeast Queens, fear God?"

"Twelve years of Catholic school and a religious mother…it is the only thing I do fear."

"But how did you justify all that you did?

"I didn't think about…until the end was in sight. I hear God can be merciful to those who repent."

"Why are you telling me all this?"

"Because if I do what I am thinking of doing, my merciful God will kick my ass all the way to the gates of hell."

"What are you going to do?"

"Don't worry your pretty little head about it. First, you must tell me that you care enough about Johnny not to want him to die. You don't have to see him again…or love him. You just have to tell me you don't want him dead."

Maria did want to see him again and wondered what would happen if that led to more. She had to know if there was something…a spark still there. She didn't answer, however, not knowing the cost of this fantasy scenario.

"Maria, I don't have long. Do you want Johnny's life spared…at all costs?

She nodded yes.

"Come closer," whispered Shea.

She leaned over and kissed him on the forehead. He slipped something into her hand and then briefly lost consciousness.

Maria left the room.

# EPILOGUE SCENE 3

**Late March 2013**

Maria had intended to be at Shea's funeral when the six o'clock news announced the death of the mob boss. However, she knew Shea would have understood that she was staying away when the 11 o'clock news followed with word of the brutal murder of his successor Dominick "D-Mon" Provenzano. The funeral could be dangerous.

She realized then what Shea had been talking about. After years of remorse and repentance for his sins, Richie Shea's last act had been to order the death of "D-Mon" Provenzano. He had done it for her and maybe even for Johnny. One final act of a penitent man...a final sacrifice that, hopefully, a merciful God would understand.

The news organizations exploded with tales of retaliation by various warring factions of the formerly united gang that Shea had led for decades. Maria didn't care. No one was coming for her or Johnny (she assumed), so let them kill each other all they wanted. Besides, she had happier things to think about.

She sat in her living room in her soft Lazy Boy lounge chair, cuddling her newborn grandson. Samantha and her husband had come down to Long Island to introduce "Grandma" to Roman Jason Reilly. Maria was touched to think that the baby's two names were those of both her and her late ex-husband. Her life finally seemed to have some meaning and direction. Roman and his parents would be heading back upstate, but she knew she would visit often.

Maria and her daughter had grown so much closer in the later stages of her pregnancy that Maria had let Samantha read her memoir. The daughter came to understand her mother so much more and to respect the strength of will that had powered her through so much adversity. She now knew everything.

Maria pawed the piece of paper in her pocket…the paper she carried with her always… the paper Richie Shea had given her on that last visit. On the wrinkled, torn sheet was simply an address… an address in Key West. Perhaps, in a while, she would go down there. She would see if the embers of love still burned.

But what if he rejected her? What if he had someone else? Shea had not been clear about what she would find if she followed her heart to the address written on the paper. She took it out of her pocket and eyed it for the thousandth time since receiving it. The baby cooed.

"What do you think, Roman?"

The baby smiled, probably having just passed gas. She heard the doorbell, and simultaneously Samantha yelled, "I got it." Maria heard a muffled conversation at the door and then nothing. Soon, Samantha stood in front of her staring with a wide-eyed expression.

"Mom, there's someone here to see you. He says his name is Johnny."

# AUTHOR'S NOTE

**Just a Song Before I Go**
*- Crosby, Stills, Nash, and Young*

In 2020, I finished the *Band in the Wind* series. I immediately started to miss the characters that I had created. They were like old friends. Actually, that is an inside joke. The characters in those books were indeed based on my old friends (and enemies). Therefore, leaving them behind left me with severe symptoms of abandonment. However, I knew that I could write no more about Johnny, Gio, DJ, and the rest. Their story was done.

It was then that my wife suggested that I write the story of Johnny Cipp's love, Maria Romano. After all, she was often referred to, but seldom did we know what had happened in her life. In the second book of the trilogy, *Sound of Redemption*, I wrote a chapter of more than twenty pages detailing Maria's plight after Johnny's abandonment.

It was left on the editing table. I was advised that it was a long diversion from the main theme of that fast-paced book. I agreed.

However, Maria's journey from an adoring teenage girlfriend to an empowered woman needed to be told. Thus, this book was born.

This book is meant to stand alone. Certain events intersect with scenes in the trilogy. However, it is not necessary to have read those books to enjoy this one. I needed to balance my presentation so that both people who had read the previous novels and those who had not could enjoy *The Other Side of the Wind* equally.

I hope that I have done justice to the character of Maria. She deserves it.

In all of my books, there are touches of the real me. I like to think of my writing as autobiographical fiction. This book is no different. As those who have read my other works know, there are always touches of "Bill" in Johnny Cipp as well as a great deal of my wife Marilyn in "Maria."

In this book, that is only found in the opening pages. Just as *Band in the Wind* was the story of what could have happened in *my* life, this is the story of what could have happened in *hers*. In the real world, we have been married fifty years and have led a rather staid life, at least in comparison to my characters. So, where is the autobiographical fiction?

In the last seventeen years, we have traveled the country in an RV. We have sought out both the traditional and the weird landmarks in our travels. If you throw in my degrees in history, you end up with the adventure "Maria" lived. It evokes the events that our country endured for the last sixty years, as well as the quirky stories of certain locations uncovered in our travels. As usual, it is impossible to detail all of the confluences between the real and the fictional, but I will highlight some of them.

- We actually did grow up two blocks from each other in Cambria Heights. However, we only met when we were fourteen. Marilyn did, however, develop a fear of my dog Rusty.
- I did play in a band called *Those Born Free* in all the locations mentioned, and it did all end in a police raid.
- It was Marilyn (not the fictional Val) who played in a band called *Hour Tyme*. That band opened for the group the *Hassles*, which did include Billy Joel and his performance of "Giving Up."
- Robert Johnson and his trip to the "Crossroads" is an oft-written story. This tale, and codicil "27 Club" story are colorful urban legends that perpetually amuse me. Variations of these yarns appear in three of my short stories.
- Events surrounding the riots at the Democratic National Convention in 1968 were correctly depicted. The MC5 concert and ensuing riot in 1968 occurred as well.
- One of the other obsessions of our travels is our tour of every major league baseball stadium in America. At the time that we visited Wrigley Field, I didn't realize I was doing book research.
- There actually is a "Viking Rune" in Lancaster, Minnesota, that claims to predate Columbus. Unlike the characters in my book, we did get to see it.
- North Dakota, with its massive sunflower fields, is the leading producer of that crop. Likewise, there is a Mandan center with the story told about the "blonde Indians" mentioned in this book.
- Our visit to Little Big Horn and the ranger talk there provided the background for Dax and Lars's interaction.

Yes, the Sioux women did exactly as described to Custer and his soldiers.

- Yellowstone was as beautiful as described. The story of the three buffalo and the jeep *did* star our Jeep as its main character. However, I did not run interference with enraged bison but simply watched and hoped for a good outcome.
- Lars and his story of draft evasion was a story that so many of us who lived through that era witnessed.
- All of the concert dates and references in San Francisco were accurately depicted as well as the "post-hippie invasion" vibe. The events at the Rolling Stones' Altamont concert are historically correct.
- All locations in Las Vegas were accurately described. Though there was no real "Veal Ranch." Unfortunately, I am sure it exists somewhere in the sordid minds of perverts.
- We really did find the Red Rock area outside of Vegas beautiful.
- Maria's encounter with Will and Sam was based on a real campground experience (actually in Roswell, New Mexico, for us). At a far distance, we saw a young homeless woman going from RV to RV, trying to obtain the code to the bathroom. She was whisked away by police before we ever got a close look. In my mind, I wrote the story that I hoped would have been our response if she had reached us.
- Maria's experience *in school* when the Twin Towers fell was my real-life experience. Teaching in a school with students whose parents could have been in the towers, we were instructed not to tell them of the unfolding events. That was a surreal experience that haunts me to this day.

- On September 11, 2001, one of my own children had just started a job that was supposed to be in the World Trade Center. He was out of contact for a while before actually running over a bridge to get to Queens and calling us. His training had been moved to the Empire State building at the last minute.
- And finally, Key West has been our winter home for almost two decades. Fort Zachary Taylor Beach is a favorite of ours. As such, it has found its place in all of my novels.

I was greatly concerned that the revelation of events in each of my novels would affect reading the others. Indeed, *Band in the Wind* (and its sequels, *Sound of Redemption* and *Brotherhood of Forever*, as well as, *The Other Side of the Wind* cover personal and public events that correspond chronologically to this book However, each has a different plot line and altered point of view. I recommend reading the other three books if questions are left unanswered. How's that for an unabashed commercial plug to buy my other writing?

# PRAISE FOR WILLIAM JOHN ROSTRON

"An extremely engaging book that kept me hooked. We usually say, the devil is in the details and this book made for one compelling read thanks to its vivid description and ability to keep the reader yearning for more! I do believe this book has everything it takes for it to be a *Bestseller!* "

— KATHERINE ABRAHAM, AUTHOR "EVERY SUNSET HAS A STORY"

The *Other Side of the Wind* is another hit. It is able to stand alone as the Memoir of Maria Romano, or as a fourth part of his "Band in the Wind Trilogy." Congratulations to Rostron for creating a very believable and heroic lead character in Maria. She was one tough lady who managed to survive some heavy stones put in her path.

— R. CAPPUCCIO

"Rostron's writing remains addictive with great emotional engagement for the reader."

— ONLINE BOOK CLUB REVIEW

"When Rostron takes you on a journey with words, you feel fulfillment."

— JAMES J. SPINA, EDITOR 20/20 MAGAZINE

# ABOUT THE AUTHOR

William John Rostron is the author of a series of novels steeped in the late 20th and early 21st centuries' music and culture. *Band in the Wind, Sound of Redemption*, and *Brotherhood of Forever* have received critical acclaim from Writers Digest, the Online Book Club Review, and many other reviewers. These books have found readership on five continents and 47 states. He has published more than three dozen short stories in anthologies with five of them receiving awards from Writers Digest this year. Most of these pieces appear in his short story compilation, *A Flamingo Under the Carousel.* Five of his stories have been produced on the New York stage and are available for viewing on the author's website. www.WilliamJohnRostron.com

www.ingramcontent.com/pod-product-compliance
Lightning Source LLC
Chambersburg PA
CBHW021139310726
48971CB00002B/393